"In this case, yes," replied Cassy wryly.

Jared laughed. "Perhaps you're right, but it needn't be." He came to her side, took her hand and led her deeper into the room.

The candlelight shed a glow that took the edges off reality. Jared caught her gaze and Cassy was pulled into the green depths of his eyes. He could be a mesmerizing man when he wished and Cassy had no experience with which to deal with him.

"I understand you told Beatrice I was in your room last night."

Cassy was pleased with the dim light for her face felt hot from the flush that rose to her cheeks. "She questioned me about being with Lord Waycross. I merely told you had come to my room to discuss it."

Jared's expression was still pleasant. Cassy breathed a sigh of relief. Perhaps they would not fight again tonight.

"She has the idea that something more took place." Jared raised his hand and stroked the softness of her cheek, allowing his hand to cup her face and raise it to his.

His touch send tiny shafts of warning throughout Cassy's body. He had the ability to turn her knees to water and to cause her stomach to spin. He leaned closer and she felt the warmth of his breath against her face. He had told the truth. She could not detect one whiff of liquor on his person.

"I cannot help what she thinks, my lord."

"So formal, when we are husband and wife," he mused, placing one finger under her chin and tipping it up until it suited him, "when we are husband and wife . . ."

A DEVILISH HUSBAND

Alana Clayton

ZEBRA BOOKS
Kensington Publishing Corp.
http://www.zebrabooks.com

ZEBRA BOOKS are published by

Kensington Publishing Corp.
850 Third Avenue
New York, NY 10022

All Kensington titles, imprints and distributed lines are available at special quantity discounts for bulk purchases for sales promotion, premiums, fund-raising, educational or institutional use.

Special book excerpts or customized printings can also be created to fit specific needs. For details, write or phone the office of the Kensington Special Sales Manager: Kensington Publishing Corp., 850 Third Avenue, New York, NY 10022. Attn. Special Sales Department. Phone: 1-800-221-2647.

Zebra and the Z logo Reg. U.S. Pat. & TM Off.

First Printing: October 2001
10 9 8 7 6 5 4 3 2 1

Printed in the United States of America

To the greatest nephew ever,
Gary Breaden,
whose intelligence allows him to
beware of things under the bed.

One

He was a drunkard. He did not shirk from the title at all. In fact, in his more sober moments—the short time from when he opened his eyes until his valet handed him his first drink of the day—he took a certain pride in it. No one of his acquaintance had fallen as far and as fast as he had, and he doubted that distinction would be equaled anytime soon. But this morning found Jared, Viscount Carlisle, more sober than he had been for the past two years.

Even more astonishing was his whereabouts, the library of his father's country home. An equally surprising discovery to his bleary eyes was that the room remained just as it had the last time he had visited it. Jared had grown up in the house and knew it well, but he had not crossed its threshold since just before he began his slide into Blue Ruin. There should have been signs of upheaval, he decided irritably. Perhaps a decline in the glossy mahogany of the carved desk, a cheapening of the gilt-edged volumes of books filling the wall shelves, or a deterioration of the fine Aubusson carpet which rested on the waxed oak floor. But it was as if he had left it only the day before. There was no fairness—no fairness at all—in a world where a man could lose his soul while everything around him remained the same.

A tremor began in his hands, and he gripped the arms of the chair in which he sat to conceal the shaking. Staring across the broad expanse of mahogany at the stern-faced man who sat behind the impressive desk reminded him of the countless times over the years his father had called him to the room as he came of age.

On occasion, they had clashed as most fathers and sons do, but there had always been an underlying degree of respect which no amount of harsh words could destroy. And in fact, at the last, it was not words that split them apart. It had taken a woman to accomplish that deed.

The silence had lengthened considerably beyond what was deemed polite before Edward, Lord Waycross spoke.

"I didn't know whether you would come," he said, fixing his piercing gaze on his only son.

"Neither did I. But then I awoke this morning with nothing better to do," replied Jared, languidly.

Lord Waycross frowned, ignoring the insult. He had heard rumors Jared was sinking in a mire of alcohol, but this was the first he had seen of his son for some two years or more. He hid his dismay as his gaze skimmed over the younger man who sat before him. Jared had lost considerable weight, and his cheekbones nearly pierced the skin beneath the green eyes that marked the Moreland men. His clothes were immaculate, as usual, but they seemed to hang just a bit too loose on his large frame. Then there was the stillness in his eyes that Lord Waycross did not like. Since Jared had first opened them to the world, they had been alert and curious to everything around him. Now they were deep pools of stagnation that revealed not a ripple of interest in what was going on.

It was difficult for Lord Waycross to know how to begin. He had considered this moment nearly continuously since he had written Jared, but had failed to discover an approach which would overcome the awkwardness of the situation. But begin he must.

He breathed deeply, then spoke. "I'm aware you're still vexed about my marriage to Eleanor," Lord Waycross said.

Jared interrupted his father with a harsh laugh. "Now why would you believe that?"

The earl's face flushed. "It is no secret that you haven't been the same since the wedding."

"You know you shouldn't put any truth in gossip culled from the *ton*," Jared replied with a lazy smile. "They dearly love to attribute scandal to anything out of the ordinary. I have merely been living up to a rake's reputation."

"Your actions in no way resemble the person you were before my marriage," argued his father.

"Of course not. I am no longer the person I was then. None of us is," snapped Jared. "Now, can we forego the discussion of my character and get on with the reason you thought it necessary to see me again?"

Lord Waycross bit back the words that sprang to his lips. Arguing with Jared now would not remedy the past, nor make his request any more palatable.

The earl took another steadying breath and met his son's gaze. "It's time you married," he stated bluntly.

Jared's mouth opened, then closed. He pulled himself up straight in the chair and suddenly burst into laughter. It was a frightening sound, for it did not spring from happiness. It sounded more like a creature experiencing a pain far too grievous to bear.

Jared continued to laugh, bending over and gasping for breath, until he finally collapsed against the back of his chair, his arms hanging loosely over the sides.

His father watched with a solemn face, his gaze never leaving the man before him.

"You want me to marry?" Jared asked when he finally regained his breath. "How could you possibly have the effrontery to demand such a thing?"

"It's my duty to see that there is an heir for our estates," Lord Waycross answered stiffly. "Since you're my only son, it's your responsibility to marry and beget the next generation of Morelands."

"It was my understanding you were heard to brag at your wedding that you would soon have a whole line of heirs instead of just one churlish one." Jared's eyes were filled with undisguised contempt as he met his father's gaze.

Lord Waycross cleared his throat, then replied gruffly. "Evidently I spoke too soon. It's been two years, and Eleanor is not yet increasing."

He seemed embarrassed, and Jared wondered whether it was for Eleanor or himself. The earl had always been a proud man, and the admission must have been extremely difficult for him. However, Jared's break with his father was too great for him to allow a trace of sympathy to seep through the facade of bitterness that encased him.

"So you see, the continuation of our family is up to you," continued the earl. "I've asked little of you, and what I ask now is no more than most men do in the normal course of their life. I am merely requesting you do it while I am here to welcome my grandchildren into the world."

Jared stood and stared down at his father. Lord Waycross had aged more than the passing of two years should have caused. He wondered what the two of them would be like if Eleanor had never entered their lives.

However, it was too late to entertain such absurd

thoughts. And now that an opportunity for retaliation presented itself, Jared was not about to let it pass. Sitting, he prepared to continue the conversation with his father in a more conciliatory manner.

As soon as Jared entered his traveling coach, he reached for his flask. As the liquor burned its way down his throat, he settled comfortably into the plush squabs and once again smiled. He imagined his father was still amazed that he had agreed to wed with so little urging. But it had not taken Jared long to realize that revenge was at hand.

He would marry just as his father demanded, but it would not be to a diamond of the first water, nor would he present Lord Waycross with a flock of grandchildren to carry on the family name.

No, the woman he selected would be not quite good enough in the earl's eyes and, to ensure there would be no children, Jared would never share a bed with her. He would not be doing the woman a disservice. She would have everything she wanted except for a family and a husband who showed her affection. As far as he was concerned, after the marriage she could follow the example of many other women of the *ton*. She could have as many cicisbeos as she wished, and he would take pleasure in seeing Lord Waycross was mindful of his daughter-in-law's activities. It could only heighten the retaliation against his father.

A fortnight later, Jared sprawled like a broken puppet in a chair at White's on St. James Street in London. His head nodded a few times before dropping forward, allowing his chin to rest in the wilted folds of his cravat.

A glass of brandy tilted dangerously between his lax fingers, threatening the rich carpet below.

Dawn wasn't far away when Jared and his group of friends had entered the exclusive men's club. They had spent the night visiting various gaming hells and brothels, spending their money as if they would never again have the opportunity of doing so. Now that it was fairly certain they would, they had come to rest at White's, where they felt safe in their drunkenness.

The men were familiar with the demands Jared's father had made on him. It had been a source of constant amusement to suggest women who would fit the requirements of his bride. While Jared dozed, his friends once again took up the discussion of his future marriage.

"It's time we made a list of serious candidates," said Viscount Brandon, a man who shuddered violently every time marriage was mentioned.

"You're right," agreed Harry, Lord Thornton. "If we leave it to Jared, he may never make a choice." Thornton's words were slurred, but he nevertheless raised a full glass to his lips.

"What is your opinion of Fiona Morrison?" asked Jack Henderson.

"Too late. She's been snapped up by Lord Carrington. Even though the Morrison money carries a hint of the shop, the amount more than makes up for it," replied Ranson, Lord Weston.

"Jane Fitzhugh?" suggested Brandon.

Thornton thought for a moment before speaking. "Don't think her parents would agree to an offer from Jared. They're particular about their daughter, and Jared's reputation is not what it was."

"I know just the lady for Jared's bride," said Henderson confidently. "The Crawford chit should do very well." He smiled, looking pleased with himself for putting forward the perfect proposal.

"I believe Jared paid her some attention at one time," contributed Weston.

"Until she indicated she wanted more than just a casual acquaintance," added Brandon. "She's nearly on the shelf, with virtually no chance for an offer of marriage. Not bad looking, but she has little dowry because her father's gambling has put him at the verge of bankruptcy. I understand his creditors are hounding him into the ground. An offer for his daughter from a man of Jared's means would be the answer to his prayers. He couldn't afford to refuse."

"He's known as a Captain Sharp and is unwelcome at all but the lowest gambling hells," said Weston.

A small silence descended over the group while they all considered the various merits of Beatrice Crawford's unworthiness.

"I believe she's the best we can do at this time," said Brandon.

The others nodded in solemn agreement.

Thornton glanced over at Jared, who still slumbered in his chair, completely unaware his future was being decided by four men who were deep in their cups.

"It looks as if it's up to us," said Thornton. "If we wait for Jared to sober up enough to make a choice, our hair will be gray."

"Your handwriting is most legible," remarked Brandon. "I vote you write a note offering for Crawford's daughter. We'll rouse Jared long enough for him to sign it, then send it off so Crawford will receive it first thing in the morning."

It took more than a few sheets of paper before the letter pleased all of them. However, it was signed, sealed, and put in a messenger's hand before the sun rose. Congratulating one another on a job well done, the men made their way home in order to rest before embarking on another evening of decadence.

* * *

In his youth, Robert Crawford had been considered a desirable *parti* by the young ladies in the neighborhood. He was tall, and although he carried a little extra weight, he carried it well. His father had left him with an estate which could readily support a family and a sum of money that should have lasted him for some time if used properly.

His first wife had also brought a considerable dowry to the marriage. Perhaps this propitious beginning had allowed him the time and funds to begin gambling.

Crawford lost his wife and gained a daughter on the same day when his wife died in childbirth. With no one to hold him on the estate except a wailing baby, he left the child in the hands of his staff and spent even more time at the green baize tables in London.

Initially, he was a high flyer, but as the years passed, he left more vowels than money on the table at the end of the evening. His estate and his manner of living suffered greatly over the years, and he had barely avoided debtor's prison on several occasions.

However, this morning, Crawford was in fine mettle as he sat down to breakfast. He hesitated briefly as he liberally spread butter over a muffin. The hours spent gambling had turned the muscles of his youth to fat, and his waist was now larger than his chest. He was not proud of the fact, but he loved the rich foods of the day. Perhaps he could wear a corset as the Prince Regent did these days.

He smiled and added another slice of ham to his plate. He deserved to enjoy his breakfast. He had enough blunt locked in his desk in the study to pay a considerable part of his debts and still have ample to return to the gambling hells.

Crawford glanced at the post, which had been positioned by his plate. He was surprised to see a letter from Jared, Viscount Carlisle, on top of the stack. The two spoke when they met, but were certainly not on any intimate terms. However, when he opened it, the contents of the missive astounded him even more. Viscount Carlisle was offering for his daughter!

A moment later Crawford moaned and buried his face in his hands. It seemed luck not only evaded him in his gambling, but also in his personal life. He had been desperate for money when his elderly neighbor, George Vance, had offered for Beatrice a fortnight earlier. Crawford had been in no position to decline Vance's generous settlement. Despite Beatrice's vigorous objections, the marriage had taken place just three days before.

To learn he would have no doubt benefited far more if he had not been so hasty took away all the relief he had felt in being able to keep his creditors at bay.

He pushed aside his plate, his appetite gone. An opportunity to become allied with a family such as the Morelands was rare for someone such as himself. There had to be a way to take advantage of the situation.

Vance was an elderly man on his last legs. A man his age with a young bride just might overindulge and . . . no, it was too much to hope George Vance would stick his spoon in the wall so conveniently. Even should he do the unthinkable, there was the mourning period to consider. No, Crawford must forget Beatrice and look elsewhere for a solution.

Crawford motioned to the footman for another cup of coffee as his brow furrowed in deep thought. He was accustomed to double-dealing, so it wasn't long before a smile stretched across his face.

"Have Miss Cassandra join me here," he said to the footman. His appetite restored, Crawford reached for his plate and continued his breakfast while waiting.

"You wanted to see me, sir?" The girl stood inside the dining room door, hesitant to enter unless absolutely necessary. She was small in stature, with a thick mass of dark brown hair, and brown eyes under finely arched brows.

"Sit down," he ordered. "I want to talk to you." Crawford studied Cassy as she chose a place across the table from him. He had never paid much attention to his stepdaughter. She had always been merely another mouth to feed, but her mother had brought enough money to the marriage to make it worth his while. Now it seemed this runt of a girl might actually be of some use to him.

"I received a message this morning," he said, tapping the edge of the letter against the dining table. "It seems somehow you have drawn the attention of a gentleman."

Cassy appeared puzzled by her stepfather's words.

"Don't act the green girl," Crawford growled. "A gentleman—and a fine one at that—wants to marry you."

"Marry? A gentleman?" parroted Cassy. "How could that be? I am not acquainted with a gentleman well enough to wed."

"I don't know how, but I'll not question our good fortune, and neither should you. Lord Carlisle has written making an offer, and it's one I won't allow you to refuse."

"Lord Carlisle?" repeated Cassy in sheer disbelief. "You are bamming me. I saw him only once or twice when he was going about with Beatrice, and he never gave me one moment's notice."

"I assure you this is no joke," replied Crawford, frowning at her. "I'm writing a letter this morning, inviting Carlisle to call and make his offer in person."

"But I've never even spoken to the man," objected Cassy, choking down the panic that rose in her.

"Makes no difference. You probably won't speak to him much after the marriage, either," judged Crawford. "Men like Carlisle only marry to set up their nursery. After that's done, I imagine you'll be free to carry on as you see fit. In the meantime, you'll be the perfect betrothed for his lordship or answer to me. This marriage should bring me enough money to pay off my debts, and I won't have you ruining it."

Cassy was outraged. "You're selling me to Lord Carlisle because of your gambling debts? Mother would have never allowed this to happen."

Crawford's face turned dark with anger. "Well, your mother isn't here, and you were left in my charge. So don't get it in your head to refuse, for your life will be worse than you could ever imagine," he threatened.

Cassy pushed back her chair and left the room without uttering another word.

Crawford smiled. The chit would do as he ordered. There was no other course open to her. No family, no money, nowhere to go. Now, if only he could pass her off to Carlisle.

There was no doubt in Crawford's mind that Lord Carlisle had meant his letter to be an offer for Beatrice. However, he had not mentioned her by name, and since Beatrice was already married, it was natural that Crawford would think it was Cassy he meant. Crawford rose and tossed his serviette on the table. He must pen a note to Carlisle before the viscount learned of Beatrice's marriage.

It was late afternoon before Jared awoke with a groan. His head was going to break into pieces any moment, and he suspected that likelihood would be a considerable improvement over his current condition. It required a few hours and several glasses of brandy before he was dressed and seated in the dining room, attempting to convince himself he should partake of the late breakfast he had ordered.

He had seen men decline until they were nothing but skin over bone when they drank heavily. He would be different, he vowed, as he helped himself to buttered eggs, ham, and muffins. While he might drink more than usual, he forced himself to eat even when food did not appeal to him. Even so, his clothes still hung more loosely than was fashionable.

While eating, Jared turned his attention to the letters stacked by his plate. His secretary attended to most of the post; however, he left the personal correspondence for Jared to peruse.

Jared opened the first letter. His fork froze halfway to his mouth as his eyes skimmed over the contents. When he reached the end, his fork clattered to the plate. He swore loud and long. "What the deuce does this mean?" he demanded to the empty room.

"I see I've arrived just in time," said Viscount Brandon, strolling into the dining room.

Jared tossed the letter onto the table. "You'll need to be a mind reader, then, for I have no idea what Crawford is up to," he said.

Brandon smiled as he read the letter. It was as they thought. Crawford had lost no time in answering Jared's offer. "Congratulations," he said, taking a muffin and buttering it. "Your worries are over."

"I have no worries," growled Jared, uneasy with his friend's manner.

"Of course not. We solved them for you, and that is the proof," boasted Brandon, gesturing at the letter with his butter knife.

"We?"

"Thornton, Henderson, Weston and myself. While you were . . . ah . . . dozing last night."

Jared's apprehension deepened. "Just what did you do?"

"Now, don't get on your high ropes. You've been dithering for the past fortnight about selecting a bride, so we discussed eligible women and chose one for you. Then, since you were not up to it yourself, we wrote a letter offering for the lady." He smiled, proud of the accomplishment.

"You what?" shouted Jared, before he could compose himself.

Brandon looked confused. "We wrote Crawford offering for his daughter. You signed the letter. But, of course, you probably don't remember. You were more than a trifle foxed," he explained. "If you think about it, Miss Crawford is the perfect lady for your needs. Her family is just low enough and touched with the scandal of Crawford's gambling to set your father's back up."

Jared motioned the footman to bring the bottle of brandy from the sideboard, and he poured a generous portion into his coffee.

"Thought you'd be happy about it," said Brandon. "Anyone can see with half an eye that Miss Crawford is just the article to send your father up into the boughs."

The liquor reached Jared's stomach, warming it. He emptied his cup, ignoring the coffee when he filled it again. By the time he finished the second cup, Brandon's explanation was beginning to seem more acceptable to him. After all, he must marry, and it didn't matter a whit to him who it was, just as long as his father disapproved of his choice.

Beatrice was the kind of blond, voluptuously figured, slightly boisterous woman Lord Waycross frowned upon as being just a bit too vulgar for good taste. Now that Jared had time to consider it, his friends had spared him considerable indecision. It was only left for him to put the question to Beatrice, but that could wait for tomorrow. This evening's entertainment was far more important than an offer of marriage.

Jared arrived later than he had planned at the Crawford house the next day. Just as he had begun dressing, his friends had invaded his dressing room, bringing several bottles of wine to fortify him for the upcoming event. They stayed during the entire ritual, making recommendations, booing or applauding his valet's selections until the poor man nearly packed his bags and left. But eventually everyone agreed Jared was complete to a shade, and he took his leave amidst much shouting of suggestions on just how to put the question.

It was a two-hour drive to Crawford's country home. From the general state of disrepair of the grounds and house, it was apparent Crawford had spent nothing at all for some time to keep his estate in order. The drive was rough, the weeds high, and the windows of the house covered with ivy. Gambling had taken Crawford over so completely that his way of life was nearly lost, but that was not Jared's concern. He had come to claim a wife, one who would scandalize his father.

Now that Jared actually stood on the steps of Crawford's home, he felt the urge to turn and run before he had gone too far. But it seemed he had already done so, for the door opened before he lifted his hand to the knocker. Robert Crawford stood in the foyer behind the butler, a welcoming smile on his face.

"Lord Carlisle, come in. Come in," he gushed effusively. "I was beginning to think you had not received my note."

"My apologies, Crawford. Some last-minute business delayed me."

"No need to apologize, my lord. I understand you have many things to manage. Come into the study and have some brandy to clear the dust from your throat," invited Crawford.

The offer was tempting, for the effects of the wine Jared had drunk at his home had dissipated, and he felt in great need of a drink to steady his nerves. What had seemed reasonable in London took on an altogether different perspective here at Crawford's crumbling estate.

"Thank you. Perhaps later," said Jared. "I have other matters on my mind which take precedence on this occasion."

"I won't keep you waiting, then. Franklin will show you to the drawing room. I'll be in the study if you wish to see me before you leave."

Jared handed over his hat and gloves and followed the butler. His cravat seemed much tighter than when he had tied it earlier in the day. The butler opened the double doors, stepped aside, and announced Lord Carlisle.

At first, Jared thought the room was empty. Then, from the corner of his eye, he caught a movement near the window of the drawing room. The young woman who stood there could be scarcely out of the schoolroom. She was small in stature and seemed to be all dark hair and huge eyes.

"My apologies," he said. "The butler must have shown me to the wrong room. I came to call on Miss Beatrice Crawford."

"Are you certain?" she asked in a soft voice.

"Of course," he answered, thinking she must be all about in the attic to voice such a ridiculous question.

"I only ask because Beatrice is not here at the moment and may never be again." She made the announcement as if she were offering him tea.

Jared wondered whether he was wrong about the wine he had consumed while he dressed. He had expected to find Beatrice waiting impatiently for him to go on bended knee before her. Crawford had certainly indicated as much when he met him at the door. Now this slip of a girl was telling him Beatrice was not even at home.

"Do you know where she is?"

"Of course. She is with her husband."

"Her husband?" he echoed, like a dim-witted sapskull.

"George Vance. He is a neighbor of ours and has been mad about Beatrice ever since his wife died. They married four days ago."

"Then why the devil am I here?"

The two of them stared at one another for a moment.

"I believe you're here to make an offer for me," the girl answered calmly.

"For you? Who are you?"

"I'm Cassandra Wallace. Robert Crawford is my stepfather. He told me yesterday you had written asking permission to call on me. I thought it unlikely, since we had never even been introduced. Oh, I've seen you on occasion from a distance, but you never noticed me. And there was no reason you should," she hastened to add. "That was why I thought it highly unlikely . . ."

"Yes, yes." Jared waved his hand to silence her. "Assuredly there has been a mistake made. I must speak to your stepfather." He stalked from the room determined to ascertain what kind of havey cavey game Crawford was playing.

"You never mentioned Beatrice in your note," argued Crawford, once Jared found him in the study.

"Since she was already married, I assumed it was Cassandra you meant."

"I'd never even met the girl until a few moments ago," Jared said, through gritted teeth. "Why would I offer for her?"

"That I can't tell you, my lord. I'm not privy to your confidences," replied Crawford, a bit too smugly for Jared's liking.

"There *is* no reason, since I did not even know she existed," he growled.

"Don't tell me you're thinking of begging off," said Crawford. "Why, it would be past all bearing for Cassandra. She would be completely humiliated."

"She didn't seem entirely enamored of the idea when I spoke with her just now."

"You know how young ladies are. She was probably overcome by your presence and turned shy."

"She wasn't at all shy," contended Jared. "She was very forthright and didn't seem a bit in awe of me. It appeared she wouldn't be disappointed if there was never a proposal made."

"As her guardian, I would consider it bad form if you withdrew your offer. I must insist you do not disappoint her."

Crawford's comments confirmed Jared's worst suspicion. The man would not easily let him go. It was no secret that he was in desperate need of money and, at present, Jared was his means to solvency.

Jared paced to the window and stared out, so deep in thought he saw nothing of the overgrown park outside. Little had changed despite Crawford's effort to hoodwink him, he decided. He needed to marry, and if he had considered Beatrice perfect revenge for his father, then perhaps the small mouse called Cassandra would be even better. Evidently she was of no consequence at all and would have remained in her stepfather's house had the opportunity to marry him not come along. He wondered how involved she was in the plot to lure him into the parson's mousetrap. She was most likely not as innocent as she looked after living under Crawford's influence. But perhaps that was all for the better, considering his reason for marrying.

He stepped to the door and opened it. "Is Miss Wallace still in the drawing room?" he asked the footman.

"Yes, my lord."

Jared gave Crawford one last sharp glance, then made his way down the hall to face his future bride.

Two

"Tell me, Betsy. Will I do? And now is not the time for loyalty. I need to hear the truth."

Betsy smoothed a strand of Cassy's long brown hair. "You are lovely as a picture."

"I knew you would say that," complained Cassy. "It's what you have said to me since I was a child."

"Because it's true," contended the maid. Betsy had been present at Cassy's birth and had watched her grow to be the young woman she now was. She had worried what would become of Cassy once her mother had died and was filled with happiness knowing she had married a man wealthy enough to keep her comfortable and handsome enough to win her heart. For Betsy had no doubt Viscount Carlisle would love Cassy once he came to know her.

"Well, there is nothing more I can do in any case." Cassy sighed. "I am so thankful to have you with me, Betsy. I don't know how I would have managed coming to a place such as this by myself." Cassy glanced around the sumptuously appointed chamber, still a little overwhelmed by the richness of her surroundings, which were far different from her stepfather's house.

The suite of rooms she occupied included a sitting room, bedroom, and a dressing room, decorated predominately in shades of green and pink. The carpet was soft and the furniture delicate, as befitted a lady. Vases filled with flowers were scattered about the rooms, scenting the air with the fragrance of a garden. It would take time for Cassy to become accustomed to such luxury, but first she must deal with her wedding night without appearing to be a widgeon.

"Don't you worry. I'll be with you as long as I can get around," promised Betsy. "Now I'm going to my room. Your young man will be here soon."

Cassy's flush was apparent even in the candlelight. "Oh, Betsy. I don't want to make a fool of myself," she cried in a sudden panic. She had not admitted it, but being alone with a strange man in such intimate circumstances frightened her. Betsy had attempted to tell her what to expect, but the account had only served to heighten her anxiety.

"Lord Carlisle is a gentleman. He'll be patient," said Betsy, hoping her judgment would prove correct. "Try not to worry. I'll bring you chocolate as usual in the morning." Giving Cassy's shoulder a comforting pat, she left the room.

Cassy returned to the dressing table and studied herself in the mirror. She was no diamond of the first water, to be sure. Her slight stature, along with her brown hair and eyes, caused her to think of herself as a small brown wren. Picking up the brush, she gave her hair one last stroke. She had often thought of having her hair cut to a more manageable length, but each time she remembered her mother's pride in the long tresses and could not carry through with it.

Again, she considered why she had not fought harder against marriage with a virtual stranger. Once her anger had cooled, she had considered her future. It was a certainty her stepfather would do all he could to force her marriage with the viscount. If she refused, she would need to find employment, and she had no experience or references to fall back on. Even if she could obtain a position as governess or companion, there would be no place for Betsy, and she could not desert the only family she had.

She had considered what she knew about Lord Carlisle. He had paid some slight attention to Beatrice when she had made her come out. Cassy had admired his bearing, and she thought him extremely handsome with his green eyes and dark hair. She had never seen him when he was not dressed to the nines, but he was never ostentatious, as some of the men were wont to be. He appeared to be courteous, and she heard no *on-dits* that he treated women disrespectfully.

At the end of her deliberations, Cassy realized the best course for her future seemed to be marriage to Viscount Carlisle.

Cassy glanced at the clock, noting the late hour. Surely Lord Carlisle would arrive soon. That morning, he had suggested they call one another by their Christian names, since they were to be husband and wife. However, she felt sure it would take time before she could become accustomed to addressing him as Jared.

She moved to the Queen Anne chair and arranged her nightgown around her, admiring the lace that trimmed the fragile fabric. She had done all she could do to make herself attractive for her new husband. Leaning her head against the back of the chair, she attempted to relax, thinking of the happy times when she, her mother, and her father were all together. Perhaps she and Lord Carlisle could build such a family of their own. As Betsy had said, he was a gentleman, a peer of the realm. Surely he would make a good father and husband. She closed her eyes, thinking of golden days yet to come.

* * *

Cassy woke slowly, wondering where she was and why her neck was stiff. However, as soon as the cobwebs cleared from her mind, it did not take her long to remember her wedding. She sought out the clock, and saw that it was three in the morning, with still not a glimpse of her husband. Evidently he did not find her appealing enough to spend their wedding night together.

What proved a greater temptation than a new bride, she wondered? Was it his friends who kept him from her? Or did he hold the same fondness for gambling as did her stepfather? Were they all gathered around the green baize table in the library placing bets on a hand of cards while she waited above stairs? Then there was the wine he had consumed like water throughout the entire wedding breakfast. Was he slumped in a chair, a bottle at his elbow, his bride merely a faint memory lost in the fumes of the liquor?

Cassy's cheeks were hot with anger and embarrassment. Taking the candle, she rose and carried it into the bedroom, where she set it on the bedside table. Climbing into the large bed, with its carved posts and numerous pillows, she made herself as comfortable as possible. If Lord Carlisle decided to join her, he would not find her sitting up till all hours of the morning waiting for him. It was not long before the activities of the day caught up with her, and her eyes drifted shut.

Jared's steps were not as steady as they should have been when he opened the door to his bride's room and walked softly across the plush rose carpet. Although he had spent his entire wedding night drinking with his friends, the liquor that had wrapped the others in a drunken slumber in the library had oddly enough left his senses clearer than usual. He questioned whether this was merely a unique experience or whether he would need to increase his alcohol consumption in order to reach the degree of numbness he found comfortable.

Reaching the bed, he looked down at his bride. He could barely make out her features by the guttering candle on the table and the dim light coming in the windows. Devil take it! It was nearly daybreak. He had meant to be gone by now.

Cassy stirred, drawing his attention to her again. Jared studied the lashes that lay long and thick on her cheeks. He had not taken the time to closely observe any of his bride's attributes during the brief ceremony that had made them man and wife, nor during the wedding breakfast that followed. He felt a twinge of shame. Except for the barest of courtesies, he had virtually ignored his wife and had turned to his guests for conversation.

However, there were no distractions in her bedroom, and he could not avoid admitting she was not unattractive. In fact, the longer he observed her, the more about her he found appealing.

The mass of dark hair that seemed too heavy for her in daylight spread across the pillow, framing the fragile bones that formed the pale oval of her face. Cassy shifted in her sleep, and her nightgown slid lower on her shoulder, baring a portion of skin that gleamed like pale silk in the dim light. She seemed somehow even smaller lying here, unaware she was being observed. A sigh drew Jared's gaze to her lips, which were slightly open, inviting him, it seemed, to taste their sweetness.

He could not refuse. It was his right. After all, he was her husband, and he had made no other demands

on her this night. Surely one kiss was small reward for
rescuing her from Crawford's household.

Jared leaned over Cassy and touched his lips lightly
to hers. The liquor, he would blame later, warmed his
blood and compelled him to allow his lips to linger
on the softness of Cassy's longer than he had intended.
Without the last bottle of port, he was convinced he
never would have deepened the kiss, nor would his
hands have sought out a more intimate contact with
the silk of his bride's nightgown.

He lowered himself to the edge of the bed and
shifted into a more comfortable position. Then he felt
Cassy stiffen beneath him. She was suddenly flailing,
her small fists striking his broad shoulders like angry
bees disturbed from their hive. Reaching for any
weapon to use against her assailant, Cassy's hand found
the vase on the table beside the bed. She landed a
solid blow on Jared's back, soaking both of them with
water and sprinkling the bed with roses.

"Damnation, woman. What are you doing?"

"Get away from me, you beast, or else I'll scream.
My husband will dispatch you quickly enough," she
threatened.

"I am your husband, madam," roared Jared. "And
I'll thank you to let loose of my coat so I can heed
your command."

"Oh . . . I . . ." Cassy stammered as she released
the lapels of Jared's coat from her grip.

Jared stood up, straightening his clothes and brushing rose petals off his shoulders. "Why in God's name
did you raise such a ruckus?"

"Why shouldn't I?" shot back Cassie, giving as good
as she got. "I was awakened from a deep sleep with
someone attempting to smother me. What would you
have done?" she demanded.

Jared could feel the water soaking through to his

skin. He was embarrassed to be found in such a position, but made the best of the matter. "I came to advise you I've been called back to London."

"You mean this morning?"

"I'm afraid so. I'll be leaving as soon as the coach is brought around."

"I can be ready in a short time," she said, swinging her feet over the side of the bed.

"No, no," said Jared, holding his hands palms up toward her. "I did not mean you should accompany me."

Cassy stared at him. He had not spent the night with her, and he did not want her to travel with him to London. Just what did he mean to do with her? *Please,* Cassy prayed, *don't let him be the kind of man who leaves his wife buried in the country while he takes himself off to Town.* She had endured more than enough solitude in Crawford's home after her mother's death. She yearned to experience all that London offered.

Jared immediately recognized the confusion in Cassy's expression. By Heaven! It seemed he could do nothing right when it came to his bride. She looked like a disappointed child whose doll had suddenly lost its head.

"It is not that you would be unwelcome, but I must travel quickly, and such a trip would no doubt cause you to suffer some discomfort. Also, there are improvements being made to your suite at the town house that aren't finished yet. As soon as it's completed, I'll return to escort you to Town," he promised.

Cassy began picking flower petals off the sleeve of her gown. "If that is what you wish," she replied, as if it was of no import to her.

He suddenly realized the water from the vase had caused her gown to become nearly transparent. Even though she was small in stature, it was readily apparent she was a mature woman. Stifling a groan, he cursed the events that forced him to consider his wife as no more than a mere answer to his father's demand. He shifted on his feet, uneasy with his thoughts. It was time he escaped before he broke his vow never to sleep with his bride.

"I must go." He backed away as if a poisonous snake were poised before him, ready to strike at any moment.

Jared reached behind his back when he neared the door, grappling for the handle. Profound relief poured through him when he realized the hall was only a step away.

"The staff has been ordered to honor your every request," he said, feeling the need to break the silence. "You need only ask."

"Thank you, my lord, but put it from your mind. I'm certain I shall be extremely comfortable here."

Her very agreeableness irritated Jared. She should be railing at him for leaving her alone on her wedding night. And for him to traipse into her bedroom at dawn, smelling like a brewery, and forcing himself on her while she was asleep would have been more than enough for most women. But there she was, sitting on the side of the bed with her bare feet dangling above the floor, brushing roses off her gown. Her hair was a dark cape, covering part of the wet spots that had caused Jared such mixed feelings only moments earlier, but it did not conceal her expressionless face. Anger would have been more natural, thought Jared. However, he would not question such an undemanding escape.

"I shall write as soon as the house is ready to be occupied and give you the arrangements for your travel."

"Very well, my lord," she said, but he had already closed the door on her reply.

Cassy had little opportunity to reflect on what had

happened with her husband, because the door had no more closed behind Jared than it opened to Betsy carrying a tray. The abigail had seen Jared leave the room and, though it was early, decided Cassy might welcome a cup of hot chocolate.

Betsy's brows rose when she spied Cassy sitting on the side of the bed, her gown wet and roses scattered everywhere. It must be some new ritual inspired by the gentlemen to celebrate their wedding night, she speculated. The peerage had some strange notions in their head, but as long as it made Cassy happy, she would not object.

Cassy spent the following days reflecting on the events which had taken place in her bedroom. Although she was inexperienced in what should occur between husbands and wives, she did not believe her wedding night and the following morning were commonplace.

Jared had made no apologies for his absence the night before. Nor had he made any explanation for kissing her while she was asleep. And she could not at all understand his reaction after she had awakened. It was only right that she would have been alarmed to find a man lying nearly on top of her without her knowledge. Surely he could understand that. But why had he run away? And she could not tie it in clean linen and call it anything else. Had he been so appalled at her appearance that he could not bear to be in her presence? She longed to ask Betsy, but was too embarrassed by the situation to confide in her dear friend.

She wondered where he was now. Jared had said he would return for her, but it had been nearly a fortnight without a word from him. Perhaps he had decided to

leave his gawky wife at his country estate after all. He
no doubt had numerous lovely women at his beck and
call in Town, and she would wager none of them had
broken a vase over his back, drowning him in flowers
and water. Was he with one of them now? Had she lost
her husband before she had even won him?

At the moment of Cassy's reflection, Jared was at
Gentleman Jack's, sparring with the great man himself,
hoping to forget for a moment the memory of the last
time he had encountered his bride. Although he finished the round in much the same mental state as he
began, his inattention had caused his body to take a
pounding.

Wincing as he shrugged into his coat, he was determined to attend to the matter that had occupied his
attention since he had returned to Town.

He had written to his father informing him of his
marriage, sorry he could not be there to see his father's
face when he learned the name of his daughter-in-law.
In return, he had received a perfunctory note of con-
gratulation which had done nothing to alleviate his
need for a more visible revenge. It seemed he must be
more obvious with his intentions. He would bring his
wife to Town. After that, his father would soon learn the
true state of Jared's marriage.

That evening, Jared and his friends set a new stan-
dard of decadence for every rogue who took pride in
his reputation. However, even with such a night, the
memory of his bride and their brief kiss lingered in
the back of his mind.

Jared was not an unfeeling man, just one who had
allowed what he considered to be a wrong to fester
until all reason was lost. And truth to tell, until Cassandra came along there had been nothing to force

him out of his self-pity. But now that he was married—albeit under unusual circumstances—his upbringing would not allow him to totally disregard his wife, no matter how he longed to be able to do just that.

He was being pulled first one way and then another when it came to his bride, and he did not like it at all. It was difficult to balance revenge against his father with the minimal respect he should accord his wife, when she was the source of his retaliation.

He would begin his marriage as he meant to continue it. He would not toady to his wife and travel to the country to escort her to Town. His coachman and some outriders would be enough to see her safely to London. She could expect no more from a man of his reputation.

Cassandra had been anticipating Jared's return. During his absence, she had convinced herself that she had misread his reactions to her. She had begun to remember the kiss in an altogether different light. If only she hadn't awakened and taken umbrage so quickly, the morning might not have ended with her groom running off to London. She had even allowed herself to daydream a bit about their reunion. So it was with cautious eagerness and great uncertainty that Cassandra awaited the arrival of her husband.

When the traveling coach arrived along with a message advising her to travel to London at her leisure, her hopes plummeted. Jared had not even taken the time to escort her to Town. For one of the few times she lied to Betsy, telling her Jared had apologized profusely, but could not take himself away from business to accompany her to London. Her trunks packed, she climbed into the coach a far more sober bride than should be expected.

* * *

Cassy had been in Town exactly nine days, and had seen her husband on only three of them. From the first, her marriage had been an unconventional one. There was no question Jared had intended to offer for her stepsister the day he came to their house and had ended up settling for Cassy. She did not know exactly how it had come about, but was certain her stepfather had a hand in persuading Jared to change his mind. It was not a flattering position for any woman. Nonetheless, Cassy had decided to make the best of it and had expected the same from Jared. However, now that she was actually in Town, it seemed her husband did not feel the need to exert even the smallest effort to make her feel welcome.

She and Betsy had walked in the park each day, and that was the extent of her outings. The carriage would be outside the door in an instant if she so desired, but where would she go? She would feel uncomfortable traveling about London by herself, and she had not one acquaintance other than Betsy to accompany her.

Wishing to break free of her solitude, Cassy was determined to confront her husband and ask why he had deserted her before they had even begun their marriage. The next day, she chose a spot in the drawing room where she could hear the comings and goings in the foyer, and informed Regis, the butler, that she wished to see Lord Carlisle before he left the house. It was nearly noon before she heard his footsteps approach the room.

He paused just inside the door. His bearing would have made any soldier proud; his dress was impeccable. Every strand of his dark hair was in place and his exquisitely tied cravat was held with a square-cut emerald. His coat was forester's green, which intensified the brilliance of his eyes, while the shine on his tasseled Hessians would have made Brummel stop and stare.

"You wished to speak with me?" he asked, without preamble.

Cassy had been waiting some time for Jared's arrival and sounded out of sorts when she answered.

"Yes, I do," she snapped, then lapsed into silence. All the memorized lines dried up, all the posturing and practicing in front of the mirror had gone to waste. She could go no further.

"And that would be?" asked Jared, looking more bored than curious.

"I wonder why you are avoiding me," said Cassy, throwing caution to the wind and jumping directly to the point. "It's true we know little about one another, but we will never learn unless we spend some time together. I don't like to complain, because you've made my life very comfortable, but I am extremely solitary and would welcome being introduced to some of your friends."

Jared had spent a restless evening thinking of his wife and blamed his dark mood that morning on her. He had left his dressing room awash in a sea of wrinkled white due to his inability to tie his cravat to his satisfaction earlier in the day. Nothing at breakfast suited him, and his cook was ready to give notice because of his refusal to take more than a bite of any dish offered. Now, he must face a complaining wife—the very wife who was the cause of his discontent.

"I am not avoiding you, madam. I am simply going about my business, as you should also be doing."

"I have no business," burst out Cassy in despair. "I have no friends, I have no place to visit, I have nothing to do but to walk in the park once a day. And while it is a pretty park, to be sure, it wears thin day after day. It would seem appropriate for you to introduce me to society so I may cultivate friends of my own."

Cassy bit her bottom lip. The frown on her husband's otherwise handsome face warned her she had said too much. But she would not retreat from her position. She was a married woman now, and should be able to voice her opinion without apprehension.

Jared was angry that Cassy was confronting him over issues he was forced to admit were legitimate. It would be unbearable to him if he were confined to the house for an entire day except for a short walk in the park. But damnation! Couldn't the woman go about on her own? Must he do everything for her?

Suddenly anger overwhelmed Jared, darkening his vision and eliminating what few reasonable thoughts remained in his aching head. He should not have tried to go the whole morning without a drink, but for some indeterminate reason he did not want his wife to know he could not make it through a few hours without a glass of liquor. What the devil! He would not be in this position if his father had not insisted upon marrying a woman nearly twenty-five years younger. The consequences had forced Jared into a marriage he did not want and had brought him to the position of being faced by a harridan of a wife who could not appreciate the life he was providing for her.

"All London is at your disposal, madam. Surely you can find some means of entertaining yourself. As for company, I shall place a notice in *The Morning Post* that you are in Town. That should bring enough invitations to please you. As for any further involvement in your life," he continued coldly, "do not depend upon it. There will be nothing between us—neither social or personal."

At the moment, Cassandra could not have halted

his speech if her life depended upon it. His words were cutting and his face was a frozen mask of contempt.

Jared stopped to draw a breath before he continued. If his wife wanted answers, then, by God, she would have them. "There is something you should know," he continued scornfully. "Perhaps it will explain the situation in which we find ourselves embroiled. My father and I have been estranged for some two years and more now. He is the one who insisted I marry. He wanted heirs and could not produce them himself."

Cassy's face grew hot at his plain speaking, and she regretted bringing up her discontent. It had led to revelations of far more than she had dreamed, revelations she was not certain she cared to hear. It was too late, however, for there was no stopping the furious outburst of words from the contentious man who stood before her.

"I did as he asked," continued Jared. "But you are not the wife he expected me to choose, and his desire for grandchildren will not be fulfilled from our union."

"What are you saying?" Cassy gasped.

"I am saying, madam, that our life together shall be no more than it has been since you arrived in London. We shall live together or apart, whichever you prefer. But we will not share confidences, nor a bed, nor children, nor anything else that constitutes a normal marriage. You should arrange your life as you see fit, madam, for I will not be a part of it." Jared took a step back and looked down his patrician nose at her.

"Now, if there is nothing else, I am late for my appointment." Taking her silence as an answer, Jared gave a brief bow, turned, and walked stiffly from the room. A few moments later, the outside door shut behind him.

Cassy remained where she was after Jared left. It was

beyond her capacity at the moment to put forth the effort to retire to her room, where she could be more private. She was totally humiliated by her husband's revelation of the reason behind their swift marriage. Cassy had been willing to accept that she was his second choice for a bride, that somehow her stepfather had convinced Jared to offer for her once he found Beatrice was married.

However, she was not prepared to learn she was being used as a means of revenge between her husband and his father. She was numb with disbelief that any gentleman of Jared's caliber would stoop to such a level. It took most of the morning, but at last the incredulity of her position passed and anger began to simmer beneath Cassy's calm surface, showing only in the darkness of her eyes.

Her life was in a muddle, and she had done precious little to change it. It was outside of enough that her husband had planned to desert her even before they were wed. She would not acknowledge it by going into a decline and allowing his enmity to make her miserable.

"I will do exactly as he suggested and make a life of my own," she said, speaking out loud. But his rejection had hurt more than she would ever admit. A part of her still yearned to have a loving bond with her husband. She had dreamed of it during all the lonely days after her mother's death. Now it seemed her dreams were only stuff and nonsense, the figments of a young girl's imagination.

"I have decided to find my mother's family," Cassy announced to Betsy several days later.

The abigail paused in repairing the hem on a pale

blue morning dress. "Whatever put that bee in your bonnet?"

Cassy had not confided in Betsy about her confrontation with Jared, nor his divulgence of the true reason behind their marriage. She had determined to keep silent on the issue for the moment. If informed, Betsy would immediately take her side in the matter and turn against the viscount. Cassy did not need Betsy's anger to further complicate the matter.

"I've been thinking of it since Mother died, but have not had the means by which to do it," she replied. In considering her future, Cassy had decided she would not willingly be Jared's cat's paw. She would leave him to grow old and bitter if that was what he desired, but she would not do so with him. He had made it clear she would no doubt turn gray and stooped if she depended upon him for a reason to leave the town house for something other than a walk in the park. It was time to take control of her destiny.

"How do you plan on going about it?" asked Betsy.

"I'm uncertain as yet," replied Cassy, a slight frown marring her smooth forehead. "Now that I have enough money at my disposal, perhaps I'll hire an agent to help. Do you remember anything that would guide me in the right direction?"

"Your mother kept her tongue between her teeth as far as her family was concerned. She said they were against her marrying your father and they had eloped. She was afraid her father would find them and harm your father, so she never mentioned him in all the time I was with her."

Cassy was disappointed. She was hoping Betsy would be able to give her a clue as to where to begin the search for her mother's family.

"I'm going to take tea downstairs today," she remarked, getting to her feet. "Even though they are pleasant, I must quit these rooms for a while."

"That you do," agreed Betsy. "It's time that handsome husband of yours took you out to make some acquaintances. You should have friends of your own to go about with."

Cassy wondered what Betsy would think of Jared if she knew the real motive behind the marriage.

Tea had been brought in when Regis appeared at the drawing room door. "Viscount Stanford has called, madam. In Viscount Carlisle's absence, he asked if you were at home."

"Stanford?" queried Carry.

"He is a long-time friend of Lord Carlisle," explained Regis.

"Show him in," Cassy replied cautiously. Since seeing the dark side of Jared, she did not know whether she could trust his judgment of friends.

She was reassured by the appearance of Viscount Stanford. He was a man of medium build, with light hair verging on red. His blue eyes appeared kind and his smile seemed sincere. His cravat was immaculate, its folds arranged in an intricate manner. The dark blue jacket he wore was decorated with gilt buttons and stretched tightly across his shoulders, topping cream pantaloons which reached to tasseled Hessians shined to perfection. All in all, he was the very essence of a London gentleman.

"Stanford. At your service, ma'am," he announced with a disarming smile.

"Please, sit down, Lord Stanford. I'm sorry my husband is not at home this afternoon."

"Regardless, my mission is accomplished. Came to

meet you, my lady, since it appears Jared is never going to do the honor of introducing us."

"He's been busy," replied Cassy, hoping to hide the true state of her marriage

"Just so," observed Viscount Stanford, as if he was aware of the truth that lay behind her words.

The viscount proved adept at putting Cassy at ease. They spent an agreeable half hour getting to know one another before he made signs of leaving.

"Been to the theatre yet?" he asked, in the clipped speech Cassy had come to accept as normal with the viscount.

"I would like it above all things, but Jared has no time for it," she confessed.

"My mother thought as much," said Lord Stanford, rising from his chair. "She has instructed me to invite you to attend with us on Wednesday next. My sister, Elizabeth, will be there also."

"I couldn't impose on your family," objected Cassy.

"No imposition at all," replied Stanford, waving his hand. "Mother will be in fine twig to be the first to entertain the new Lady Carlisle."

Cassy hesitated, dearly wanting to say yes, but unwilling to appear too eager. "Well . . ."

"It's settled then," said the viscount without waiting for her acceptance. "If there is anything else I can do while Jared is involved in business, you need only tell me."

"Why, Viscount Stanford," replied Cassy, suddenly shedding all shyness, "I believe your offer has been made at a most opportune moment."

The viscount nodded and again took a seat across from her. "What is it I may do?" he asked.

Now that she had his attention, Cassy wondered whether she should ask him such a personal favor.

However, she looked into his eyes and judged his offer was sincere.

"I never knew my mother's family and I would like to find them, but I do not know how to go about it."

"Know anything about them?" he asked.

"Just a few snippets she let slip in conversation, but I don't believe they would be much help. She was extremely careful to keep everything to herself."

"Know a good man who has worked for me before. Might be able to help you."

"Could you arrange for him to call on me? I would like to commence as soon as possible."

"Will bring him by tomorrow afternoon, if you will be at home."

"You may depend upon it," she said, favoring him with a radiant smile. Cassy was overjoyed. She was finally going to take the first step of a new way of life.

Three

"And he is going to assist me in finding Mother's family," said Cassy, ending her recital of Viscount Stanford's call.

"He sounds very gentlemanly," agreed Betsy, observing Cassy. Her face was flushed with excitement, and she appeared happier than she had since her mother's death "But shouldn't Lord Carlisle be the one to do that?"

"He's too busy for me to bother him with something so inconsequential," replied Cassy, avoiding Betsy's gaze.

"Yet you will ask a stranger?" questioned Betsy.

"Lord Stanford is no longer a stranger. He has even asked me to call him by his given name. It is Andrew, but he says his friends call him Drew. I felt as if we were old friends from the start, and it was not awkward asking for his help."

"What is wrong?" asked Betsy, putting an end to Cassy's chatter. "I know you better than you know yourself, and something is amiss between you and Lord Carlisle."

Betsy had caught her off guard and tears gathered in Cassy's eyes, a weakness she could not abide. "Oh, Betsy, I've struggled to keep it from you. I didn't want to destroy the respect in which you held him, but I'm afraid Lord Carlisle was not entirely forthcoming in his reason for marrying me."

"What do you mean?" asked Betsy, her eyes narrowing as she put aside the dress she was mending and gave her full attention to Cassy.

"I have only known a few days myself," revealed Cassy. Then she launched into telling of the confrontation with her husband.

When she finished, Betsy's hands were clenched in her lap, but she would much rather have had them around Lord Carlisle's neck. "It's too late to do anything about the marriage. And besides, you are still better off here than with your stepfather," she stated, rationally. "However, it would be much better to have a husband who at least had a thought for your welfare."

"I can have anything I want," replied Cassy. "Except for attention from him. He made that abundantly clear. And now that I have thought on it, I do not want it. I will not beg him for attention. Though I would dearly love to have children of my own, I would not want any of them to grow up as heartless as Lord Carlisle.

"That is why I accepted Lord Stanford's offer to assist me. Lord Carlisle has left me to make my own way. He did say he would place a notice in *The Morning Post* announcing I was in Town, but I do not know whether I can rely upon even that. In any event, without his support, I must depend upon others until I have learned the ins and outs of my new position. Lord Stanford's mother has invited me to the theatre on Wednesday next. They have a wide variety of acquaintances, and he vows it will not be long before I meet every one of them."

"I'm happy you are finally going out. A young lady your age should not be sitting at home alone, but it should be your husband showing you around."

"He has told me to expect nothing from him," Cassy reminded her. "And I have accepted that. I am living in a beautiful house and can afford anything that money can buy. There are many women who would say that is more than enough."

But will it be enough for you? wondered Betsy. However, she did not voice her question. Instead, she turned their conversation toward what Cassy should wear to the theatre.

As promised, the next afternoon Drew appeared with a gentleman by the name of John Martin. It seemed Mr. Martin had once been a Bow Street Runner before setting up his own business.

Martin was a nondescript man. He was shorter than most men, but his stocky build insured that no one would take advantage of him. His clothes were of good quality, but not ostentatious. All in all, his appearance and manner inspired confidence that he was a man one could trust.

Cassy did not want Jared to happen upon her while she was with Drew and Martin, so she met with the two men in the small sitting room at the back of the house.

"Lord Stanford tells me you desire to find your mother's family, my lady," said Martin.

"That is true, but I'm afraid I know very little about them."

"Tell me what you know," he said, his dark eyes watching her intently.

"My mother's maiden name was Howard, Dianne Howard. Her mother's name was Anne, of that I'm certain. She never mentioned her father. I think he was a harsh man who felt my father was too lowly for his daughter. I know she blamed him for driving her to elope."

"Did you get a sense of where her home was located?"

"I remember a few things. Mother mentioned a town that had a river flowing through it. She said there were five stone bridges over it, and she enjoyed standing on them, watching the flow of water beneath, when she was a child. There was an Assembly room located on the marketplace. They attended an assembly there once a month."

"Can you remember anything else?" urged Martin.

"She mentioned that lovely things were made there. Decorations from marble and alabaster, and a porcelain manufacturer. I'm not certain, but I believe I remember her mentioning silkworks and a woolmart in or near the town."

"That should help a great deal," said Martin. "Did she say anything about siblings?"

"Not that I remember. During all those years, she never told me anything of substance. It was a habit by then, I expect, and one she stuck by."

"I'll search for a town that is similar to the one you mentioned. I don't know how long it will take me, but I'll keep you advised."

"Thank you, Mr. Martin. You've been very good to come so quickly."

"It's my pleasure, my lady. If you think of any other detail, no matter how small, get in touch with me. What seems to be inconsequential to you might be the very thing we need to lead us to your mother's home."

"I will," she promised. "There is one other thing. It may not be of help to you at all, but she often told me of a special tree near the entrance to their home. It had been bent over when it was a sapling and had grown level along the ground, then upward. She pretended it was a horse and she sat there watching people pass by on the road. That's all I can remember," she said apologetically.

"You've given me more than you realize," Martin replied. "I don't want to build your hopes, but I feel there is a genuine likelihood that I will be successful."

Tears sprang to Cassy's eyes and she clasped her hands tightly together. "Thank you, Mr. Martin."

"Don't thank me yet. Even if I find her home, there is no assurance any of the family still remains."

"I am willing to take that chance. In any case, I will have more information than I do now."

He rose and gave a small bow. "Then I shall begin immediately," he replied, turning to leave.

"Drew, I am prodigiously thankful for your assistance."

"No need. Drive tomorrow afternoon?" he asked.

"I'd be delighted," she said, thankful she had a dress fit for a ride in the park.

The next afternoon, Jared stepped out into the upstairs hall at the same moment his wife appeared from her room. She was dressed for the outdoors in a blue dress and bonnet which flattered her small figure. There was an awkward moment of silence as the two stared at one another.

"My lady, you're looking well," he said, feeling compelled to say something pleasant.

"As are you, my lord," replied Cassy shortly.

"Are you going to the park?" he asked, as they turned to walk down the hall.

"No, I am going driving with Lord Stanford."

"Drew?" said Jared, unable to keep the surprise from his voice. "How the devil did you meet him?"

Cassy began pulling on her gloves. "It astounds me

that you ask. You made it abundantly clear at our last meeting you had no interest in my activities, nor did you wish to be involved in any way." Her voice was sharp, and she made no pretense of being cordial.

"That does not mean I shouldn't have some knowledge of what you're doing."

"Make up your mind, my lord. You can't have it both ways. I am only doing as you requested: taking control of my life."

They had reached the top of the stairs and Jared reached out to put a detaining hand on her arm. "Drew is an old friend. I won't have you poisoning his mind against me," he warned.

"How little you know of me to think I would expose our situation even to your best friend. If anything is revealed, it will come from your own lips. And by the way, your old friend wonders why he hasn't seen you for some time. You might do well to keep in touch. Friends are difficult to come by."

She pulled away from his hand and descended the stairs, arriving at the bottom just as Drew knocked.

"Drew," called out Jared as he followed Cassy down the stairs. "It's been far too long."

"Just so," agreed Drew. "Understand you've been busy."

"Er, yes," said Jared, abashed at being caught by someone who knew the truth of his circumstances.

"Offered to show Lady Carlisle around Town since your time is limited. Hope you don't mind."

Jared fixed a jovial smile on his face. "No. No, of course not. I appreciate it, and I'm certain Cassy does, too."

"My pleasure," said Drew. "Best go to beat the traffic in the park."

Jared watched as his wife walked through the door, smiling up at another man. Then he turned and made his way to the library. He needed just one small drink to appease the craving that pulled at his nerves until he reached White's.

Jared had been unable to keep Cassy from his mind since he had revealed the truth about their marriage and the bitterness that existed between him and his father. Although it was a certainty she would have eventually discovered it, there was no doubt he could have been gentler in the telling.

It was true he deplored his father's marriage to Eleanor, but in all good conscience, Cassy was an innocent caught up in his family's conflict. When he had first devised his plan, he had thought the security of marriage to him and all that he could offer a wife would be enough. He had not given any thought as to how she would feel being the means of revenge toward his father, nor how much his absence from her life would mean. She would be forced to make excuses when he was never with her, and there would be no doubt she held no interest for her husband.

It was not only guilt that caused him to think of Cassy. He often remembered how she looked lying in her bed, her hair spread across her pillow, the morning after their wedding. And when he had touched her lips, they were just as soft and inviting as they looked. He wondered whether it was too late to salvage some small part of their marriage or if he truly wanted to do so. If he did, it would mean his father had won again, and he didn't know whether he could accept that.

That evening, for only the second time since Cassy had arrived in London, Jared dined at home.

"I did not expect you for dinner this evening," said

Cassy, as the footman hastily set another place at the table.

Jared shook out his serviette and spread it across his lap. "It was a sudden decision," he answered.

Cassy nodded. "You made a wise choice. Cook has outdone herself tonight."

An oyster stew was served, thick with oysters, seasoned with herbs, and served over toasted bread with poached eggs and fried oysters. They both silently applied themselves to the dish, neither initiating conversation.

Jared at first felt decidedly uncomfortable facing Cassy, but when she showed no effort to make his way easier, traces of irritation began to nibble at his good intentions. He had meant to attempt to settle the ill feelings that lay between them. He had thought to escort her to an evening's entertainment and see that she met enough people to settle her into the social whirl. It was the least he could do after dragging her into a family dispute. However, her demeanor was not a welcoming one, and it took an effort for him to begin.

Jared cleared his throat. "I have received an invitation to Lord and Lady Ashfords' home tomorrow evening. They are well known for holding excellent musicales."

"Viscount Stanford mentioned it to me this afternoon. He invited me to attend with him," Cassy said, taking a serving of chicken fricassee.

"You are going, then?" asked Jared, surprised as an unexpected surge of disappointment flooded him.

Cassy looked across the table, considering her answer while her dark eyes critically appraised him. He acted as if the harsh words he had thrown at her just a few days before had never passed his lips. In fact, it seemed as if he were on the edge of asking her to the musicale. Cassy did not understand him at all, but she decided to make the best of things.

"I have no gown that is suitable."

Jared studied his wife's attire. Her gown was brown with a pattern of small yellow flowers. While it might be adequate for an early walk at a country home, it was by no means acceptable for an evening in Town. If viewed by anyone in the *haut ton*, it would be judged *du vieux temps*, completely out of fashion.

This was a problem he could easily solve. "You must have an adequate wardrobe for the Season. I did not think . . . that is, I thought your father . . ."

"Stepfather," she reminded him.

"I thought your stepfather would have provided for you."

"In the normal course of events, that would be the case. However, my stepfather only allowed me three new gowns, and everyday ones at that."

Jared was astonished. "After the settlement I made?"

"And you thought he would spend something on me?" Cassy laughed. "Robert Crawford cares nothing for me," said Cassy. "I was merely a minor irritation which refused to go away, but as long as I stayed out of his way he did not overly complain. Then you came along with your offer and he realized I was worth something to him."

"I did not mean . . ."

". . . to offer for me?" she finished for him.

"No. To force you into something you did not want," he corrected her.

"There is no reason to avoid plain speaking, my lord. I knew you did not want to marry me. We were not acquainted, and I had seen you with Beatrice more than once. You were offering for Beatrice, but since she was already wed, Crawford somehow tricked you into asking me. I thought then that marriage to you would be preferable to staying with my stepfather and perhaps being forced into something far worse. So I suppose I cannot complain no matter what I am served up."

Dinner had been forgotten. The tempting courses cooled on the table between them.

"However, I am not so certain now that my judgment was correct," she continued. Her gaze lowered and she remained silent while Jared sat staring at her.

Jared did not like the turn their conversation had taken. He had married Cassy because he was convinced it would humiliate his father. He had not meant to liberate an orphan whose stepfather would not furnish her with an adequate wardrobe, and he did not intend to be trapped into feeling sorry for her. That could only lead to a greater involvement with Cassy than he wished.

Damnation! Where was the time when a man could marry and carry on as he had before? Life would be much more simple if that were the case. Well, he would not allow himself to become more concerned with Cassandra than he was. If he did, it would ruin his plans for revenge.

"You must order some gowns tomorrow," he said, breaking the silence and changing the subject.

"But I really don't need . . ."

Jared held up his hand. "I'll hear no more about it. Even though our marriage may be an unconventional one, your appearance nevertheless reflects on me. I won't have people surmising that I can't afford to dress my own wife fashionably."

Cassy did not mean to brangle with him. "As you wish, my lord."

"Once you have an adequate gown, there is a play I think you would like . . ."

"Excuse me, my lady," said Regis, stepping into the room.

Thank God for the interruption, thought Jared. He had almost invited his wife to the theatre. Why was he acting like such a rattle-brained green-head? He had nearly invited her out twice in one conversation when it was apparent she had no desire to be with him. It just wouldn't do.

"There is a person at the front door who says she is your sister," continued the butler.

"Beatrice?" said Cassy, in astonishment.

"I do not know, madam. She said she was Mrs. George Vance."

Cassy's mind was in a whirl. What was Beatrice doing showing up on her doorstep at this hour of the evening? She had not heard from her stepsister since her marriage to Vance and had never thought to see her again. Beatrice had always held her in small regard, and after Cassy's mother had died, Beatrice had used her stepsister as little more than a maid, having her fetch and carry whenever the spirit moved her. Now Beatrice was here, and Cassy did not look forward to hearing the reason behind her arrival.

"If you will excuse me, my lord," said Cassy, rising from her chair.

"I'll accompany you," Jared offered, beginning to rise.

"No," she replied. "I think it best if I see Beatrice alone first. You may join us later if you like."

Jared lowered himself back into the chair. "As you wish," he said, a slight scowl on his face. He did not know what Beatrice wanted, but from his limited knowledge of her, it could not bode well.

Cassy was surprised by her stepsister's appearance when she first entered the drawing room. Beatrice's hair was mussed and her gown wrinkled. The skin beneath her eyes appeared bruised, as if she hadn't had a good night's sleep in a sennight.

"Oh, Cassy. I'm so glad I caught you at home. At first I thought you would already be gone for the evening, and I didn't know what I was going to do. The servants, of course, would not know me, and I did not relish sitting on your steps until all hours of the morning."

Cassy could tell her stepsister she could have found her at home any hour of the night or day, but there was no sense in embarrassing herself when it wasn't necessary.

"I'm surprised to see you," replied Cassy. "I can never remember Mr. Vance traveling to London, but I suppose you were able to convince him." Cassy smiled, and attempted to compose her face in a pleasant expression as she settled into a chair across from her stepsister. It was a decidedly odd time of evening to be paying a call, but Beatrice did not always follow the rules. Cassy would bide her time until Beatrice told her the reason behind her visit.

"I did not convince George to do any such thing, and I never shall again," Beatrice said, her features twisting in distress.

Cassy had seen Beatrice cry on command whenever it suited her. However, this time she seemed genuinely agitated. "Beatrice, what is wrong?"

"George is dead," she announced baldly.

"Dead!" repeated Cassy in dismay. "But how could that be? He seemed in such good health at your wedding."

"The doctor said his heart just gave out and, of course, his children blame me." Beatrice touched the corner of one eye with a lace-edged handkerchief. "I have been left with a mere pittance on which to live. The remainder of his estate was inherited by his children, and they ordered me from the house and from their lives forever."

"I can't believe this," gasped Cassy.

"Well, believe it you must. I have been on a coach that has jounced and jostled me until my head is spinning. I was given little time to eat or freshen myself from the time I got on until I got off. I have been cruelly treated by everyone since George's death, and I cannot bear it if you turn me away." With that she burst into huge, gasping sobs, burying her face in her hands, her shoulders heaving.

Cassy stared at her stepsister, wondering whether her tears were real and, if so, whether she would welcome consolation.

"What is going on in here?" asked Jared, entering the room, serviette still in hand. "I can hear the commotion all the way to the dining room."

"I'm sorry you were disturbed, my lord. I believe you are acquainted with my sister, Mrs. Vance. As you can see, she is extremely upset. Her husband recently passed away, and from what I can understand she was left without a roof over her head."

Beatrice's sobs quieted once she realized Jared was in the room. "My Lord Carlisle," she said, looking up at him with a tear-stained face. "What Cassy says is true. The fates have been cruel to me." Her hand crept up to lay over her heart. "I had nowhere to turn except to my beloved sister in hope she would extend a helping hand."

"My wife's family is welcome anytime."

Cassy glanced at Jared in surprise, she then remembered Jared and Beatrice had once almost been a couple until Beatrice pushed a little too hard, a little too soon.

"Is there anything we can do?" he asked.

"I am so at sixes and sevens, I can't think straight."

Once again she touched her eyes with her handkerchief.

"You must stay with us until you get matters straightened out," Jared generously invited.

Beatrice's tears ceased flowing and she smiled up at
Jared. "My lord, you are too kind. I would never impose on your hospitality if I had any other choice."

"Think nothing of it. You must get settled in, then
have dinner. I'm certain whatever fare you encountered
on your journey could not compare with our table."

Beatrice made a delicate moue. "You would not believe what I was offered. I could not eat a bite during
the entire journey."

"Then I won't keep you," replied Jared. "I'll be
gone by the time you finish dinner, so I will bid you
a pleasant night's rest."

"You are going out?" Beatrice said in surprise, looking from Jared to Cassy.

Cassy wondered whether Beatrice expected Jared to
stay and entertain her the entire evening. If so, she
was in for a sharp disappointment. Jared had not once
allowed her to affect his life since the first day of their
marriage, and she did not anticipate he would change
for Beatrice.

"Unfortunately, I have already made plans," he answered, a pleasant smile on his face. "I hope you understand." He raised her hand to his lips, never removing
his gaze from hers.

Beatrice smirked with pleasure. "I do, my lord."

"Good. Things will look better in the morning," he
predicted. Stepping back, he looked toward Cassy. "We
shall continue our discussion later."

Both women watched as he strode from the room,
then turned toward one another again.

"I was convinced you wouldn't mind," said Beatrice.
"My only other refuge was Father's house, and I

couldn't bear to be buried in the country all alone.
Besides, I don't believe he would welcome me, since
I have so little money at my disposal. Then there's always the chance he would try to marry me off again,
and I will not be tied to another dotty old man."

Beatrice's face was set in stubborn lines, and Cassy
knew there was no moving her for the present.

Cassy rang for the housekeeper. "Let us get you settled in a room," said Cassy, attempting to make the
best of the situation. Her husband had invited her stepsister to stay, and Cassy could do nothing about it.

"I hope it will be large and well furnished," said
Beatrice. "George's house was so dark and dismal, and
the furnishings—well, you wouldn't credit it."

"I expect we'll be able to find something that will
satisfy you," said Cassy, leading the way out of the drawing room, past the trunks in the hall, and up the stairs.

Beatrice approved of her room, which was furnished
mostly in blue and gold and had large windows which
allowed ample light to enter. There was a sitting area
around the fireplace and a rosewood desk near one
of the windows.

"This is more like it," Beatrice said, turning in a
circle to inspect every corner.

"I think you'll be comfortable here," said Cassy, remembering her own room in Crawford's house. It had
been small and shabby and cold in the winter, a far
cry from what she was offering Beatrice. She wondered
whether her stepsister would consider the contrasts
and feel the least bit of contrition.

"I will require a maid," said Beatrice, tossing her
shawl and reticule on the nearest chair.

Cassy nearly laughed out loud. It was obvious Beatrice had not given a moment's consideration to the

difference between what Cassy had been given at Crawford's house and what Beatrice was experiencing in Cassy's home. Beatrice had not had an abigail of her own at home, but she expected one here.

"I'll speak to the housekeeper and have her assign one of the maids to see to your needs."

"Good. Now, I am starving. Let me freshen up and then we can go down to dinner."

Cassy felt a chill run over her. Beatrice had been in the house less than an hour and already she was issuing orders.

"I cannot believe you are staying home this evening. There must be dozens of events going on in Town."

"More than a person can attend in one evening," agreed Cassy.

"Once I get settled, I intend to try," revealed Beatrice.

"Do you mean to stay long?" asked Cassy, the chill returning.

"Well, I must get my affairs straightened out. Surely there is some way I can get more from George's estate. I will confer with Jared tomorrow and see if he has any suggestions."

"And how long do you think that will take?"

"Why, I have no idea. You cannot wish me gone already after all the years you lived under our roof."

"My mother married your father," Cassy reminded her. "It was none of my doing."

"Regardless, you were there, and long after your mother died, too."

"My mother brought enough to the marriage to save your father from ruin with his creditors. I remember he was enormously thankful at the time."

Beatrice waved her hand. "That is long past. Jared has welcomed me, even if you don't, and I believe he said for me to stay as long as I wished."

A wave of despair swept over Cassy when she realized Beatrice intended to settle in for an indefinite stay. While she had not yet enjoyed the Season as she should, she had basked in the privacy her new life offered. She did not think that would continue with Beatrice in the house. She remembered how it was living with her stepsister before her marriage and shuddered.

As the two women made their way downstairs, Cassy straightened her shoulders, determined she would not allow Beatrice to run her life again. She was a married woman now, not the girl Beatrice had run roughshod over whenever she felt the need. However, she acknowledged it would not be a smooth transition, one she looked forward to not at all.

While they were at dinner, Beatrice once again raised the subject of why Cassy had not accompanied Jared that evening. "I cannot understand why you choose to sit at home when all London is filled with such gaiety."

Cassy did not wish to admit the truth to her stepsister. "As you know, I am accustomed to a quiet life. It is taking some time for me to become adjusted to such a fast pace."

Beatrice laughed. "It would take me no time at all," she bragged.

"But you have had a Season and are familiar with the *ton.*"

A scowl appeared on Beatrice's face. "I am, and I remember that the women did not welcome me. I believe they were jealous of the men I attracted. However, you won't have that problem once you begin going about."

Cassy glanced at Beatrice, but her stepsister was cutting up a piece of chicken and did not even look her way. Evidently, she considered her observation to be unremarkable. Cassy kept quiet. There was no reason to come to daggers drawn over a comment that was very likely the truth.

What concerned her was Beatrice's behavior now that she was in London. Cassy could not see her stepsister wearing black and sitting at home while everyone else danced their way through the Season.

Cassy's fears concerning Beatrice's behavior proved correct the second day of her visit. She could not believe what she was hearing from her stepsister.

"Oh, my lord, surely you can find time to attend the Thorntons' ball. I would dearly love to attend, but I dare not do so alone and Cassy has refused to accompany me."

"Beatrice, your husband has recently died. You cannot go to a ball so soon," said Cassy. The three of them were seated around the luncheon table, and Beatrice had used the occasion to approach Jared.

"Oh, piffle! George and I were barely married, and look at the state in which he left me. I owe him nothing, and I do not intend to waste a year of my life over the man. There will be no black gloves for me," she boasted. "How many people even know I was married? It was never announced in the newspaper, and I have been gone from London for a year. If the news gets out, people will assume I've already ended my period of mourning."

"People will know," insisted Cassy, hoping Jared would agree with her. "Someone will uncover it and won't be able to keep it to themselves."

Jared called for a glass of wine. It wasn't that he could no longer go without it, he assured himself, but it would enhance the grouse he was consuming. He had no idea why he had decided to have luncheon at home today. He had come downstairs just as the women were going into the dining room and made a spur of the moment decision to join them.

He had avoided his wife and her stepsister for the last two days for similar reasons. He did not mean to be drawn into their lives. He was determined to remain aloof from Cassy because of his inconsistency whenever he was around her. One moment he was swearing she would never be a part of his life, the next he was on the verge of asking her to the theatre. The only way to avoid these contradictions, it seemed, was to stay away from the woman.

As for Beatrice, he had firsthand experience with her grasping ways. Even though he was married, he did not trust she wouldn't try to capitalize on more than a slight family relationship.

As the two women continued discussing Beatrice's availability to attend entertainments, Jared's thoughts took a new twist. Beatrice was a newly widowed woman, stepsister to his wife, and her reputation was not what it should be. His father was not reacting nearly as unfavorably about his marriage to Cassy as he had expected. But what would his father say if his son formed a close association with Beatrice, particularly when he was so recently wed to her stepsister and should be concentrating on setting up his nursery?

Jared smiled and silently toasted his latest idea. "I shall be happy to escort you to the ball this evening," he said to Beatrice, interrupting her argument on why she should go about as she chose.

Beatrice's mouth was agape. "You will?" she asked, not believing what she had heard.

"Of course. Take a nap this afternoon, for we will be out most of the night," he advised her. Finishing his wine, Jared dropped his serviette beside his plate as he stood. "I must be off, but I shall be back in time to change for the ball," he promised.

"Did you hear that?" said Beatrice as soon as Jared left the room. "We are going to a ball tonight."

Cassy rose. Her mouth was a firm straight line, her face an expressionless mask. "*You* are going to the ball," she said. "Not I."

"What do you mean? Of course he meant the both of us. You are his wife."

"Just so," replied Cassy, and walked from the room.

Cassy made herself scarce that evening. Even though her marriage was far from what it should be, she would not allow anyone to see the humiliation she suffered when her husband and stepsister departed for an evening's entertainment.

A few days earlier, she had ordered several new gowns with the promise one would be ready for her night at the theatre. She would find her way on her own with the help of Drew and his family. Jared and Beatrice were welcome to one another.

Four

Beatrice concealed her smirk of satisfaction as Jared helped her into the coach. She had never gotten over her infatuation with the viscount and was devastated when she heard Cassy had married him. When her husband died, she was determined to take advantage of the situation. After all, Cassy was only a stepsister. Family loyalty did not enter into it.

So, although the *ton* might frown on her for not mourning her husband, Jared would soon set them straight. And if society also disapproved of any relationship she might have with her brother-in-law, there was nothing illegal in it. She might even marry him if he asked, for she and Cassy were not related by blood. But first, Cassy must be gotten rid of before Jared would be free to marry again.

What Cassy did not know was that Robert Crawford had insisted Beatrice go to her stepsister for shelter after the death of George Vance. He expected her to form a liaison with the viscount in hopes of deriving additional funds to once again relieve his gambling debts.

Beatrice smiled as Jared settled onto the seat beside her, mistakenly thinking she had won the first skirmish.

Jared prayed his being with Bernice would have the desired effect on his father. He was sacrificing his peace of mind to be with the woman, and he should receive something in return.

"You are in particular good looks this evening," he said as the carriage rolled over the cobblestones.

Beatrice laid her hand on his arm. "I wore this dress especially for you. I hoped you would like it."

Jared's gaze traveled to the gown's low neckline, just as she had planned. "I like it very well," he said, laying his hand atop hers.

Jared was fully aware of Beatrice's machinations. He had seen them all before. But it fit his plans to play her game in order to heighten his revenge. He would see word reached his father that he was spending more time with Beatrice than with his wife. Before Jared was finished, Lord Waycross would believe his son would never have a legitimate child by Cassy, but that there was a distinct possibility he would produce a bastard with Beatrice.

Jared smiled at Beatrice and tightened his hand over hers. Retribution was at hand.

The ball had attracted even more of the *ton* than Jared had hoped. He stood at the edge of the dance floor, his eyes scanning the crowd, searching for his father's tall figure.

"Where is your lady?" asked Viscount Brandon, appearing at his side.

"She's not my lady," growled Jared, then nodded toward the dance floor. "She is dancing with some dandy who fancies every woman in the room finds him undeniably handsome."

"Perhaps you shouldn't have allowed her to dance with him, then," observed Brandon.

"If it weren't that I have use for her, I would gladly

wish the young cub luck with her," said Jared. "Have you seen my father tonight?"

"Not yet. But he could be anywhere in this mob," replied Brandon, as the music ended. "I will leave you to it, then, and will speak with you tomorrow to discover if you were successful."

Jared saw Beatrice and her partner approaching. "Are you certain you can't stay for a while?"

"I mean no insult, but I heard enough from Mrs. Vance when you first arrived to last me the remainder of the evening."

"I don't blame you. I only wish I could escape so easily."

"Where the devil's your wife?" asked Brandon. "I expected to see her this evening."

"She is not as easily led as I first believed," admitted Jared. "I am hoping that escorting her stepsister will cause my father even more irritation than an unworthy wife. However, if he is not here to observe firsthand, I am sacrificing an evening for nothing." Jared frowned and searched the room again with no success. His father was nowhere to be seen.

"I must go. Mrs. Vance is nearly here. I'm meeting up with Weston to visit Harriette Wilson," Brandon revealed.

"Then I don't need to wish you a good evening," replied Jared, thinking with envy of a congenial evening with the well-known Wilson sisters. The women were the most sought after Cyprians in London. A man could always find witty conversation, a buffet supper, and a bit of dalliance at the Wilson establishment.

"I will give Harriette your regards," offered Brandon. "Will we see you at White's tomorrow, or has your time been spoken for by Mrs. Vance?"

"I am not so poor spirited as to be led around by

a woman such as Beatrice both day and night. I am with her for a specific purpose, which evidently will not be accomplished this evening. If I can persuade Beatrice to return home early, then I may see you at Harriette's."

"I will not count on it," said Brandon, as he disappeared into the mass of humanity surrounding them.

Jared did not get to see Harriette Wilson that evening. Beatrice insisted upon staying at the Thorntons' ball until the very last strain of music faded. By then Jared had more than enough of Beatrice and polite society in general. He hoped his father would begin attending the *ton's* events so he would not be forced to endure too many more evenings such as the one just finished.

Beatrice sat close by his side in the coach, winding her arm through his and laying her head on his shoulder, feigning fatigue. The scent she wore seemed stronger than when they had begun the evening, and he wondered whether it would seep so deep into the material of his jacket that he would need to discard it.

It was with a great sense of relief that Jared reached his bedchamber and allowed his valet to help him out of his evening clothes. "Air that jacket as best you can," he said, as Thomas removed the garment. Thomas sniffed, then wrinkled his nose and carried the jacket out of the room.

Jared reached for the bottle, which was a constant fixture of his rooms. He had consumed only enough liquor to see him through the evening, and his nerves were telling him they needed the calming influence of a drink. Pouring a large glass, he propped up against the pillows in the massive bed that occupied his room, considering his plan of revenge. He wondered whether he should revise it, for his effort thus far was a distinct failure. He emptied his glass, closed his eyes, and relaxed his head against the pillows. He would think about it tomorrow when he was with his friends. Perhaps they would have a suggestion.

Cassy was alone in the drawing room the next morning. Exhaustion had finally forced her to sleep the night before without hearing Jared and Beatrice return. She had promised herself she would not think about the two of them together, and was looking for a distraction when Regis announced Mr. Martin was in the foyer.

Her spirits immediately lifted. "Show him in, Regis."

"My lady, I may have news," said Martin, as soon as he stepped into the room. There was a sparkle in his eyes, and Cassy took it as a sign of success.

She crossed her fingers for luck, then quickly dispensed with the childish gesture. "What is it, sir?"

"I believe the town your mother spoke about may have been Derby. The river and bridges seem to match what you've told me. I am going to travel there first thing in the morning."

Cassy burst out with a laugh of sheer delight. "I am so excited," she said.

"Don't get your hopes up yet," he warned her. "There's a possibility this isn't the town we seek. I merely wanted you to know why you wouldn't be hearing from me for a few days."

"Thank you. Thank you very much. You will come to me straightaway upon your return?"

"As soon as I clean away the dust of my travel," he promised, smiling.

"Do not even wait for that," she said effusively, walking with him to the door and wishing him well.

* * *

Brandon, Thornton, and Henderson were already gathered around a table at White's when Jared arrived. "Where's Weston?" he asked.

"Haven't seen him since last night. He was with a new ladybird," Henderson informed him.

"He's probably still with her," said Thornton. "He's always head over heels for a few days. Then we'll see him creep back."

"You missed a grand evening at the Wilsons'," said Brandon, his eyes still heavy-lidded from such a late night. "Did you run into Lord Waycross last night?"

"Luck was against me," Jared replied with disgust. "I suffered through an entire evening with society's finest for nothing."

Thornton poured him a glass of port. "Does that mean you're giving up on your plan?"

"My tactics have changed slightly." He then went on to tell them how he planned to take Beatrice about, encouraging his father to think a serious dalliance was going on.

"But what of your wife?" asked Henderson.

"She can carry on as she sees fit. You remember, my intentions from the beginning were to avoid any semblance of a marriage with her. I will not give my father the joy of grandchildren," he spat out.

"Will we meet her?" asked Brandon.

Jared laughed and drank down half the liquor in his glass. "I hope not. I don't want you feeling sorry for her and thinking I'm a scoundrel for using her as I am. If you do meet her, however, remember that she is far better off in my household than with Crawford."

"Saw Crawford last night. He was going into the Pigeon Hole," said Brandon, mentioning one of the infamous gambling hells located on St. James's Square in London. "Looked pleased with himself."

"Gambling away the settlement I made," speculated

Jared. "He had better enjoy it, for it will be the last he'll get from me." His face was grim for a moment as he recalled how Crawford had been too tightfisted to buy Cassy a few gowns.

"Bring us a new bottle," said Jared to a nearby footman. He turned back to his friends, his face an undisguised mask of distaste. "I must make good use of my time today, for I am promised to another mindless *ton* event this evening."

A round of drinks was poured and the men lifted their glasses, toasting the future success of Jared's revenge.

Beatrice joined Cassy for tea that afternoon, full of information about the night before. "You may depend upon it being the event of the Season," exclaimed Beatrice. "I've never seen such a crush. The decorations were of the first stare and surely cannot be equaled. There were even bowers made of flowers where a couple could have a few private words." She tittered and glanced at Cassy from beneath her lashes. She hoped her sober-faced stepsister was imagining her with Jared in a private, flower-enclosed alcove.

"And the gowns," she went on. "One was more lovely than the others. I could immediately see that I need to refurbish my wardrobe. What I have just won't do."

"I'm happy you enjoyed yourself," said Cassy.

Beatrice accepted a cup of tea and filled her plate with a various assortment of cakes. "I had forgotten how lively London can be. I was simply danced off my feet and did not rest the entire time, except for when we went in for dinner." Beatrice's eyes glistened with the memory. "We are going out again tonight," she said.

Cassy concentrated on keeping her face expression-less. She couldn't imagine Jared attending a *ton* function two nights in a row.

"Jared says he will take me whereever I want to go," confided Beatrice. "Of course, I'm certain he meant to include you."

It was the last thing Beatrice wanted, but she felt she must extend herself until she found out the true state of affairs between Jared and Cassy. Theirs did not seem a particularly close marriage. However, it was possible to misjudge these situations.

"Thank you, but I believe I will refuse your kind invitation," replied Cassy.

Beatrice was unsure as to whether Cassy was teasing her. "You should get out more," she advised. "You must find it deadly dull to sit here day after day."

"I am making do," said Cassy. "I am not accustomed to continual rounds of entertainment, so I do not miss it."

Beatrice shrugged her shoulders. "It is your decision, of course, but I don't understand it at all." Her face brightened. "I am going to the modiste this afternoon. Perhaps you would like to help me choose my new gowns."

Cassy could imagine spending an afternoon selecting material and patterns with Beatrice. "I have an appointment of my own," she said. "But I will give you the name of an excellent modiste."

"I have already selected someone. So many of them do not have the imagination I require."

Cassy raised her eyes to heaven, whispering a small prayer that Beatrice would rein in her imagination.

Cassy was thankful to have the possible discovery of

her mother's home to occupy her mind, for the next few days nearly sent her into a fit of the dismals.

Since Jared had taken Beatrice to the ball, she hung onto his every word as tightly as she hung on his arm. The two left each evening for some entertainment or another, and Beatrice no longer put forth the effort to inquire as to whether she would like to join them.

One morning, Cassy was in the small sitting room at the back of the house embroidering when Beatrice strolled in. She covered a yawn with her hand, then dropped into a chair near Cassy.

"What an evening we had," she said, watching for Cassy's reaction. "I danced until I wore holes in my shoes. I am unable to understand how you can sit around sewing while there is so much to do."

"I will move at my own pace, and it is not the same as yours," replied Cassy, her needle moving evenly in and out of the material.

Beatrice was still attempting to judge the true circumstances of her stepsister's marriage. She could not coax one word from Jared about his wife, and Cassy was not any more forthcoming.

"Don't you feel it's your duty to accompany Jared on occasion?"

"If Jared feels the need for my company, he will tell me so," said Cassy.

"I can't imagine that you don't insist," said Beatrice. "He is such a handsome man and knows just how to treat a woman. He took my eye immediately when I came to Town for my Season. I'm certain he was nearly ready to propose when father insisted I return home."

Cassy's anger was rising, and she could not accept Beatrice's version of happenings. "You mean when he decided he'd rather spend his money on gambling than on your come out."

Beatrice appeared surprised at her plain speaking.

"No matter," she said. "It doesn't alter the fact that Jared exhibited considerable interest in me."

"I wonder why he didn't offer for you, then?" asked Cassy, unable to sit still and accept her stepsister's barbs without some retribution.

"In fact, Father believed he meant to offer for me until he found I was already married," continued Beatrice, ignoring Cassy's question.

"Did he?"

"Yes. He said Jared seemed disappointed, then accepted that you were the only other choice. I'm surprised your pride would allow you to take second place."

"Do you truly believe Jared did not have other women who would wed him? Or that he would be forced into a marriage he did not want?" Cassy stuck her needle into the material and placed it into the sewing basket beside her chair, then leaned back in her chair awaiting Beatrice's answer.

Beatrice could not say yes, for that would make Jared appear weak. However, if she answered no, she would be admitting Jared had wanted to marry Cassy. "There could have been circumstances of which we do not know."

Cassy attempted to give her a triumphant smile. "In any case, I am his wife," she said.

"That does not mean he cares one whit about you," hissed Beatrice, unable to hide her venom. "He is never in your company, and I doubt he has even shared your bed."

Cassy felt the heat in her face. She had never given over to her temper in front of Beatrice, but enough was enough. She rose and looked down at her stepsister. "You had best concentrate your energy on something other than my personal activities, for they are none of your business," she advised, her body tight with tension. "I might also remind you that this is my home as well as Jared's, and you are a guest in it. I will not be spoken to as if we were still in Crawford's house." Cassy moved unhurriedly out of the sitting room, closing the door softly behind her. As she reached the upper hall, she wondered why she had allowed herself to pull caps with Beatrice over a man who had married her only for revenge.

Beatrice sat quietly until Cassy had enough time to be away from the room, then gave a shriek of anger. She pounded a pillow, then sent it flying across the room to hit the wall and fall to the floor. How dare Cassy speak to her like that! After all she and her father had done for the chit. They had given her a roof over her head after her mother died, which was more than many would do. She would ensure that Jared heard of his wife's rudeness. From the way he was treating her, he would not allow Cassy to speak to her in such a manner.

Jared was in the library when Beatrice ran him to earth. He was not at all happy about having his peace disturbed, but realized he still needed to keep Beatrice appeased if his plan was to work.

"Jared, I am so relieved you are at home. You know I am not one to complain, but I have been treated so rudely that I cannot keep it to myself."

There was a high blush on Beatrice's cheeks and, indeed, she did appear to have been at odds with someone. "I can't imagine any of the servants being impertinent, but tell me who it was and I will deal with it."

"It was not a servant," Beatrice corrected him. "It was Cassy."

Jared hid his impatience. "Surely it was merely a sisterly spat, and is nothing in which I should be involved."

"You are entirely mistaken. This was more than a squabble. Cassy was cruel without a cause, and nearly ordered me from the house." Beatrice modestly lowered her lashes. "I believe she is jealous that we are going about together." Whatever Beatrice expected, it was not that Jared would burst out in laughter.

"I'm sorry, Beatrice," he said, when he had regained control of himself. "I assure you Cassy is not jealous that I am escorting you around Town."

"How can you be certain?" she questioned, disappointed that he was not taking her complaint seriously.

"It is not something I wish to go into," he answered, "but believe me, it must have been something else that caused her to get into a row with you."

"Whatever it was, she is certainly acting strangely. She's nothing like she was when she lived with us."

"She's a married lady," replied Jared. "That can certainly change a person."

"Then you intend to do nothing?" Beatrice asked.

"I will not be drawn into it," he replied firmly. "Now you must allow me to finish this letter if you expect us to attend the theatre this evening."

He knew his threat would work, and a few moments later, unappeased but silent on the subject, Beatrice closed the door behind her as she left the room. He stretched his legs out before him and contemplated his tasseled Hessians. It was odd, but Jared experienced what felt like pride in hearing that Cassy had nearly tossed Beatrice out bag and baggage. If only an evening at the theatre with Beatrice did not loom before him, he might have thoroughly enjoyed the moment.

Cassy went for a walk in the park, attempting to clear her mind of Beatrice and her vindictiveness. Her new gowns had arrived the day before, and this evening she was to attend the theatre with Drew, his mother, and his sister. By the time she and Betsy returned to the house, she was looking forward to the evening.

Before she knew it, the time had arrived. The gown she had chosen to wear was blue, with a modest neckline and small puff sleeves. Betsy drew her hair to the back of her head and fashioned it into a smooth chignon. Cassy again thought of having her hair cut. It was heavy and thick, took forever to dry when she washed it, and was difficult to fashion into anything but the simplest style. But it was too late to do anything now, since Drew would be arriving any moment.

She felt suddenly shy as she walked downstairs to greet Drew. He complimented her until her cheeks grew warm, and she was in an agreeable mood when she climbed into the coach to join his family.

Cassy was immediately drawn to both Drew's mother and sister. Lady Stanford was a lovely woman with just a few silver strands visible in her blond, stylishly arranged hair. Elizabeth was a near copy of her mother. Both women were fashionably dressed, and Cassy envied them their style.

Before they reached the theatre, they were all chatting away as if they had been friends for years instead of mere minutes.

"It is regrettable Jared is unable to show you around Town," remarked Lady Stanford, as they joined the line of carriages moving slowly toward the theatre entrance. "He is highly knowledgeable, and there is no doubt you would enjoy it vastly. We will be poor replacements, but I hope you'll agree to go about with us until you become established in the *ton* and form attachments of your own."

"I could not impose," objected Cassy.

"Please say you will," exclaimed Elizabeth. "I would

like it above all things to have someone more my age to attend the entertainments."

"Usually gets her way," remarked Drew, smiling at his younger sister. "Better to agree and be done with it."

"If you're certain it isn't an inconvenience, I would be happy to join you," said Cassy.

"Then it is agreed," said Elizabeth, clapping her hands. "If it is amenable, we shall call tomorrow and plan which events we will attend. There are so many diversions, and we shall enjoy as many as possible."

Elizabeth's happiness was contagious and Cassy was smiling as their carriage reached the entrance of Covent Garden.

When they entered, Cassandra was struck silent by the magnificence of the theatre. The vestibule staircase ascended between two rows of Ionic columns, between each of which was suspended a beautiful Grecian lamp. The box in which they sat was separated from the others by slender, richly gilt pillars. Cut glass chandeliers lit up the seats, which were covered with light blue cloth.

"The audience is as entertaining to watch as the play," observed Cassy, after the first act was over.

"Many only come to see and be seen," said Lady Stanford, applying her fan vigorously to stir up the still air in the box.

"Look at the box directly across from us," instructed Elizabeth.

The box Elizabeth indicated was filled with women whose cheeks and lips were brightly painted and whose dresses showed nearly all of what nature had endowed them.

Elizabeth held her fan before her face as she spoke. "Those are the Fashionable Impures," she informed Cassy. "We are not to know about them, or at least not to acknowledge that we do. However, I think they are the most interesting people in the theatre."

"You would not say that if you were forced to live their lives," remarked Lady Stanford. "I would not wish that on any woman."

"Look, isn't that . . ." began Elizabeth, before her mother tapped her arm with her fan.

But it was too late, for Cassy had already followed the direction Elizabeth had indicated and saw Jared in a box to the right of the stage. Beatrice was by his side, wearing a gown nearly rivaling the courtesans' finery.

Jared's dark head was bent close to Beatrice. They were so caught up in one another, they were oblivious to everything about them. They shared a laugh and Jared straightened in his chair, his gaze drifting over the pit, then on to the opposite boxes. It would only be a matter of moments before he would see her, Cassy realized. Loath to be caught staring at him, she quickly looked away, commenting to Elizabeth about the ceiling, which was painted to resemble a cupola. Only then did she allow herself to glance at Jared's box again.

As she suspected, his dark gaze was fastened on her from across the width of the theatre. However, she did not know how to interpret it. Surely he was not irritated because she had attended the theatre with the Stanfords. He had made it plain she should go her own way and he would go his, but perhaps he thought she was spying on him. Averting her eyes, she began a lively conversation with Elizabeth and Lady Stanford. *Let him stare all he wants,* she decided. *I will not be intimidated.*

Jared watched as Cassy laughed and talked and appeared to have a very good time indeed. But that was what he wanted, wasn't it? He did not want to be responsible for her other than supporting her. She had done what she had promised. She was making her own way without any help from him. Yes, it was exactly what he wished, exactly what he had told her to do when he had exploded in anger. Then why couldn't he look away? What kept his attention riveted to her? He was so engrossed, Beatrice resorted to tugging on his sleeve before he turned to her.

The next day Cassy was up early, despite her visit to the theatre. She did not want to attribute her restless night to seeing Jared and Beatrice together, but she hadn't been able to get them out of her mind. As morning approached, she chastised herself for being such a goose, fluffed up her pillows, and forced her mind clear of the two. She had slept peacefully until Betsy arrived with her chocolate, curious to hear all about her evening.

"I had such a wonderful time," Cassy said, her eyes glowing. "The theatre was beautiful, and the plays were more than I ever imagined." She went on to describe her experience in detail, never mentioning Jared and Beatrice.

Betsy was happy to see Cassy was finally enjoying herself. "And tonight you will dance the night away."

"I don't expect that," replied Cassy. "But I hope I will meet some agreeable people and hear music and watch others dance."

"Pish! You will be right among them," predicted Betsy. "A lovely young woman like you will have plenty of partners."

"I don't aspire to being all the rage," Cassy said laughing. "But I would like to dance once or twice. Perhaps Drew will take pity on me."

"You don't need pity. You are pretty enough and smart enough to attract any man."

"And you are highly prejudiced," accused Cassy, still

smiling. "But it certainly helps to know someone has confidence in me."

"You should have it in yourself," declared Betsy.

"There are things that make it impossible," replied Cassy, recalling Jared and Beatrice so close together at the theatre the night before. Her anticipation of the ball that evening was suddenly marred by the memory.

"I'm going downstairs to the drawing room and wait for Lady Stanford and Elizabeth to arrive," Cassy informed Betsy. She had not even had time to sit down before Beatrice followed her into the room.

"There you are," said Beatrice. "I thought you might still be abed after attending the theatre last night."

Cassy hoped they would not get into another brangle today. "I am well rested," she replied pleasantly.

"That is more than I can say," remarked Beatrice. "We were out till nearly dawn."

"Then it appears the surprise is that you are not still abed."

"I had no choice. We are promised this afternoon for a picnic with Jared's friends." Beatrice watched Cassy closely, waiting for her reaction.

Cassy glanced out the window where the sun was shining brightly."It should be a fair day for a picnic," she commented. "Cook will fix an excellent basket to take with you."

"Is that all you have to say?" asked Beatrice, frustrated with Cassy's reaction to her announcement.

"No, it isn't," replied Cassy firmly. "Don't forget the wine. You know how much Jared likes his wine."

Cassy's continued detachment nettled Beatrice. "Don't you care that Jared is taking me instead of you?"

"Haven't you noticed that husbands and wives go

their own way every day in the *ton?* It is not done for a gentleman to appear to be in his wife's pocket."

"Of course, I've noticed," sputtered Beatrice.

"Then why should I allow myself to be thrown into a flutter over such a common practice?" she inquired innocently.

Cassy smiled as Beatrice whirled and stomped from the room. Perhaps she was learning how to play the game after all.

Five

The Stanfords had come and gone. The women had drawn up a list of events they wanted to attend, had taken tea, and enjoyed a considerable gossip about the people Cassy would meet in the coming days. Lady Stanford finally persuaded Elizabeth they must take their leave, promising they would be back that evening to convey her to the Manvilles' ball.

As soon as the door closed behind them, Cassy climbed the stairs. Elizabeth's inconsequential chatter had taken her mind from Beatrice and Jared for a time, but once she was left alone with her thoughts, she could not stop thinking of her husband with her stepsister.

Cassy straightened her shoulders. She would not allow Beatrice to ruin her first ball. It was time to stop thinking of herself as someone who had no other recourse than to suffer in silence. That was what Beatrice expected, for Cassy had done just that since her mother's death. But now she was a woman of means who held a place in society despite her husband's inattention. Beatrice might have Jared, but she couldn't legitimately take a place at his side as long as Cassy was alive. Cassy reached her room, closed the door, and leaned back against it with a sigh of relief.

"You should rest this afternoon," suggested Betsy,

entering from the dressing room. "You have a long night ahead of you."

"You're right," said Cassy. "I want to be at my best this evening." She wondered whether she would see Jared and Beatrice at the ball. She hoped fate did not bring them together again, for she did not enjoy the encounters nor Beatrice's remarks afterward.

"I'll introduce you around," said Drew, pulling her arm through his as they entered the Manvilles' ballroom.

"And I shall make you known to the important hostesses later in the evening," promised Lady Stanford, before she and Elizabeth left to join a group of their friends.

As promised, Drew and Cassy strolled around the edges of the dance floor, stopping every few steps so Drew could acquaint her with the people he knew. She was warmly welcomed and felt she was finally beginning to make a place for herself. However, they had not traversed halfway around the room when Drew abruptly halted.

He hesitated a moment, then indicated a couple not far away, saying, "That is Lord and Lady Waycross." He was aware she had not yet met her father-in-law and did not want her surprised by his presence.

Cassy followed his gaze and discovered a very handsome couple. The man's hair was going silver, but she could see the resemblance Jared shared with him in his tall, erect figure and proud bearing. The lady was lovely in a gown of deep rose that made Cassy aware of the inadequacies of her own dressmaker. Her light blond hair was dressed in a cluster of curls at the back of her head. Cassy wondered how Jared could object to his father marrying such an elegant lady.

Drew hesitated for a moment, then realized he had no time to be subtle. He drew Cassy aside. "Don't take offense, but has Jared told you about the reason behind your hasty marriage?"

Cassy lowered her gaze and a flush of color rose to her cheeks. Was everyone aware of the circumstances of her wedding? If so, how could she hope to hold up her head in public?

"Jared said there were ill feelings between him and his father. He acknowledged he hoped to get a measure of revenge by marrying someone not quite suitable," she admitted.

Drew cursed silently at Jared's unfeeling comments. "What he said is only a half-truth. Jared and his father are at daggers drawn, and have been since the earl's marriage, but you are as respectable as anyone in this room, and don't let anyone convince you otherwise."

Cassy gave him a brave smile, and straightened her shoulders. "I'll keep that in mind," she promised.

"There's something more you need to know," he began, but got no further because they were suddenly face-to-face with Lord and Lady Waycross.

"Lord Stanford, perhaps you will do the honors and introduce me to my daughter-in-law."

"It is a pleasure to finally meet you," said Cassy, before Drew could utter a word.

"Thank you, my dear. And I am equally gratified to make your acquaintance. May I introduce my wife, Lady Waycross?"

"Not so formal," insisted Lady Waycross. "After all, we are family. My name is Eleanor," said the woman Cassy had been admiring just a moment ago.

"You're right," said Lord Waycross jovially. "We should not stand upon formality, but should be on a more familiar standing."

Cassy thought it would be difficult to address such

a distinguished man by his Christian name, but perhaps it would become easier once they were in one another's presence more often.

"You must call me Cassandra or Cassy, whichever you prefer."

"I wish to apologize, Cassy. My son is remiss in his duties and should have seen we were introduced long before this," said the earl.

Cassy did not want to be the cause of any more trouble between father and son. "Please don't blame him, my lord. He has been extremely busy as of late. In truth, he could not escort me this evening because of pressing business that could not wait until the morrow."

"Yes, I can see," replied Lord Waycross, staring at the door.

The small group turned their gaze in the same direction. Jared and Beatrice had just entered the ballroom. Beatrice wore a dress cut so low Cassy wondered how she managed to keep it from falling from her shoulders. Perhaps Jared and the men who quickly surrounded them also worried for her discretion, for they could not keep their eyes from her décolletage. Cassy was struck speechless with embarrassment.

Lord Waycross turned to Cassy and took her hand. "Don't worry, my dear. I know my son far better than most people. There is no need for you to be put to the blush by his deplorable manners. I've learned it's best to ignore him when he disregards civility. Why not go in to dinner with us so we can become better acquainted?"

"I . . . I don't know," stammered Cassy, still unnerved by the arrival of her husband and stepsister.

Lord Waycross offered her his arm. "Trust me," he said. She took his arm, and he led her in to dinner chatting amiably, while Drew followed with Lady Waycross.

* * *

"Isn't that your father and his wife with Cassy?" asked Beatrice, looking across the ballroom.

"It is," Jared answered shortly.

The last thing Jared wanted to see was his father and Cassy chatting in such an agreeable fashion. He had expected Lord Waycross to give his wife the cut direct, considering her family and the speed with which they were wed.

"I understood that you and your father were not on good terms," remarked Beatrice.

"You understood correctly," he replied. "However, it seems my wife has not yet heard the news."

Jared's temper rose considerably the longer he watched Cassy, his father, and Eleanor clustered in such an intimate grouping. Observing that Drew had made the introduction only made matters worse. The chit was turning his own friends against him. Just when he thought things could not go more astray, Cassy took his father's arm and they strolled into the dining room, followed by Drew and Eleanor.

"Dance with Weston," he growled, nearly thrusting Beatrice into Ranson's arms. He stalked through the French doors, across the terrace, and into the small garden. His temper was so near the surface he was not fit to be with people. Stepping into the shadows, he pulled a slender flask from his jacket and took a soothing drink, easing his anger in the only manner he knew.

"Will the two of you bring us plates?" asked Lady Waycross, once they had chosen a table.

Lord Waycross met her gaze, then gave an almost imperceptible shrug. "Shall we wait on the ladies, Drew?"

"My pleasure," he replied, holding the chair for Cassy to be seated before he left.

"I'm happy we finally met," said Eleanor, in a manner which seemed sincere. "And I don't want to appear bold, but I felt it important that we talked. I would have called, but Edward felt we shouldn't intrude. Men are sometimes guilty of having very little common sense when it comes to people and their feelings." She smiled, and Cassy could not help but respond to her affability.

"I agree with you completely," she said, returning Eleanor's smile.

"There is no way we can avoid Jared's feelings toward me and his father. He is angry beyond all reason that I married Edward. I cannot say he is not justified to a certain extent, but I believe he and his father should have settled their dispute long before now." She glanced over her shoulder and saw her husband and Drew approaching.

"Oh, dear, I have much more to relate and they are almost here. Above all things I wish us to be friends, but first you should hear the full story of the break between Edward and Jared, and my part in it from my point of view." She looked over her shoulder again, and found Lord Waycross and Drew were nearly upon them. "Will you call on us soon so I may continue?"

"What is it the two of you are gossiping about?" teased Lord Waycross.

"I was inviting Cassy to take tea with us," replied Eleanor. "And you must come, too," she said to Drew.

"Delighted," responded Drew.

"Good! We shall settle on a date later," said Eleanor.

"I shall look forward to it," said Cassy.

The dinner continued pleasantly. It was as if everyone at the table had decided that nothing troublesome would be discussed that evening.

* * *

"I wonder," said Cassy, when they were on their way home, "why we were the focus of so many eyes. Certainly it was unexceptional that we should all dine together, even though Jared chose to spend his time elsewhere."

Drew had taken his mother and sister home first, as their home was nearer. He and Cassy were now alone in the carriage and could speak frankly.

Drew had become fond of Cassy. He admired the way she carried on under the most difficult circumstances, circumstances even more unusual than she understood.

He also sympathized with Jared's plight and worried that his friend had immersed himself in bitterness too long, using liquor to numb his resentment in order to carry on as usual. But Jared's actions this evening had swung Drew's support to Cassy. She deserved to be aware of the events shaping her life. Lord Waycross might eventually tell her once they became well enough acquainted but, left alone, Jared would never explain the entire circumstances surrounding their marriage.

"There's something more you should know," said Drew.

"I'm not convinced there is a need to know more," she said in a small, quiet voice. "Married life is not turning out to be anywhere near what I thought it would be. And it has not been for the better. If it is something that I can do without hearing, I would appreciate your not sharing it with me. Or, if I must hear it, can we put it off until I am more rested?"

"I'm afraid not," said Drew. "After tonight, there will be even more talk, and I think it's important you know the full story before you face any of our social termagants."

"Now I'm certain I'm not going to like what you are about to say."

"Probably not, but it must be said. Better from a friend than from someone who wants to embarrass you."

Cassy sighed. "Go again, then," she said in a resigned voice.

"There is no easy way," he said. "Before she met his father, Eleanor was to marry Jared."

The coach rolled over the cobblestones as the silence built inside.

It had gone on too long for Drew's comfort. "Cassy?"

"What happened?" she whispered.

"Jared met Eleanor during the Season. He was taken with her almost immediately, and she seemed to reciprocate his feelings. It only lacked the announcement to make their engagement official. Then Jared invited Eleanor and her parents to Waycross House in order to meet his father. I expected to see him back in Town bragging about being betrothed to a diamond of the first water, but weeks went by and I didn't once catch sight of him.

"The next time I saw him, Eleanor was married to Lord Waycross and Jared was too drunk to recognize me. I've rarely seen him fully sober since then. He's learned how to handle his liquor until he can function even when drinking heavily. Then there are days when he disappears completely, and I know he's probably locked in his rooms emptying one bottle after another."

Silence hung heavy in the coach for several minutes. So this was what Eleanor was so anxious to explain, thought Cassy.

"Is that all of it?" she asked, unable to keep her voice entirely steady.

"I think that's enough."

"Why didn't you tell me earlier?"

"Jared is your husband," said Drew. "It was up to him to explain, but after tonight I saw he wasn't going to tell you anything more. Jared is no longer the man I once knew. Unremitting anger and liquor have changed him, and until he comes to his senses, it isn't at all fair keeping you uninformed."

"Why hasn't anyone mentioned this to me before? From what I understand this is exactly the kind of scandal the *ton* lives for."

"The *ton* can keep its collective mouths closed when the denouement appears to offer more entertainment than the first telling," observed Drew.

The coach drew to a halt in front of the town house. Drew helped Cassy down and walked up the shallow flight of stairs to the door with her.

"I'm sorry I had to be the one to tell you," said Drew.

"I would rather hear it from you than anyone else," replied Cassy.

Drew was concerned that she showed no outward distress. "I can come in and keep you company, if you like."

"Thank you," said Cassy. "But I am tired and I have a great many things to think over."

"May I call on you tomorrow?"

"You are always welcome," she said, touching his arm before turning and entering the house.

Cassy was grateful she had told Betsy not to wait up for her. She didn't think she would have been able to face her with the knowledge she now carried. She needed time to adjust to what Drew had told her.

She tossed her gloves and reticule onto a chair and draped her shawl over the back before dropping to the settee in front of the marble fireplace. Suddenly she buried her face in her shaking hands, thinking of the humiliation Jared had heaped on her without her knowledge.

Cassy finally raised her head and stared into the empty fireplace. The tears dried on her face and her anger began to build. Jared should have fully explained why he and his father were at daggers drawn. It was apparent he wanted to punish his father for taking Eleanor from him, but he should not have used Cassy in such a way. She had done nothing to deserve the degradation he had caused her.

And what was it Eleanor wished to say to her? Surely nothing she could add would wrap up the whole affair in white linen. Did she think to absolve herself from what had happened? She seemed to have more character than that, but Cassy was seriously beginning to doubt her own judgment.

She thought back on the kiss she and Jared had shared the morning after their wedding. Until this moment she had seen it to be an honest kiss, but now she considered it as just another deceit among many. If Jared could not offer her love or respect, he could at least have been honest with her. There was no reason for him to pretend passion, no matter how slight.

Cassy's attention was drawn to noise in the room next to hers. If it was Jared, it was the first time since their marriage that he had returned home while she was still awake.

A knock sounded on the door between their rooms, and Jared entered before she could answer.

"What do you think you are doing?" he demanded. He stood over her, his fists clenched at his sides, his face contorted with anger.

Cassandra felt enough anger herself to ignite a fire if one had been laid in the fireplace. She would not be bullied by this man who coveted his father's wife. "I am sitting here wondering why I ever allowed Robert Crawford to browbeat me into marrying you."

"Don't attempt to feed me that pap. You were happy to be rid of Crawford and his pap of life," accused Jared. "You jumped at the chance to marry into this." He gestured around the room.

Cassy considered his allegation before answering. "It wasn't the money that prompted me to accept your offer. It's true I was extremely unhappy with my stepfather. It is also equally as true I was apprehensive about marrying you. However, I remembered the happiness my mother and father shared and convinced myself you were sincere in wanting a real marriage. I thought we might achieve at least a small measure of their contentment."

"Then you're a fool," he asserted ruthlessly.

"Perhaps so, but at least I am not fool enough to waste away yearning for someone who is married to another."

"You don't know what you're talking about," he charged.

"Oh, don't I? How long did you think you could keep it hidden from me? Did you think I could spend time with your father and stepmother without learning your secret?"

"She is not my stepmother," snarled Jared.

Cassy uttered a laugh which caused Jared to stop and study her carefully. "After all this time, you still cannot face the truth."

"You should have stayed away from my father," he said, ignoring her denunciation.

"You made no effort to guide me into society. You even advised me to continue on my own because you would not be part of my life. I followed your advice, and it led me to cross paths with Lord Waycross this evening. Perhaps if you had not been so absorbed with Beatrice you might have been able to keep me from him, but you could not tear yourself away. That was your downfall."

"I knew you would bring up Beatrice's name. She told me you had always been jealous of her, and now my friendship with her has caused you to side with my father."

"I am not siding with anyone," Cassy stated firmly. "And, as a warning, Beatrice does not have friends. She has acquaintances who are her friends as long as they are useful to her. It seems to me the two of you deserve one another."

"What I don't deserve is a wife who turns against me at the slightest whim."

"The slightest whim," repeated Cassy, in total disbelief. "Sir, you are too much in your cups to hold a reasonable conversation. Please go back to your room. If you so desire, we can continue this conversation at a time when your faculties are not befuddled by too much liquor."

"I am not drunk," he objected.

Cassy stood, her hands on her hips, staring at the man with whom she had hoped to build a life. "You reek of liquor, sir. So much so it is offensive to me. I will need to raise the windows and air out my room when you depart, which I hope will be immediately. If not, I shall call your valet and have him help you back to your suite."

Jared had never had a woman order him out of her presence, and he found it humiliating beyond all reason. As much as he would have liked to continue to argue the merits of whether he was completely castaway or not, he did not want to risk the embarrassment of Cassy's carrying out her threat. He turned on his heel, but before he could take a step, his wife spoke.

"Jared," she said softly. "In case you're curious, I intend to see more of your father and Eleanor in the future. Much more."

Jared stomped out, slamming the door behind him.

Since his marriage, Jared had fought to control his drinking. He was able to drink with his friends without notice because they imbibed as frequently as he did. However, there were times when he was unable to do anything but give in to an unbridled need for liquor. At those times, he would have his valet bring bottle after bottle to his suite of rooms until he could no longer lift a glass to his lips.

The night of his argument with Cassy was one of those nights. His revenge was not working out as he had hoped. His wife, upon whom he had counted his father to disapprove, had instead spent a large part of what was evidently a pleasant evening with Lord Waycross. And if that wasn't outside of enough, she had rung a peal over his head as it had never been rung before. The final humiliation came when she had declared him a drunk, ordered him from her room, and advised him she had future plans to see his father.

It was all too much. It was essential he escape the devils that pursued him. "Thomas. Thomas," he called impatiently.

"Yes, my lord," said the valet, entering the room.

"Bring me a bottle," demanded Jared, pulling the cravat from around his neck and tossing it across the room.

"There's one here, my lord."

Jared crossed to the table and poured himself what would be the first of many glasses. "Then bring me another," he ordered, gulping down the fiery liquid to quench his consuming thirst.

* * *

Beatrice was worried. It was nearly noon, and she had not seen Jared all day. She had knocked at his door, but his valet said his lordship was resting and insisted he could not be disturbed.

Jared had acted strangely since he had observed Cassy and his father together at the ball. He had left her abruptly and reappeared later, bringing the smell of liquor with him. He had been rude and inattentive to her the remainder of the evening, which she had not appreciated at all, yet she had been afraid to complain.

Beatrice could not coax him to dance with her even once. He stood where he could watch Cassy and her father at dinner, and continued to brood and watch the group until they had taken leave of one another. They had left immediately after Cassy did and had come straight home.

Beatrice assumed he was going to take Cassy down a peg for spending so much time with his father, and she longed to hear what he said. She had left her room meaning to listen at the door, but that interfering valet came and went with bottles until she was forced to abandon her idea. Beatrice was fairly certain that Jared and Cassy did not share a bed, and, seeing the number of bottles the valet carried, Beatrice was convinced Jared would be too much in his cups to be with Cassy. So much the better for her plan. She would sweeten Jared up on the morrow.

But here she was with nearly half the day gone, and Jared had not yet left his rooms. There had been a Venetian breakfast she had yearned to attend today, and she was sorely vexed he had not appeared in time. She should have known better, though, for he had evidently spent the night drinking heavily. She had enough experience with her father to know the aftereffects.

As if he had materialized with her thoughts, Regis announced her father.

"How are you progressing?" he asked without greeting her.

"I am having an enjoyable time," replied Beatrice, knowing exactly what he meant and attempting to irritate him.

"Damn it. You know that is not what I mean. Have you found out how to get your hands on some of Carlisle's blunt?"

"You mean you are short of funds again?" she asked sweetly.

"Don't play with me, girl," he warned. "My position grows more perilous by the day. I am forced to sneak around town like the veriest blackguard in order to avoid my debtors."

Beatrice laughed. "But you are a blackguard. Do you expect never to be called to book?"

"It is only a run of bad luck," he huffed. "The next time I'll win enough to pay off all my debts."

"I'm in no position yet to ask Jared for any more than a roof over my head. He and Cassy are not getting along, but the break isn't complete yet. If only she would return to the country estate and leave Jared here, I'm certain I could make better progress."

"Or if she would disappear altogether," said Crawford. "And I might be able to arrange that."

"What do you mean?" asked Beatrice.

"Accidents happen every day," he explained. "It would be a tragedy for someone as young as Cassy to be involved in one serious enough to fatally injure her. Yet think how opportune should you be there to comfort her grieving husband."

Beatrice smiled at her father. "Yes, how opportune," she agreed.

Cassy went in to luncheon hoping she would be the only one at the table that day. However, her hopes were ruined when Beatrice arrived a few minutes later.

"I can only take time for a bite," said Beatrice. "My gowns were just delivered and I am anxious to see whether they are all I expected."

"I'm certain they will be exactly what you wanted," replied Cassy.

"I hope so. I would not like to tell Jared I spent his money unwisely."

"What do you mean?" asked Cassy.

"Why, didn't he tell you? Jared offered to pay for my gowns. I attempted to talk him out of it, but he insisted. He's such a generous man," Beatrice gushed.

Cassy considered her sparse collection of gowns and wondered why she had not bought more. If Jared could give Beatrice carte blanche to dress herself, then why shouldn't Cassy take advantage of the opportunity also?

Cassy felt the heat of anger begin to rise and fought it down. It wouldn't do to allow Beatrice to see how she felt.

"I was surprised to see you last night," said Beatrice, sitting across from Cassy. "You gave me to understand you did not go out to entertainments."

"I told you I would do things at my own pace, not that I would never go out in the evening," Cassy corrected her calmly. "Um. You really should try the rolled fish fillets. The filling is seasoned just right."

Beatrice placed a fish fillet on her plate, took a bite, looked pleasantly surprised, and took another. "Jared was not happy to see you with his father," she said, once she swallowed.

"He told you so?" asked Cassy, wondering whether he actually confided in Beatrice. "The asparagus in cream is the best I've tasted. I highly recommend it."

Beatrice was having difficulty in keeping track of the conversation and tasting the dishes Cassy directed toward her. "He didn't need to. I could tell he did not like it."

"Thank you for your concern, but you needn't worry. We discussed it last night after we returned home." Cassy served herself with an artfully shaped croquette. She cut into the crisp brown outside and a delicious scent wafted across the table to Beatrice. "Croquettes of chicken and ham," Cassy said, closing her eyes in obvious enjoyment.

Beatrice accepted a croquette, then cast her mind about to remember Cassy's last comment regarding Jared. "Last night?" she finally asked.

Cassy nodded. "I didn't know he had returned until he came to my room. He stayed so long, I had to practically drive him back to his suite. I was exhausted by then, and could scarcely keep my eyes open. But, as you know, Jared is a gentleman, so he reluctantly honored my request and returned to his room so I could get a few hours of much needed sleep."

Beatrice could not believe her ears. Could she have been so wrong about Jared and Cassy? She had not seen even a hint of affection pass between them. Had Jared returned home and gone directly to Cassy's room? Did he actually prefer this slip of a girl to a mature woman? She could not believe Cassy held any sway over Jared.

"And he's no longer angry?"

"Jared angry with me?" Cassy asked, as if the question were absolutely absurd.

"But we are going out this evening." Beatrice looked thoroughly confused.

"Of course you are," agreed Cassy. "Have some cheese-cake. I had cook make a raspberry sauce to go over it. It's my belief that fresh raspberries can't be equaled as a sauce for dessert."

Beatrice liberally spooned sauce over the cheesecake and tasted it. "Jared should never do anything to lose his cook," she said.

"We don't intend to," Cassy answered. "However, these were my mother's recipes today. Crawford would never allow her to use them. He always said he was a beef and potatoes man. I'm glad you enjoyed the dishes." Cassy rose and placed her serviette beside her plate. "I hope you have a pleasant time this evening. I certainly intend to do so."

"You're going out again?" said Beatrice surprised.

"Of course. I'm just beginning to enjoy the Season."

Beatrice watched her stepsister leave, then returned her attention to dessert. The conversation had not gone as she had planned. She had intended to embarrass her stepsister, but her continual interruptions with comments concerning the food had kept Beatrice's concentration just a little off kilter, until it was difficult to keep track of what Cassy had said.

Cassy stood in the hall deliberating what she should do next. She did not know how much longer she could bear to live in the same house with Beatrice. Just when she thought she had conquered her temper when it came to her stepsister, something else occurred to prove that she was still susceptible to Beatrice's connection to her husband.

She had taken the wind out of Beatrice's sails by speaking of Jared coming to her room the night before. She only hoped Jared would be discreet if Beatrice asked him about the visit.

Six

That evening Beatrice paced the drawing room. She was dressed in a new gown that her dressmaker advised was just the thing. The tiny sleeves barely hung on her shoulders, and the neckline revealed far too much of her generous bosom. She lacked only jewels to be what she considered complete to a shade. She wondered whether she could convince Jared to allow her to wear some of the diamonds she knew were in his family. Perhaps he would see her and offer them without her asking, she thought. If he ever arrived downstairs.

"I see you are ready to go," said Jared from the doorway.

Startled, Beatrice turned, her skirts swirling around her ankles. "I was beginning to wonder whether you were still going."

"Why wouldn't I?" he asked, surveying her gown.

"Well, you *were* deep in your cups last night, and I . . ."

"I was not drunk," he said between gritted teeth.

"Of course you weren't," she quickly agreed.

"I was merely tired. It had been an exhausting day."

"Are you certain you are up to going out this evening?" she asked, hoping beyond hope that he would insist upon continuing with their plans. She did not look forward to spending the evening at home alone.

"I am fine as fivepence," insisted Jared.

"No doubt due to your late-night rendezvous with Cassy," she said, vexed beyond all bearing by thoughts of the two of them together.

"How did you come by that knowledge?" he asked, his voice as cold as his eyes.

"She told me," spat Beatrice.

"Cassy is my wife. What we do behind closed doors is private, and I do not wish to discuss it." He stared at Beatrice just long enough to make her feel distinctly uncomfortable. "Shall we go?"

Beatrice did not like to give up so easily, but the cold light in Jared's eyes told her she had nearly pushed him to his limit. "I am looking forward to tonight," she said as she took his arm.

Jared did not look forward to the evening's entertainment. The Winthrops were old friends of his family and, while he wanted revenge, he did not like to appear a rapscallion in their eyes. However, Beatrice had insisted upon attending their ball, and he could not afford to alienate her yet.

She had arrived downstairs wearing a pomona green gown with a lemon yellow overskirt; neither shade flattering her at all. The neck was low cut with a tiny strip of material on each arm passing for sleeves. The hairdresser who had arrived earlier in the day had used hair pieces to fashion a bun on top of Beatrice's head, woven round with small braids and finished with curls falling from around the concoction. It looked as if the hairdresser could not decide on an appropriate style and had used as much as possible in order to cover every demand Beatrice might make. Jared rationalized that the overabundance of hair was brought about because it would produce a larger bill for him to pay, rather than making Beatrice more stylish.

"I have always desired to meet Lord and Lady Winthrop. I consider them the most fashionable of *le beau monde*," she gushed.

"I would not count on seeing them this evening," said Jared. "There will most like be such a crush that the Winthrops will be swallowed in the crowd." He hoped he was right, because he did not relish the idea of two of his family's oldest friends seeing him with Beatrice. He felt a flash of guilt that he was using others so shamelessly for his own benefit. But things had gone too far for him to regret his decision or attempt to halt what he had started. He had, after all, married only to antagonize his father, and that was far worse than going about with Beatrice. He was not such a dupe as to believe she had appeared as an innocent on his doorstep. She was there to ingratiate herself and derive whatever benefits she could for herself and her worthless father. He could clear his conscience of using Beatrice, he decided.

Jared's prediction proved to be true. As they approached the Winthrop house, they joined a line of carriages that inched slowly toward the brightly lit entrance to deposit their richly dressed passengers at the end of a strip of red carpet that led into the town house. They had arrived too late to be welcomed in the receiving line and edged directly into the crowded ballroom.

"Oh, how wonderful," said Beatrice, her eyes shining with excitement. "This is beyond all comparison."

Jared had to admit Lady Winthrop had gone to considerable lengths to transform her ball room. In addition to the masses of blossoms which were *de rigueur* for any entertainment, flowering trees had also been positioned around the edge of the room, and a fountain sparkled in one corner.

"Look who's here," said a voice from behind Jared.

He turned and found his coterie of friends, who had just arrived.

"What are you doing here?" he asked.

"Thought we'd drop by and see what was drawing you to these events," said Brandon.

"Apparently it's the lovely ladies," added Weston, looking at Beatrice, who simpered at his compliment.

"Gentlemen, may I present Mrs. Beatrice Vance? She is stepsister to my wife and is currently visiting us."

The men all murmured greetings, taking her hand and saluting it.

"Mrs. Vance," said Brandon, "if this dance has not already been claimed, perhaps you would care to dance."

"I would like it above all things," said Beatrice, placing her hand on his extended arm and accompanying him to the cramped dance floor.

"Remind me to do something extraordinarily extravagant for Brandon when this is all over," said Jared.

"We have come to save you this evening," said Henderson. "To show you that we are friends beyond all compare."

"We are each going to take a turn at entertaining Mrs. Vance," added Thornton.

"Then I will be forced to do something extraordinarily extravagant for each of you," said Jared.

"No need," said Brandon. "We felt we should do something to help since we wrote the note that got you into all of this."

"I would probably have done no better myself," replied Jared. "When you begin to feel guilty, remember that the idea was to embarrass my father. If we meet tonight, I believe I will have accomplished that end."

"Go find yourself a bottle and someplace private in which to enjoy it," advised Thornton. "We will keep Mrs. Vance so busy she will never even miss you."

Jared took his friends' advice and chose a secluded alcove at one of the many windows lining the room. He caught occasional glimpses of Beatrice as she danced, and silently thanked his friends for allowing him an evening free of her incessant praise of all that comprised the *ton*.

As for himself, society as a whole had little to recommend it when they gathered for the Season. Taken individually, most of the men and women of the upper ten thousand were quite congenial. However, when they assembled in London, sharing one another's company every day and night, competing for the title of best host and hostess or firing off their daughters to bring a gentleman up to scratch, the results were not always pleasant.

Jared grinned wryly. How could he criticize anyone in this room when he was involved in such a scheme against his father? Before he could answer, he had company.

"Man after my own heart, hiding behind the draperies," said Drew as he edged into the alcove beside Jared. "Saw Mrs. Vance. Knew you had to be here somewhere."

"I don't know whether I like the reasoning behind that deduction," said Jared. "But I suppose I can't blame the connection on anyone else but myself."

"Not finding it comfortable?" asked Drew.

"I never expected to be comfortable with Beatrice as my companion," revealed Jared, " but I did not expect it to be so wearing. I keep reminding myself it will all be worthwhile if it will serve to mortify my father to the greatest degree."

"Lord Waycross is a strong man. Will take something outrageous to overset him," judged Drew.

Jared considered his words. "His desire for a continued line of Morelands is great, and I am the only one able to give him that. If he feels his expectations for grandchildren are threatened, he will be galled to the quick. Once he sees me with Beatrice and knows she is also living beneath my roof, he will begin to question the credibility of my marriage."

"And what of Cassy?"

Jared had avoided thinking beyond the culmination of his revenge. However, each time he saw his wife, it prodded at his consciousness more insistently.

"Cassy will be well taken care of. She will have anything she desires, more than she ever had with Crawford."

"To be sure," Drew agreed, "but what of family? Most women want children. Will you deny her that in order to punish your father?"

"She should have known . . ." began Jared.

"But did she?" insisted Drew.

Jared had not even considered advising Cassy before they were married as to what she should expect. He had been so wrapped up in his own misery that he had considered little else than the satisfaction he would gain in thwarting his father's ambitions. Should he have revealed his plans to Cassy and allowed her to choose whether she wanted to spend her life childless?

"No," he admitted to Drew. "She did not know what I had planned for our marriage. I doubt whether she or any other woman would have agreed to wed me if she had."

Jared poured himself another drink from the bottle he had brought to the alcove, swallowing half of it in a single gulp. "It is too late to undo what has been done," he said.

"Have come to know family means a great deal to Cassy," said Drew.

"Then she will need to make do devoting time to

an orphans' home," snapped Jared, tired of feeling guilty.

"Might look elsewhere for their father," suggested Drew.

"What do you mean?" he asked, his voice hard. "Is Cassy having an affair with someone?"

"Not that I know of," responded Drew. "But wouldn't be surprised if in a few years, when she has learned the way of the *ton* and is yearning for a child, she does so. Look around you. Common enough occurrence."

Jared did as he suggested and saw several women whose children bore their husbands' names, but were rumored to have been fathered by one of their cicisbeos. Surely Cassy would never subject him to that embarrassment. But how would she feel in a few years' time with their marriage remaining an empty one? Would she choose to fill it with another man's children, or would it seem important to her that her legal husband be their father? Jared was only beginning to realize what he might have set in motion with his hasty decision to marry.

"Speaking of Cassy," said Drew, nodding at the dance floor.

Jared followed his gaze and saw his wife dancing and laughing up at another man as if she had not a worry in the world. And why shouldn't she? he thought. Hadn't he gone his own way since their marriage with seldom a thought to his wife? Jared was distinctly uncomfortable with the eye-opening insights Drew's remarks had sparked, and he took comfort in the only manner he knew, by tipping the bottle and filling his glass once again.

"Looks as if you might get what you've been wanting for so long," remarked Drew. "Lord and Lady Waycross are here."

"Where?" demanded Jared.

"Just at the door now," Drew responded.

"Take this," said Jared, thrusting his bottle into Drew's hands. "And for God's sake, don't try to be peacemaker this evening."

"Wouldn't think of it," said Drew, watching him closely.

Jared stepped from the alcove and scanned the room, searching for Beatrice. He saw her sipping a cup of punch with Harry Thornton and made his way through the throng to their side.

"It's time we danced," he said to Beatrice, taking her cup and handing it to Thornton, who looked at him oddly.

Jared led Beatrice across the room until their paths crossed with Lord and Lady Waycross. "What a surprise," he said, stopping in front of them.

"Jared, it's good to see you," said his father.

"My lady," said Jared, giving a slight bow toward Eleanor, who nodded in return.

"I don't believe you know Mrs. Vance. She is my wife's stepsister," he revealed, watching his father's face. "I have been showing her about London."

"How very cordial of you," said Lord Waycross. "I am certain Mrs. Vance appreciates it."

Beatrice uttered a nervous giggle. "Jared has been more than generous to me. He even furnished me with a new wardrobe," she revealed, lifting the material of her overskirt.

Jared could not have been more pleased with Beatrice's response if he had written it for her himself.

"I could not refuse her," he said, looking at Beatrice fondly, hoping he appeared to be sincere.

"It is very nice," said Eleanor, appraising Beatrice's gown with critical eyes. "Such an unusual color combination."

"I chose it myself," confided Beatrice. "I must admit

that the modiste attempted to talk me out of it, but I insisted on the pattern and material being exactly as I instructed. I believe the result proves my taste is much superior to hers."

"Indeed, it is, madam," agreed Lord Waycross, before turning his attention to Jared. "And is your wife here?"

"I believe I saw her here earlier," he said in a dismissive tone. "I do not question her engagements, nor she mine."

"I found her to be altogether charming," remarked Lord Waycross. "You made an excellent choice in choosing your bride."

Jared did not like his father's compliment at all, and decided to draw his attention once again to Beatrice. "And she has such a lovely stepsister, too," he said, smiling at Beatrice, who simpered exactly on cue.

"There is Cassy," said Eleanor, looking over Jared's shoulder.

"Come and join us," said Lord Waycross, reaching out toward Cassy as she approached them. "We had hoped to see you again."

"Thank you, my lord."

"Are you alone?" asked Eleanor.

"I came with the Stanfords," said Cassy. "They have been all that is amiable since I have come to Town. I would still be sitting at home if they had not insisted I join them in their rounds."

Jared kept his face expressionless as all eyes focused on him. He would not allow himself to look ashamed of the way he had treated his wife, particularly in front of his father and Eleanor.

"If we had known, we would have been happy to have introduced you to society," said Eleanor.

"We certainly would have," said Edward, casting a stern glance at Jared. "It isn't proper at all for a lady to be left at home during the Season." He did not mention a name, but Jared felt his father's words were directed at him. Jared's only reaction was to place his hand over Beatrice's.

Everyone in the small circle noticed the movement. Much to Jared's delight, a look of disapproval passed over his father's face. Perhaps he was getting back some of his own after all.

"Don't feel sorry for Cassy," said Beatrice. "I've invited her to come with us time and again, but she has refused."

"Incomprehensible," remarked Eleanor, her comment falling heavily in the silence that followed Beatrice's remark.

"It's far past time that I danced with my daughter-in-law," announced Lord Waycross. He turned to Eleanor. "My dear, as soon as I return, we shall all go in to supper."

"I believe I will go claim a table for us," said Eleanor, disinclined to be left with Jared and Beatrice.

"We will meet you there," replied Edward, offering his arm to Cassy and leading her onto the dance floor.

In a matter of moments, Jared and Beatrice found themselves alone.

"They did not even invite us to join them," complained Beatrice. "I cannot say much for the manners of your father and stepmother."

"She isn't my stepmother," said Jared, through clenched teeth. "You will do well to remember that."

"In the legal sense of the word, she is," argued Beatrice, oblivious to the emotion boiling around Jared.

Lord Weston arrived at that moment to claim a dance with Beatrice. Jared's face was dark and thunderous. "Trouble?" he asked, out of Beatrice's hearing.

Jared nodded, not trusting himself to speak.

"Go with them," he instructed, nodding toward the door where Brandon, Thornton and Henderson waited.

"I'll see Mrs. Vance home. She won't know you're gone until it is far too late," he advised.

"I owe you," replied Jared, relieved he would soon be out of this infernal circus.

"Where is Jared going?" asked Beatrice, watching him disappear into the crowd.

"He needs some fresh air," said Weston. "And I desire to dance with the loveliest lady at the ball."

Beatrice giggled and tapped his arm with her fan. "Gammon. There's no need to tip over the butter boat," she said, enjoying every word of his flattery.

"I would never offer Spanish coin to you," he said, placing his hand over his heart. "Every word I said is well deserved." He placed her hand on his arm, and they joined the couples already on the dance floor.

Drew had watched the entire episode from the safety of the alcove where Jared had left him. He could not hear what was being said, but judging from the expressions and from Jared's hasty departure from the ball, Drew could tell things had not gone completely to his friend's liking. He shook his head and glanced at the bottle he still held in his hand. He could see how Jared would be tempted to drown his unhappiness in a bottle, but it was not for him. He set the bottle on the floor and made his way out of the room. He would go to White's, take possession of his favorite chair, and consider how lucky he was to be free of encumbrances.

Cassy was at breakfast the next morning when she received an invitation from Eleanor to take tea with her that afternoon. She had heard more than enough about Jared's disappointment, and she had no desire to sit though an hour or more of confessions from her husband's past betrothed. However, she did not feel she could refuse, since both Lord and Lady Waycross had been so cordial to her when they had met.

Beatrice entered the dining room and made her way to the sideboard to fill her plate. "I was simply overwhelmed last night," she said, not even taking time to bid Cassy good morning. "Did you see the attention Jared's friends paid to me? And Lady Waycross complimenting me on my gown? I vow, it was more than I ever expected. I do believe Jared was pleased I was readily accepted by his friends and family, don't you?"

"I'm certain he was," agreed Cassy, continuing with her breakfast. She would not allow Beatrice to ruin her morning.

Beatrice had piled her plate high with buttered eggs, ham, tongue, and two muffins. As she was returning to her seat, she passed behind Cassy, and her eyes lit on the note. "What is this?" she asked, picking up the invitation before Cassy could stop her.

"It's none of your concern," replied Cassy, reaching for the letter.

Beatrice held it out of her grasp, and continued reading it. "Why, it's an invitation to take tea with Lady Waycross," she exclaimed. "I suppose you meant to keep it from me."

"It was not addressed to you," said Cassy, forcing her tone to remain even.

"Lady Waycross would not be so ill mannered not to include me in her invitation. Not after being so congenial just last night."

"Examine the direction, if you do not believe me," instructed Cassy.

"It is merely an oversight," insisted Beatrice, after she observed only Cassy's name appeared on the note. "She no doubt assumed I would consider myself invited."

"I cannot presume that," said Cassy. "If you wish to

visit Lady Waycross, I cannot stop you. However, you will do it on your own. You will not accompany me this afternoon."

"You cannot keep me away." Beatrice stomped her foot in anger.

"I have no intention of doing so. I am going to take tea with Lady Waycross. If you wish to call as well, you must find your own way. Perhaps you should ask Jared if he will take you," suggested Cassy, firing her final shot in the battle.

"I am so glad you accepted my invitation," said Lady Waycross, once they settled into chairs in the elegant drawing room.

"I had my reservations," Cassy admitted. "I had known, of course, that Jared opposed his father's marriage to you, but since we first met, I have learned the rest of the story."

Eleanor seemed to pale, and she clasped her hands in her lap. "I hope it did not turn you against me."

"The person who related it gave me just the basic facts of what happened. There was no explanation as to why it happened."

Eleanor leaned toward her, sincerity etched on her face. "Will you allow me to tell you my side of the story before you come to any conclusions?" she pleaded.

"I imagine I shall hear it more than once from many different people. You may as well be one of them. I should warn you, however, that it might be best if you speak quickly. Beatrice found your invitation and insisted that you had meant to include her. While I strongly discouraged her, it is not unlikely that she will appear any moment."

An expression of distaste appeared briefly on Eleanor's face. "I hope she heeded your warning. I would not take kindly to being interrupted, and since she is no real relation, I would not think it necessary to be kind."

"She was hovering around Jared when I left, so perhaps he will distract her," said Cassy.

"I cannot believe he is spending time with that woman."

"I believe it to be an effort to offend his father."

"Then he is doing a good job of it," said Eleanor. "Edward does not outwardly display his feelings, but he is thoroughly disgusted with Jared's way of life."

"It's nothing to write up in *The Morning Post*," declared Cassy drolly.

Both women laughed. Tea was brought in and several minutes were spent pouring tea and accepting cakes before Eleanor began to speak.

"I will make this as brief as possible. Then you may ask me anything you wish." She drew a deep breath and launched into her story. "It wasn't long after I came to London for my come out that Jared began paying court to me. I think he was ready to settle down, and I happened along at the right time. I looked forward to going about more with other people and enjoying everything that a young lady should, but my parents considered Jared perfect for me. I argued with them as best I could, but they were adamant. I had never defied my parents before and found I could not begin at such a late date. Before the betrothal was officially announced, Jared insisted we travel to the Waycross estate to meet his father.

"I cannot adequately describe the immediate impression Edward made on me. It was as if someone had cut out my tongue, for I could not say a word. He overwhelmed me with his presence. When we came to know one another, I found that our souls touched. I

know I sound like a sentimental fool, but those were
my exact feelings.

"At first, I did not know that he felt the same. I
only knew marrying Jared would be the greatest mistake I could ever make. In truth, I was determined not
to marry anyone unless it was Edward.

"One afternoon Edward found me hiding in the garden, tears pouring from my eyes because of the bumble
broth I had made of my life. He coaxed and pleaded
until I confessed I did not want to marry Jared. He
asked me why, and I could not stop myself from admitting that I wanted nothing else but to marry him.

"He laughed out loud. I thought he was laughing
at me, but he was quick to assure me it was from pure
joy. He admitted to thinking he was an old fool for
loving me so quickly and I, of course, hastened to assure *him* that he was not." Eleanor smiled, remembering the scene.

"And that left Jared," said Cassy.

"It was a problem we didn't consider at the moment. However, when our jubilation lessened, we realized that our joy would bring pain to Jared. We never
dreamed it would be so deep nor last so long.

"When he married you, we thought he might forgive us, but it has made little change. Oh, he speaks
now when our paths cross, but it goes no further. I
don't know what it will take to bring Jared and Edward
together again, or if it is even possible. I hoped you
might be able to help."

Cassy could not prevent a harsh laugh from escaping
from her lips. "Do not depend upon me," she said.

Eleanor appeared disappointed. "You do not believe
what I say," she murmured sadly.

"It isn't that," replied Cassy. "I'm certain your version of the story will do as well as anyone's, but I cannot help because I have no influence at all with Jared."

"Surely he would at least listen to you," said Eleanor.

"Allow me to be blunt," Cassy remarked. "Jared married me for no other reason than to get revenge against his father for taking you from him. He meant to offer for my sister, but she was already married, so he settled for me. I was to be just low enough to offend Lord Waycross's sensibilities."

"What?" Eleanor gasped, putting her hand to her breast. "I did not think Jared could be so callous."

"I have learned never to underestimate a man in love," said Cassy.

"Or his desire to possess someone merely because they are desired by another," offered Eleanor.

"You don't think he loves you?" asked Cassy incredulously.

"Perhaps at first," said Eleanor, waving her hand as if shooing away a fly. "But he still cannot be head over heels after all this time, or he does not have the intelligence I once thought he possessed."

"I'm certain you realized during your short betrothal . . ."

"It was never a betrothal," protested Eleanor.

"I'm certain you realized during your short . . ."

"Acquaintance."

". . . acquaintance," repeated Cassy, "that Jared is a stubborn man. It took only a short . . . acquaintance on my part to realize it. What happened between the three of you is as fresh in his mind as if it was yesterday. While you and Lord Waycross have built a life together, Jared has been mired in the past."

"How lamentable," mused Eleanor. "There must be a way to help him through this."

"You are welcome to try, but do not depend upon me to aid you, for my pleas would have no impact at all upon him. And I do not even know whether he wants to get over it. He seems to be enjoying going about as he is."

"And I thought we could invite you to dinner, make an emotional apology, and be done with it," remarked Eleanor with a wry smile.

They both laughed, and Cassy felt a bond with Eleanor. She was the first woman with whom Cassy could speak freely about Jared.

"I'm sorry you wasted your afternoon," said Cassy still smiling.

"It wasn't at all a waste," objected Eleanor. "We have become acquainted, and I believe we can become good friends if given the chance. I hope you'll visit again soon. Edward will be disappointed he missed you."

"I would like that," Cassy answered simply.

"Then come tomorrow for dinner. I shall invite Drew to fill out the table."

Cassy hesitated, wondering whether this was what she wanted.

"Please say you will. If you have a horrid time, then I shall never invite you again," Eleanor promised.

"All right. If Drew accepts, so will I."

"Then I shall see you tomorrow evening," Eleanor said confidently.

Seven

Cassy did not see her stepsister and husband leave the house the next evening, for she had left earlier with Drew to have dinner with Lord and Lady Waycross. She was glad to have Drew's support. He was such a staunch ally, she did not know what she would have done without him since she came to London.

Dinner was filled with light conversation and humorous anecdotes. Afterward, Lord Waycross and Drew elected to join the ladies in the drawing room rather than stay at the table for port and a cigar.

When they were seated, Lord Waycross turned to Drew. "Would you keep Eleanor company while I show Cassy the terrace?" he asked.

"Pleased to," replied Drew.

Lord Waycross led Cassy onto the terrace, where they looked out onto the small garden at the back of the house. "Do you mind if I smoke?" he asked.

"Of course not," replied Cassy. She was convinced he had not asked her outside merely to see the terrace, and she was apprehensive about the reason they were alone. She had heard two accounts of Jared's estrangement from his father and wondered whether she would be subjected to Lord Waycross's perspective.

"I wanted to talk with you about Jared."

Cassy kept quiet, uneasy with the subject.

"I don't expect you to say anything against him,"

said Lord Waycross. "I only want you to know that it's my desire to be on good terms with my son again. I miss him."

His words were simple, and Cassy believed they were sincere.

"I should have foreseen what would happen when I married Eleanor," said Waycross. "But I was so much taken by her, I was oblivious to everything about me. I suppose I couldn't imagine anyone's objecting to a marriage between two people who were so right for one another.

"I conveniently forgot my son felt the same way when he brought Eleanor home to introduce her to me. I considered Jared a young man with years in front of him and ample time to find another lady. And Eleanor responded to me so readily, I could not believe she was truly in love with Jared. At least those were my arguments whenever I felt guilty about marrying Eleanor.

"I found out too late Jared did not agree with me. We had an argument that nearly came to blows. Jared accused me of stealing Eleanor from him only to brag that I had a young wife. He said Eleanor's parents were looking for rank and fortune for their daughter, and that was the reason they encouraged her betrothal to me.

"If he hadn't had the sense to leave at that point, I don't know where our anger would have led us, and I'm glad I never found out. Jared didn't come to the wedding. At the time, I was relieved he chose not to attend. The wounds were still too fresh for us to begin any kind of healing.

"I hadn't spoken to my son until I called him home to ask him to marry, and we've barely spoken since then. He did write to tell me of your wedding, and he speaks to me when we meet, but that is all. I feel he's waiting for something from me, but I don't know what he wants. I wondered if you knew."

Cassy had no desire to be dragged into the argument between Jared and his father, but the two men seemed determined to involve her just the same.

"I can't speak for Jared," she said slowly. "It is no secret he blames you for his unhappiness, but I cannot tell you how to settle the matter. I am a near stranger to your situation, and am unaware of all the nuances of the problem. I know that you asked him to marry and he wed a stranger."

"I am not sorry I did so," Lord Waycross responded. "I'm surprised he chose such a levelheaded young woman as you. I had thought he would choose a goose-cap for his bride just to annoy me. However, he has done himself proud in selecting a wife."

Cassy blushed in the darkness of the night, wishing she could agree with Lord Waycross. Instead of confessing the true state of affairs in her marriage, she changed the subject.

"It may be that Jared will not hold a grudge forever. Perhaps he will come about soon."

"Do you think you could help?" he asked.

"I don't know that he would listen to me," replied Cassy, thinking that Eleanor must not have told her husband of their conversation. "Have you tried to speak with him yourself?"

"He hasn't indicated he was ready to make amends any time that I've seen him."

"Be patient," counseled Cassy. It was the only thing she felt safe in saying.

"They are truly in love, aren't they?" said Cassy, when she and Drew were on the way home in the coach.

"Seem to be," agreed Drew.

For the first time, Cassy found herself feeling pity for Jared. To love a woman as beautiful as Eleanor and then to lose her to his father must have been far more taxing than she could ever imagine. "It must be difficult for Jared to see them together."

"Time for Jared to quit his brooding and get on with his life," said Drew, much to Cassy's surprise. "Thought his marriage to you was just the thing until I found out why he did it. Not that you're wrong for him. He just doesn't know you're right."

Tears gathered in Cassy's eyes. It was rare that a woman could find such a friend in a gentleman.

Cassy was emotionally drained by the time she reached home, but the evening was not over yet. When she entered the house, Regis advised her that Lord Carlisle was in the drawing room and would like her to join him before she retired.

Remembering their confrontation the night before, Cassy approached the drawing room warily. She was not up to another clash with Jared. She wanted only to seek her bed and enjoy a good night's rest.

"Come in," Jared said, as she hesitated at the doorway. "I promise I have not been drinking and am as reasonable as soberness will allow me to be." He smiled reassuringly, and Cassy stepped into the room.

"Regis said you wished to see me. Is something wrong?"

"Must something be amiss for me to want to see my wife?"

"In this case, yes," replied Cassy wryly.

Jared laughed. "Perhaps you're right, but it needn't be." He came to her side, took her hand, and led her deeper into the room.

The candlelight shed a glow that took the edges off reality. Jared caught her gaze, and Cassy was pulled into the green depths of his eyes. He could be a mesmerizing man when he wished, and Cassy had no experience with which to deal with him.

"I understand you told Beatrice I was in your room last night."

Cassy was pleased with the dim light, for her face felt hot from the flush that rose to her cheeks. "She questioned me about being with Lord Waycross. I merely told her you had come to my room to discuss it."

Jared's expression was still pleasant. Cassy breathed a sigh of relief. Perhaps they would not fight again tonight.

"She has the idea something more took place." Jared raised his hand and stroked the softness of her cheek, allowing his hand to cup her face and raise it to his.

His touch sent shafts of warning throughout Cassy's body. He had the ability to turn her knees to water and to cause her stomach to spin. He leaned closer, and she felt the warmth of his breath against her face. He had told the truth. She could not detect one whiff of liquor on his person.

"I cannot help what she thinks, my lord."

"So formal, when we are husband and wife," he mused, placing one finger under her chin and tipping it up until it suited him.

"I . . . I don't know what Beatrice believes happened last night, but I didn't offer any details."

"Of course you didn't, you little minx," agreed Jared, smiling. "You allowed her to think what she wished, and for Beatrice that was the worst that could happen in her eyes."

He leaned closer, his lips barely touching hers. Cassy's eyes closed and her lips parted slightly in order to receive his. He allowed his lips to linger, pulling his wife closer to meld her body with his. She gave no indication she wished to be free, so he slipped his arms around her, his hands caressing the softness of her body beneath the silk of her gown.

Cassy had not known a kiss could be all that it was. She was floating, tasting a sweetness she had never experienced before. The touch of Jared's hands left trails of sensation in their wake. With a forwardness she did not know she possessed, she pressed herself against him, reveling in the hardness of Jared's body against hers.

"Shall we give her something real to consider?" he murmured in her ear.

"What do you mean?" replied Cassy, opening her eyes and staring up at him.

"Let us go upstairs." he suggested. "There is no anger between us now. We can be man and wife in the true sense of the word."

Warmth enveloped Cassy when she thought of lying beside Jared in his large bed. She snuggled deeper into his arms and he held her tighter.

"Come with me, my love," he whispered.

This time, Cassy kissed him. All the pent-up loneliness turned to desire for the man who held her. She was finally going to have someone with whom to share her most private thoughts.

"What a pretty scene." The bitter voice of her stepsister caused Cassy to jerk away from Jared.

"And you said you wished to retire early," continued Beatrice to Jared. "But perhaps you were going to do that—just not alone."

"It is none of your concern," replied Jared stiffly.

"None of my concern?" repeated Beatrice, her shrill voice rising. "Am I to believe I mean nothing to you? Do you expect to have a wife and mistress under the same roof?"

Cassy felt sick at Beatrice's words. She turned and

fled the drawing room without another word to either Jared or Beatrice. She doubted either knew when she left.

As she climbed the stairs, Cassy silently cursed her treacherous body. Jared had told her too many times he wanted nothing to do with her. Despite that knowledge, his slightest touch had made her forget everything that had transpired since their wedding.

Now there was no doubt that Beatrice was Jared's mistress. She had admitted it, and Jared had not denied her claim. Cassy fought to keep the images of Jared and Beatrice together out of her head.

Cassy wondered what had made Jared approach her this evening. Was he becoming bored with Beatrice? If so, surely he could command the attention of nearly any woman he chose. Why her? Cassy stepped into her room.

"There you are," Betsy greeted her. "Did you have a good time?"

Cassy's thoughts were so jumbled from her encounter with Jared and Beatrice that it took a moment for her to remember where she had been that evening. Had it really been such a short time ago she had said good night to Drew? So much had happened in such a few minutes.

"Lord and Lady Waycross were all that anyone could wish. Dinner was excellent, and Drew was the perfect escort," said Cassy.

"Too bad it wasn't your husband," grumbled Betsy, undoing the buttons on her gown.

"Perhaps one day Jared and his father will reunite," said Cassy, unwilling to allow Betsy to witness her disgust with her husband.

"A body can only hope," agreed Betsy, hanging Cassy's gown in the armoire, then returning to take down her hair.

"Forget the one hundred strokes," said Cassy, when Betsy picked up the brush. "You can catch up in the morning. I want only to lie down."

"No wonder, with the hours you've kept the last two days," scolded Betsy. "It will take you some time to get used to Town life."

Cassy climbed into bed. Betsy pulled up the covers, then tiptoed from the room. There was no need to be so quiet, thought Cassy, for she doubted her eyes would close before dawn.

Downstairs, Jared and Beatrice stared at one another.

"What do you mean by intruding on a private discussion?" he inquired coldly.

"Is that what you call it? A discussion? And I thought you were making love to her," scoffed Beatrice.

"Call it what you may," said Jared, "it was still none of your concern. You are only a guest in this house. You have nothing to say about what happens in it."

"You have treated me as if I do," she argued. "You have chosen to spend your time with me rather than your wife. Then suddenly she tells me you visited her room, and the very next night I find her in your arms. What am I to think?"

"Think what you usually do—nothing," snapped Jared. "You are here because you want to be. Because you chose it. You can just as easily choose to leave if you so desire. I'm certain your father will welcome you back.

"And while we are on the subject, if I ever hear you claim to be my mistress again, you will wish you had never heard my name."

Things were not going as Beatrice had planned. She had expected Jared to deny anything had gone on with

Cassy and to reassure her she was most important to him. She could not believe he actually wanted her to be gone, leaving him alone with her little nothing of a stepsister.

"You know I do not want to leave here," she cooed, attempting to coax him into a more genial humor.

"Then act like it," Jared advised, stalking from the room.

Beatrice's faced burned at his chastisement. She would make Cassy pay for this night, she vowed.

The next day, Cassy was reliving the disastrous events of the past evening. She had played least in sight that morning and evaded both Jared and Cassy by having breakfast in her room. Then she used the back stairs to reach the small sitting room where she now sat having a fortifying cup of tea.

She was not yet ready to confront either of them. She could face down Beatrice, for her sister had no right to comment about what went on between her and Jared, no matter if she was his mistress, as she claimed. However, seeing her husband again left her apprehensive. She did not quite know how to act toward him after their kiss of the night before. Perhaps it meant nothing to Jared, perhaps he was using it to make Beatrice jealous, but it had certainly exposed Cassy to the desires of a woman.

She was happy for the distraction when Regis announced that Mr. Martin had called. Anxious to learn the results of his visit, she asked the butler to show him in.

Cassy greeted him with a radiant smile. "Mr. Martin, I am so happy to see you have returned. I hope you have good news for me."

"I think you'll be pleased," he announced, modestly. "When I reached Derby, I found it fit the description of the town your mother had mentioned. After some questioning of the local people, I was able to locate a family by the name of Howard who had resided there for some years. The house was located several miles outside of town near a small village called Littleover. I asked directions at the inn and learned from the innkeeper that James Howard still occupied the property. His parents have been gone for years and he has one aunt who has married and moved away.

"I felt I had the right Howard family, since the clues you gave me led me straight to Derby. When I traveled to the estate the next day, I was certain this was your mother's home, for directly by the drive leading to the house was a tree which could greatly resemble a horse in the eyes of a child."

Tears filled Cassy's eyes. She was becoming a watering pot of late. "Tell me you found that James Howard is my relative," she begged, her hands clasped before her.

"He is your cousin," said Martin.

"Thank you," she said, wiping away the tears she could not hold back from spilling over onto her cheeks. "Thank you so much."

"I couldn't have done it if you hadn't remembered what you did," he replied, sharing the success with her.

"How did he react when you told him I was searching for him?" she asked, her words tumbling out in a rush.

"He was absolutely speechless for some minutes," recalled Martin. "Then he had so many questions about where you were, what you were doing, where you had been all your life. I couldn't answer them all and didn't feel I should. I told him your name and that you were presently in London. He wanted to come immediately, but had to make arrangements to be away from the estate. He plans to arrive in Town in a few days. He is to contact me. Then I will bring him here and introduce the two of you."

Cassy could hardly restrain herself from leaping up and dancing around the room. "I am so excited. I don't know how I will pass the time until then."

"Keep busy," he advised. "The days will go by before you know it."

"You will bring him to me as soon as he arrives?" she asked.

"As soon as he cleans the dust from his boots," Martin promised.

"I do not care about dust at all," replied Cassy.

Jared's appearance almost as soon as Martin disappeared nearly destroyed Cassy's joy.

"We should talk about last night," he said, closing the door behind him.

A private interview with Jared was exactly what Cassy craved to avoid. "I have nothing to say," she remarked, putting some distance between them.

Jared followed her across the room until there was very little space between them. "But I do, and I would like you to listen," he said, stretching out his hand to her.

Unable to judge how she would react to his touch, Cassy moved out of his reach. "I would prefer to forget about last night," she said. "What we . . . what happened was a mistake."

"I told you, I was sober," he said, interrupting her. "I knew exactly what I was doing."

"Evidently Beatrice did not think so," snapped Cassy.

Jared's mouth formed a thin line of distaste. "It is none of her business, and I told her so."

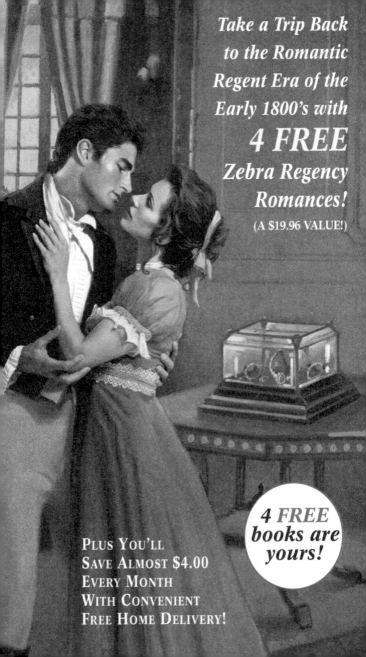

We'd Like to Invite You to Subscribe to Zebra's Regency Romance Book Club and Give You a Gift of 4 Free Books as Your Introduction! (Worth $19.96!)

If you're a Regency lover, imagine the joy of getting **4 FREE Zebra Regency Romances** and then the chance to have these lovely stories delivered to your home each month at the lowest price available! Well, that's our offer to you and here's how you benefit by becoming a Regency Romance subscriber:

- **4 FREE Introductory Regency Romances are delivered to your doorstep**
- **4 BRAND NEW Regencies are then delivered each month (usually before they're available in bookstores)**
- **Subscribers save almost $4.00 every month**
- **You also receive a FREE monthly newsletter, which features author profiles, discounts, subscriber benefits, book previews and more**
- **No risks or obligations...in other words, you can cancel whenever you wish with no questions asked**

Join the thousands of readers who enjoy the savings and convenience offered to Regency Romance subscribers. After your initial introductory shipment, you receive 4 brand-new Zebra Regency Romances each month to examine for 10 days. Then, if you decide to keep the books, you'll pay the preferred subscriber's price.

It's a no-lose proposition, so return the FREE BOOK CERTIFICATE today!

Say Yes to 4 Free Books!
Complete and return the order card to receive this $19.96 value, ABSOLUTELY FREE!

If the certificate is missing below, write to:
Regency Romance Book Club
P.O. Box 5214, Clifton, New Jersey 07015-5214
or call TOLL-FREE 1-888-345-BOOK
Visit our website at www.kensingtonbooks.com.

FREE BOOK CERTIFICATE

YES! Please rush me 4 Zebra Regency Romances without cost or obligation. I understand that each month thereafter I will be able to preview 4 brand-new Regency Romances FREE for 10 days. Then, if I should decide to keep them, I will pay the money-saving preferred subscriber's price for all 4...that's a savings of 20% off the publisher's price. I may return any shipment within 10 days and owe nothing, and I may cancel this subscription at any time. My 4 FREE books will be mine to keep in any case.

Name _____

Address _____ Apt. _____

City _____ State _____ Zip _____

Telephone ( ) _____

Signature _____
(If under 18, parent or guardian must sign.)

RN101A

Terms and prices subject to change. Orders subject to acceptance by Regency Romance Book Club.
Offer valid in U.S. only.

PLACE STAMP HERE

ll..l.l.lll...llll.l.l.l.l..l.lll.l.l..l.ll.l..lll..l

REGENCY ROMANCE BOOK CLUB
Zebra Home Subscription Service, Inc.
P.O. Box 5214
Clifton NJ 07015-5214

"And what the two of you do together is not mine."

"We have done nothing beyond mixing with the *ton*," he said firmly. "She is not my mistress."

"It is of no matter," said Cassy, although relieved at his denial. "We have both agreed we should go our own ways."

"After last night you can still say that?" he asked, his green eyes glinting as he stared at her.

"Particularly after last night," she replied.

"You are afraid to face your feelings," he said accusingly.

"Perhaps I am," she agreed. "If you will think back over our short betrothal and marriage, you will surely see ours has been a highly unconventional union. You have never thought of me as a person, only as a means of revenge. I will tell you now it is not a comfortable position in which to find oneself. Now, if I'm not mistaken, you expect me to fall into your arms and be grateful you have noticed me." Cassy ignored Jared's attempt to interrupt her. "I am not as green as all that. If you are bored with Beatrice, then I'm certain there are any number of demi-reps who would welcome your attention."

"Devil take me! I am not interested in demi-reps," Jared exclaimed.

"Then you had best try to turn Beatrice up sweet, for I will not be used any further." She hurried from the room before he could attempt to convince her otherwise.

Cassy returned to her room to rest for the evening and to avoid further arguments with Jared, but she had forgotten Beatrice. As Cassy reached her door, Beatrice sailed down the hall toward her.

"I want to talk to you," she announced.

"Not another one," moaned Cassy.

"What do you mean?" asked Beatrice.

"It isn't important. We'll talk later," she said, hoping to put Beatrice off.

"Now," insisted Beatrice. "I want to know what you hoped to accomplish last night."

Cassy forced an expression of puzzlement on her face. "I don't know what you mean. I was merely kissing my husband." Cassy could have sworn she heard a growl emanate from Beatrice's throat.

"You have not gone about kissing him before," charged Beatrice.

"And how do you know?" asked Cassy. "Can you see through walls? Did you have a spy in the household before you arrived?"

"No," admitted Beatrice, sullenly. "But Jared would have told me."

Cassy laughed. "Do you truly believe Jared would confide his most personal moments to you? He has informed me you were mistaken in claiming you are his mistress. Perhaps you have him confused with someone else," she suggested.

Beatrice flushed an ugly red. "The two of you do not at all act like newlyweds, and it will not be long before he succumbs to me," she bragged. "Why would he spend all his time with me if he does not mean for us to be lovers?"

"I do not attempt to explain my husband's actions. If you want to know, you must look to him for answers. Now, I am fatigued." Cassy put her hand on the doorknob.

"You will not get away with this," hissed Beatrice. "Jared is mine. He has always been mine, and he would have married me had he been a few days earlier."

Cassy looked her directly in the eyes and smiled sweetly. "But he wasn't, was he?" Cassy opened the door and slipped inside, leaving Beatrice seething in the hall. She breathed a sigh of relief. She had faced them both and was little the worse for the wear. Was she maturing, or had she become as ruthless as Jared and Beatrice?

While waiting to greet her cousin, Cassy made good on her promise to make a life for herself. Between Drew, Lady Stanford, and Elizabeth, her days and evenings were full. She made friends easily and was soon receiving more invitations than she could accept.

Jared would admit to no one but himself that he was unhappy his wife was successful in the *ton*. He was surprised by his feelings of anger when he thought of her in another man's arms waltzing around a ballroom or strolling through a dimly lit garden. He continuously thought of the night Beatrice had interrupted them and wondered what would have happened if she had not shown up.

He learned Cassy had continued seeing his father and was furious, but he forced himself not to show it. He imagined his father had lured his wife into plotting against him. Perhaps that was why she had rejected him. Well, he would not allow her to get the best of him again. If she wished to be left alone, that was what he would do.

His drinking escalated, and he abandoned his usual measures to conceal it. His rage grew at the circumstances in which his life seemed to be mired. He felt a great need to strike out at someone to appease his temper, and the very person appeared in the doorway of the drawing room at a time when his discontent with life was at a high point.

Cassy had come to the drawing room in search of her embroidery when she unexpectedly came across

Jared reading the newspaper, a glass on a small table near his elbow. She immediately stopped, hoping to withdraw before he noticed her. However, her luck did not hold.

"I'm grateful we are not going about together," remarked Jared spitefully, as he looked at Cassy standing in the doorway. "My sensibilities are offended by your gown. I wish you would take some advice from someone knowledgeable about how to dress."

Cassy was aware that she would never be a diamond of the first water, nor did she aspire to be a fashion plate. However, she believed her clothes were acceptable and his remarks were uncalled for.

"And whom should I ask for advice?" she said, wondering whom it was he admired.

"Consult Beatrice," he suggested, hiding the wicked smile that threatened to spread across his face. "She is awake on every suit when it comes to fashion. I can find no fault with anything she has worn since she arrived."

"I will consider it, my lord," replied Cassy evenly. "However, as you say, since we seldom find ourselves in one another's company, the matter should not be of importance to you."

Returning to her room, Cassy studied herself in the mirror. It was as she thought. She observed a respectable woman in a respectable gown with respectable hair. She did not believe Jared when he said she should be ashamed of her appearance, but she could not deny there was room for improvement if she aspired to be dressed to the nines.

That evening, Cassy attempted to ignore her husband's cruel remarks on her appearance as she dressed for a card party which she would attend with Viscount Stanford. When they reached the party, Drew became involved in a game while Cassy strolled through the rooms watching play at various tables.

A small alcove and a partially drawn hanging sheltered one table, giving it a degree of privacy. Cassy was nearly upon it when she recognized the men there to be friends of Jared's. She quickly drew back behind the heavy velvet wall hanging in order to avoid drawing their attention. She could not greet them with even a hint of courtesy after the incident with Jared. Considering their closeness with her husband, it would be logical to assume they shared his views toward her, and would probably raise their quizzing glasses to inspect her from head to toe.

"Shame Jared can't be here tonight," said the man Cassy recognized as Harry Thornton.

"Don't forget we are partly responsible for him being in such a pickle," remarked Henderson.

"It would have happened anyway," said Weston. "But, lord, would you ever believe we fixed him up with the wrong bride?"

Thornton had just taken a sip of port. He choked and sputtered before becoming able to speak. "Remember, he was out cold and couldn't make a decision, let alone put pen to paper. And I had no idea that Beatrice Crawford had a stepsister when I wrote the letter. I was surprised he went ahead and offered for her—a woman he had never met."

"You heard him. He said it really didn't matter who he married. After all, he does not mean to live with her as man and wife," Henderson reminded them.

"And she such a little thing," said Weston. "With all that hair, you'd think she would tip over."

"Do you think there's anything to the saying *more hair than wit*?" asked Thornton, laughing.

Weston threw down his cards. "If there is, I pity poor Jared."

The men were still laughing when Cassy tiptoed away from the alcove, her face flaming. This time it proved true that a person never heard anything good when eavesdropping. She should not have tarried behind the wall hanging once she realized who occupied the table.

But then she would not have discovered the truth about Jared's mistaken offer for her. Every day added a new detail to her marriage story. Now she knew he had been drunk while other men made a game of selecting his bride, and Cassy had no doubt it had been a constant source of amusement since then for the men she had just overheard. They, in turn, had been so foxed they didn't even include the bride's name in the letter, and had no idea that two women resided in Crawford's household. That was the answer to how Jared came to call expecting to find Beatrice waiting for him.

Cassy had come to accept that Jared had taken her as second choice and had decided she must learn to live with the fact. But what she had discovered this evening was nearly more than she could bear. She was completely humiliated and wondered whether the tale had spread to society at large. Was everyone laughing behind her back when she entered a room?

A combination of anger and rebellion flared, igniting a desire to retaliate against the man who had held her up for ridicule. He had made her his wife out of his own selfish desire for revenge, and in such an aberrant manner that those who knew could also judge in what worth he held her.

"You must be tired. You've hardly spoken a word since we left the party," said Drew. The two were in the coach on their way to the town house, and Drew wondered what was consuming Cassy's attention so completely.

"I'm thinking about how many lovely women were at the Venables' this evening."

"Have nothing up on you," replied Drew.

Cassy smiled at him in the dim glow of the carriage lights. "Thank you for your loyalty, but I am hardly any competition for them. Drew, how do you think I would look with my hair cut short?"

"No expert on women's hair styles, but suppose it would do quite well if done by the right person."

"And who would that be?" asked Cassy.

"Have no idea, but my mother would. Be glad to ask," he offered.

"Thank you. And while you're doing that, ask her about gowns. No, better yet, perhaps I should speak to her myself. I want to change my style and would like her to assist me, if she is willing."

"Nothing better she likes than buying gowns and all those fripperies. She and my sister are constantly shopping. Don't see how they do it, but they seem to thrive on it." He shook his head in bewilderment.

"Will you see if she is free tomorrow?" asked Cassy. "I'd like to commence as soon as possible. I've wasted too much time being a country mouse."

Drew laughed. "And spend as much of Jared's money as you can in the effort," he advised.

Cassy joined in his laughter, feeling better than she had all evening. "And a horse, Drew," she demanded.

"A horse?" he questioned.

"Yes. I know Jared has a stable full of fine animals, but he's chosen all of them for himself. I want a horse all my own. I rode every day in the country and longed for a horse better than the poor examples Crawford kept in his stable. Will you do it, Drew? Will you buy me a horse?"

"Be pleased to. Will visit Tattersall's tomorrow. Find you the best they have," he promised.

"Thank you, Drew. If it weren't for you and your family, I would still be sitting at home alone."

"Think nothing of it," he replied.

The coach pulled to a stop and Drew escorted her to the door. It did not surprise her in the least that neither Jared nor Beatrice was home when she entered. Cassy wondered whether her plans for the next few days would catch Jared unaware or whether he would continue to barely acknowledge her existence.

She would have his attention one more time, she vowed, thinking back over the evening. It was time her husband learned she fully understood how their marriage had come about. She would not have him think her a bird-witted simpleton any longer.

Eight

Jared was surprised to find his wife seated at the table when he came down for breakfast late the next morning. He had returned home earlier than usual the night before because Beatrice had nearly driven him out of his mind by clinging to him every moment of the evening. He wondered again if the price he was paying for revenge on his father was too much.

"Good morning, my lord," said Cassy, drawing his wandering thoughts back to the present.

"Good morning," he answered shortly. He filled his plate from the warming dishes on the sideboard, while the footman poured his coffee. Keeping his back to Cassy, Jared quickly poured sherry into a glass and drank it down. He was tempted to pour a second, but decided one would suffice until after breakfast.

Cassy sat quietly until Jared took his place and lifted his serviette. "That will be all, Regis," she said firmly. "And close the door when you leave. We would like some privacy." Cassy wanted to be certain they would not be interrupted during what might be the last meaningful discussion she would have with her husband.

Jared lifted his cup to his lips as if this was the morning's normal course of events, yet his eyes were watchful beneath his dark brows. "I did not know we had anything to discuss that required such solitude," he remarked as the silence grew.

A single cup of tea rested on the table in front of Cassy. She followed Jared's actions and took a sip before she spoke. "But you would have known had you attended the Venables' card party last night. I know Beatrice abhors card parties because she cannot play well at all, but at times it might do well for you to insist upon being with your friends, particularly when they are mixing with the *ton.*"

A flicker of apprehension caused Jared to set his cup firmly in its saucer. "Just what is it you wish to discuss?" he asked.

"Nothing," she said, meeting his gaze and holding it.

"Then why are we locked in the dining room together?" he asked, raising a brow quizzically.

"I merely said I didn't wish to *discuss* anything, not that I had nothing to say."

"Ahhh." Now Jared understood. She meant to ring a peal over his head about Beatrice. It was understandable. Most wives would have done so long before now. But he would not stop his campaign to draw his father's ire. It was unfortunate Cassy had to bear the brunt of the gossip, but there was nothing to be done if his plan worked as it was meant to. After all, his wife knew theirs was not a love match.

Cassy leaned slightly over the mahogany table toward Jared and spoke in a confidential tone. "I overheard the most unusual bit of gossip at the card party last evening."

"You are now spreading *on-dits?* It certainly hasn't taken you long to be caught up in the *ton.*"

Cassy sat up straight, her demeanor stern, her voice cold and crisp. "The *ton's* rumors are of no interest to me, but this was something which I learned of firsthand. I found it extremely enlightening and thought I should share it with you."

Jared's apprehension returned, and he could not shrug it off. "Then tell me what it is and be done with it," he demanded crossly.

"As you wish, my lord," she said, in such a biddable manner that for a moment Jared thought he had control of the conversation. That is, until she spoke again.

"At the card party I came across a table of men whose names, I believe, were Thornton, Henderson, and Weston."

Jared nearly groaned aloud. What had his friends gotten him into now?

"They were enjoying themselves tremendously. In fact, it was their very gaiety itself that drew me to them. I wondered what it was they were laughing about so uproariously. And would you believe, my lord, it was me." She looked at Jared, brightly expectant.

"What? Nothing to say, my lord?" she asked as Jared remained silent. "Then I will continue." Cassy could not swallow a drop, but she lifted her cup and pretended in order to gain some time to restrain her temper. It would not do to stomp her foot and cry, or even to throw her cup at his head. He would only discount her as an hysterical woman, and she wanted to survive this confrontation as a strong person who knew her own mind and could control her destiny.

"Perhaps I shouldn't have listened, but when I heard my name mentioned I could not resist. I learned you had nothing at all to do with writing the letter offering for me. You were totally castaway—slumbering in a chair, if I remember rightly—when the selection of your bride was made. Your three friends evidently discussed a list of unworthy women and decided Beatrice was just low enough to do. But your friends were unaware there were two females in Crawford's house, so they didn't bother to mention Beatrice's name. Of course, you were too drunk to read what your friends wrote when you scrawled your signature on the letter, and events were set in motion that have brought us to this point."

The story, falling from Cassy's lips, sounded worse than it had been, he thought. "You must realize . . ." he began, thinking to tell her so.

Cassy raised her hand to interrupt him. "No, it is my time to talk. I thought I had heard all the details concerning how our marriage had come about, and they were cruel enough, but I came to accept them as inevitable and worked to build a life despite them. And I have been fairly successful." She lifted her chin proudly.

"Then last night I was degraded even further by hearing a story that has probably made the rounds of every scandalmonger in town. It is beyond all bearing that I must endure the disgrace you have heaped upon me. I was not involved in the rift between you and your father, yet you have used me unjustly. You have made a mockery of marriage, most particularly ours, and I have had enough.

"This is what I am going to do," she said, red spots of anger burning bright in her pale face.

"Madam, you forget yourself," interrupted Jared in a stiff voice.

"No. *You* have forgotten me," she accused, looking him directly in the eyes. "It is time I remembered myself, and you have helped me do it. I intend to do exactly as you advised me when we first married. I am going to live my life without a single thought of you. You and Beatrice have made a life together and, for all I care, you may continue to do so."

Good Lord! He could not allow her or anyone to assume that Beatrice was a permanent fixture in his life. "I told you, Beatrice and I are not . . ." he began, but once again she cut him off.

"I am nearly finished, my lord. There is little more to say but that I suppose we should attempt to be civil to one another in public. However, I shall leave that to you. It matters not one whit to me whether we should ever speak again. I will be happy to write notes when we need to communicate, if that is your wish."

The door was pushed open and Beatrice stood on the threshold, watching the two with suspicious eyes.

Regis stood behind her, attempting to close the door again. "Madam, please come away. I'll serve you in the small sitting room."

"I will have breakfast here," responded Beatrice, moving slowly into the room while keeping her gaze fastened on Cassy and Jared.

"It is of no matter, Regis. We are finished here," said Cassy smiling at the butler.

"I would like to speak with you further on this matter," said Jared.

Cassy rose from her chair. "I believe we have said all that is necessary, and if I linger any longer I shall be late for an appointment." Cassy pulled out her chair and looked toward her stepsister. "Here, Beatrice, take my place. It is exactly across from Jared, and I'm certain that is where you want to be."

Cassy strode from the room with a firm tread and her head held high. She paused to tell Regis to have the carriage brought around, then proceeded upstairs to ready herself to take the first step in becoming the woman she wanted to be.

Damnation! thought Jared, as he listened to the conversation between Cassy and Regis. What had gone so wrong when it had seemed so simple? Marry a woman who would welcome a husband of his standing and extract the revenge he needed from his father. But it had not worked out as he had planned.

His friends and their interference had caused the first problem, and it had grown more complicated as the weeks passed. If he allowed himself the weakness, he would agree with Cassy that her situation had been appalling from the very beginning. But he could not permit himself to feel sorry for her, or the whole plan would fall apart. He silently cursed everything that had happened since his father demanded he marry.

"I don't know," mused Cassy, as she stood before the cheval mirror in her room that evening, wondering whether she had the courage to descend the stairs. She must make up her mind quickly, for Drew and his family would soon arrive to take her to the Elderwoods' ball.

Betsy's anxious face peered over her shoulder. "You're a picture, child. There's no reason not to go," she insisted.

"I feel . . . strange," said Cassy, reaching to pat hair that was no longer there. "My head is so light."

"You've been carrying that hair around all your life. It's natural you should feel different. But in a few days, you'll wonder why you didn't do it years ago," Betsy predicted.

"Are you certain I don't look too forward? This dress isn't like anything I've worn before."

Betsy stepped back and scrutinized Cassy from head to toe. Her hair had been cut short and was pulled to the back of her head in a profusion of curls. Her dress was made from an ivory silk lutestring with a daring neckline and tiny puff sleeves. Ivory roses of the same material were tucked among her dark curls, and a pearl necklace and earrings—the only jewelry her mother had saved from Crawford—glowed against her skin in the candlelight.

"You'll steal every man's heart," predicted Betsy.

"I'll settle for making it through the evening without becoming an object of ridicule." Cassy grimaced.

Betsy handed Cassy her gloves. "There is no chance of that. Now, you had best go down. Viscount Stanford should be here any minute now," she advised.

Cassy sighed. "I suppose so. Hiding in my room for the evening will not do."

"That man is downstairs, too," said Betsy.

Cassy did not ask who she meant. Betsy had always called Robert Crawford *that man*.

"He's forever underfoot now that Beatrice is here," complained Betsy. "They're up to no good, you can count on that. They've always got their heads together whispering."

"Beatrice is not my concern any longer. I have washed my hands of her. Jared invited her to stay, and she is his responsibility, no matter what kind of game she and Crawford are playing."

Cassy gave one last look in the mirror, allowed Betsy to drape a shawl over her arms, then made her way downstairs. As she reached the top of the stairs, Beatrice and Jared, followed by Crawford, entered the foyer from the drawing room. They were also dressed to go out for the evening.

As usual, Jared was perfectly attired, while Beatrice wore another of her favorite bright colors, this one a blue so brilliant and shiny it was nearly blinding. Beatrice had gained weight from Cook's excellent meals, and the expanse of exposed flesh was not at all attractive, to Cassy's way of thinking. She examined Beatrice's gown and wondered how Jared could ever think Beatrice was an example of the perfectly dressed woman.

Crawford was the first to spy Cassy. His eyes went

wide and his mouth dropped open. "What the devil!" he exclaimed.

At another time and place, Cassy might have lost her courage, but she was no longer under her stepfather's control. Ignoring his outburst, she continued down the stairs in what she hoped was a graceful and dignified manner.

"For the love of heaven, Cassy! Where is all your hair?" burst out Beatrice.

"In the dustbin by now, I suppose," replied Cassy as she reached the bottom of the stairs.

"You look like a . . . a skinned rabbit," said Beatrice still staring at her. "And that gown looks utterly ridiculous on you. Surely you are not going out looking as you do."

Jared could not believe Cassy had undertaken such an extreme change. Somewhere in his mind he still held the image of her as a quiet country miss, but all that had changed. She was a polished London lady who would turn any man's head.

He had used her enough. It was time he gave a little back. He could support her even though he selfishly did not like to think of his wife, looking as she did, being the object of other men's desires.

"Lady Carlisle looks charming," said Jared stepping forward to raise her hand to his lips, reminding everyone that she was, after all, his wife.

Beatrice's face was filled with astonishment. "Don't tell me you approve of this . . . this display? Why, you will be a laughingstock if you allow her to appear in public like this!"

"Cassandra is perfectly capable of deciding these things for herself. I hardly think it is a subject to send you into the boughs." His green eyes settled on Beatrice with an intensity that defied anyone to disagree with him.

"You're right, of course," said Beatrice, attempting to appease him. "I'm only thinking of you."

"Do not stress yourself, madam. I am capable of dealing with my wife, if need be. However, I see nothing wrong with her appearance. On the contrary, she seems to be taking on some town bronze extremely well."

"Thank you, my lord," replied Cassy. A tight smile appeared on her face, as if she doubted his comments.

They were spared any further conversation by the arrival of Drew's carriage. Cassy departed, somewhat shaken by her encounter with the three, particularly her husband. She prayed the rest of her evening would be less stressful.

"In looks tonight," commented Drew, as they descended the shallow steps to the cobblestones.

"Thank you, Drew. I believe that's my first sincere compliment from someone other than Betsy."

"Won't be the last," he predicted.

"You look absolutely wonderful," said Lady Stanford, when Cassy entered the carriage.

"Your hair is so lovely in that style," declared Elizabeth.

"It certainly feels odd," said Cassy, reaching up to touch the curls again.

"You will be overwhelmed by partners," predicted Elizabeth. "Drew will be forced to protect you from the onslaught," she teased.

"My pleasure," replied Drew

"You are embarrassing me," Cassy said. "Let's talk about something else before I become too full of myself."

"I know just the thing," Drew remarked. "Went to Tattersall's this morning."

"Did you find an acceptable mount?" Cassy asked, excitement brightening her eyes.

"A good one," said Drew. "A mare near the color of your hair."

"I have seen her," broke in Elizabeth. "She's beautiful."

"I had a mare nearly like her when I was your age," said Lady Stanford.

"Where is she? When can I ride her?" demanded Cassy.

"Left her at my stable. If you're up to it, we can ride in the morning."

"I will be ready at whatever hour you suggest."

"Early," he suggested. "You can become accustomed to her before the park is crowded."

"I can hardly wait until morning," she said, smiling. "This is the happiest I've been for quite some time."

"Should be happy after the ball," he said.

"And why is that?"

"With your new looks, you'll cause a sensation," he concluded.

"I hope you are wrong, for I don't know what I would do."

"Every woman is born with the knowledge," he assured her.

As Drew predicted, Cassandra's appearance created a stir when she entered the Elderwoods' ball that evening. She was soon surrounded by gentlemen wishing to claim a dance. She arrived home still humming a tune and looking forward to her first ride in the park the next morning. But as she stepped through the door, her gaiety was cut short.

"Come in and have a bit of brandy with me," called Beatrice from the drawing room door. Her dress was wrinkled and her hair was mussed. She looked as if she had sampled more than a little of the potent liquor while waiting for Cassy.

"I have no desire for brandy," Cassy replied, ready to ascend the stairs.

"But I have a desire to talk to you, so come in anyway," snarled Beatrice.

Cassy sighed, straightened her shoulders and walked toward the drawing room. She hated to end such a lovely evening like this, but Beatrice was stubborn and would not rest until she said what had built up inside of her. Cassy had been the object of her wrath before and had always suffered through by merely allowing Beatrice to wear herself out.

"I'm surprised you were gone so long. I expected you to be laughed out of whatever simple event you attended."

"It was the Elderwoods' ball. The one you aspired to attend, but to which you did not receive an invitation," revealed Cassy. "And I had a delightful evening. My card was full before I could turn around, and the gentlemen flattered me outrageously."

"And you believed them?" scoffed Beatrice. "They were merely making sport of you. There were probably bets on who could make you simper most." Beatrice emptied her glass and immediately filled it again.

"I suppose you meant to impress Jared with your new looks. Well, you didn't. After you left, he laughed so much that he had to take a seat to recover. You will never keep him, you little mouse. Remember, if my wedding had been a few days later, I would have married him instead of Vance," she hissed.

Cassy would not allow Beatrice to browbeat her any longer. The reaction to her new appearance that evening had only served to reinforce her resolve to live her life as she saw fit.

"You have repeated that so often you are boring, and it means nothing. You are not married to Jared," taunted Cassy. "And as long as I am alive, you will never be. You may go out with him each evening and spend every day with him, you may even become his mistress, but you will still not be his wife."

Beatrice's face turned red with anger. Her eyes bulged and her mouth twisted with hate. "You hussy! You're nothing but a brazen-faced tart! You think a new hair style and gown will change a mouse like you? If you do, you're mistaken. You will never be more than Jared's wife in name only, no matter how many hair styles you affect. It would do you good to remember that accidents occur frequently, and if one should happen to you, I will be the next Lady Carlisle."

Cassy would not have been human if Beatrice's malice had not affected her. However, she managed to keep her face expressionless while her stepsister ranted. She wanted nothing more than to escape from the evil that emanated from Beatrice.

"Beatrice, you are mistaken in one thing. You are welcome to my husband, for I have no desire to claim either his time or attention." Then inspiration struck. "The only value he has to me is his fortune. He denies me nothing. I am able to purchase anything I desire and simply send the bill to him. It is a delightful change from my former life."

Cassy had the good fortune to see Beatrice become too angry to speak. She had hit on the very thing Beatrice wanted more than Jared, and that was money. Her stepsister might be living in Jared's house and enjoying his company, she might even be cajoling some money from him now and again, but Cassy doubted she would ever have carte blanche to Jared's funds.

"I am extremely fatigued," Cassy said in a languid

voice. "I must be rested for my engagements tomorrow."

She retained her composure until she reached her room, where she collapsed on the settee to examine her feelings. Perhaps it was wrong, but she experienced an unladylike exhilaration from striking back at Beatrice. Her stepsister had said hurtful things to Cassy in the past, but never anything as vicious as tonight. In a roundabout way, she had even threatened Cassy's life. Beatrice deserved everything she had gotten, thought Cassy. Most wives would not have been as generous as Cassy had been thus far.

Betsy had been napping in the small dressing room attached to Cassy's suite of rooms. She emerged, drowsy, but ready to hear about the evening's events. Cassy forced a smile, disinclined to dampen Betsy's joy in her recent triumph of the *ton*.

The next morning, Cassy abandoned good manners and watched from the window for Drew to appear. He arrived with a dainty sorrel mare prancing by his side. Cassy rushed from the house, and before long they were trotting side by side in Hyde Park.

"How wonderful to be riding again," said Cassy. "And on such a perfect mount. Thank you so much for selecting her for me. I could not have made a better choice myself."

"You make a good pair," said Drew, glancing at Cassy. She was looking inordinately charming this morning in a blue habit trimmed in black. A small hat perched forward on her head with a single black feather curling down past her cheek.

"I would dearly love to see how she goes," said Cassy. "Is it permitted?"

"Not many in the park," observed Drew. "See no harm in it if you are able."

"There was one thing my father taught me, and that was how to ride." She loosened the reins, and the mare leaped forward, seeming to want to impress her new owner with her speed. Cassy felt the wind against her face and the strength of the animal beneath her and was once again a carefree girl.

Suddenly she saw a horse moving up beside her. She laughed, thinking Drew was challenging her. The horse pulled even and Jared's stern face came into view, his hands reaching for her reins.

"Stop it," she yelled, attempting to turn her mare away from his reach.

But it was too late. His large hand gripped her rein near the bit, and he began pulling them both to a halt. They were side by side, their knees touching, when they came to a complete stop.

"What, for God's sake, do you think you are doing?" she cried, tempted to use her riding crop on him.

"Saving your life." He spoke sharply, a dark expression covering his face.

"I do not need to be saved. I was having a perfectly fine gallop when you interfered," she railed.

"Gallop? You were dashing headlong down the path. What was I supposed to think but that the animal was out of your control?"

"I am an excellent rider, sir, and I do not need your help." Cassy's cheeks were pink, and tendrils of her hair had escaped and were curling about her face. She made an appealing picture, which was not lost on Jared.

"How was I to know?"

"If you had taken time to inquire, I could have told you. But you have never asked whether I would like to ride, just as you didn't question whether I would like to dance or visit exhibitions or attend soirees. In truth, the only thing you have asked since we met is whether I would marry you, and I was foolish enough to say yes."

Jared was held speechless by her tirade and sat astride his horse, staring at her.

Cassy closed her eyes and breathed deeply, attempting to control her anger. When she opened her eyes, Jared was still there.

"I am leaving now," she announced through gritted teeth. "And I don't want you anywhere near me. Continue to go your own way, as you have done since we were wed. Why you chose this morning to exhibit any sign of concern for my well-being is beyond me. But please don't repeat your mistake, for I am able to take care of myself, and have been doing so for years." She turned the mare and rode toward Drew, who had stopped to wait some distance away.

Jared watched the two disappear down the path. He reached for his flask and found he had forgotten it that morning. He couldn't return home, he decided. Not only because of his wife being up in the boughs, but because Beatrice was probably up and attempting to run him to ground by now. He would go to White's and have a drink, where a man could be confident he would not find himself beleaguered by a woman.

Nine

Cassy's day would have been ruined had she not received a note from Mr. Martin advising her that James Howard had arrived in town and they would call upon her at two o'clock in the afternoon.

Cassy was pacing the drawing room an hour before they arrived, wondering what she should say to her cousin when they met. Perhaps he would be a dour man who did not want a new relative, or someone vain enough to think she was beneath him. Cassy did not want to be too coming, but, on the other hand, she did not want to appear stiff. Having a family, she decided, was more complicated than she had thought.

But when the men were announced, Cassy found she had nothing to worry about.

"You are cousin Cassandra?" James Howard asked as he crossed the floor to take her hands in his. "I am absolutely overjoyed to see you."

"And I you," she said, smiling up at him. "I am so happy Mr. Martin found you."

"We owe him quite a bit," he said, turning to the man.

"You've thanked me enough," said Martin. "Now, I believe I'll go and leave the two of you to speak in private."

Cassy studied her newfound relation as he bid Martin good-bye. James was a little over medium height.

He looked fit, his complexion darkened by the summer sun, which would indicate he took an active interest in managing his estate. His hair and eyes were a lighter shade than hers, but a similarity in the shape of their faces and nose indicated they were of like lineage.

James turned back to her as Martin left the room. "We never thought to hear anything about your mother again," he said.

"I have attempted to keep my hopes alive, but it has been difficult with so little to go on." Cassy took a seat and James sat directly across from her. "Mother would never speak about her family, and I only had bits and pieces that she mentioned to give to Mr. Martin."

"Grandfather was a hard man," James disclosed. "He said your mother was an ungrateful chit who ran away with someone unworthy of her. You must appreciate he was difficult to please when it came to finding spouses for his children."

"But my mother and father truly loved one another," protested Cassy.

"Love didn't enter into a successful marriage, according to Grandfather. Your father was a soldier who had neither fortune nor title. When he wouldn't allow them to marry and they eloped, he washed his hands of her. I believe he came to regret his decision later in life. At one time, he even attempted to find your mother, but it was too late. All trace of her had disappeared. My grandmother told me your mother was the youngest and his favorite. Perhaps that was why he felt so strongly about her marriage."

"Mother was afraid he would find us and attempt to break up our family, so she took every precaution to keep our whereabouts a secret."

"How I wish she hadn't, for I believe her father would have forgiven her marrying without his consent.

Did she tell you anything about our family?" James asked.

"Nothing at all," said Cassy.

"Well, your mother had a brother, John, and a sister, Grace. Both were older than she was. John was the oldest and was my father. He and my mother died in a carriage accident about five years ago. Grace is still alive."

"You mean I have an aunt, also?" asked Cassy.

"You do. She married a widower and has no children of her own. I have written to her about you, and I know she'll want you to visit with her at the first opportunity."

"And do you have children?"

"Not even a wife," he answered with a smile. "I've been busy making improvements on the estate, so I've had little time to think of marriage. But while I'm here in London, perhaps I'll find someone suitable," he teased.

"I do hope you can stay for a time," said Cassy. She was overjoyed to find she had a family of her own and need not rely upon her reluctant husband or stepfather to provide one for her. Her spirit was renewed by her newly discovered cousin.

"I had planned on it so that we may become better acquainted. You seem to have done well for yourself," he said, glancing around the finely appointed drawing room.

Cassy found herself blushing, thinking of how she had come to be Jared's wife. "I was surprised when Lord Carlisle offered for me," she confessed.

"You should not have been," replied James. "He should count himself lucky to have won your hand."

"You must tell me all you know about my mother's childhood," she declared, anxious to shift the attention from her marriage.

Cassy listened, fascinated by the story of her ancestors, of which there was a long line on her mother's side. Finally James paused.

"As much as I'm enjoying this, I have business which I must transact this afternoon."

"I'm sorry," apologized Cassy. "I didn't mean to keep you so long. I know you must also be weary from your travels."

"It has been worth it," James said gallantly.

"Will you be able to visit tomorrow?" she asked. "I don't want to interfere with your other plans, but I would like to see you as much as possible while you are here."

"I'd be delighted, but I don't want to wear out my welcome."

"That could never happen," insisted Cassy.

"Then tomorrow it is," he agreed. "What time would you like me?"

"Why not accompany me to a soiree tomorrow evening? I'll introduce you to some of the friends I've made since I came to Town."

"It's been several years since I've been to London during the Season. I look forward to enjoying the entertainments again."

"Good," said Cassy. "Shall we say eight o'clock?"

"Eight o'clock," he agreed, then took leave of her, expressing again how pleased he was that they had found one another.

Drew made his way to White's once he saw Cassy home from their ride. Jared was sitting by himself, a bottle on the table at his elbow. Drew did not know whether he would be welcome after the morning's adventure. However, he strolled across the room and came to rest beside Jared's chair.

"Sorry about this morning," he said. "Should have told you about the mare, but Cassy was set on doing this by herself."

Jared motioned him to the empty chair on the other side of the table. "There's no reason you should have advised me. I've advised Cassy time and again to live her own life, and I have no cause to complain now that she's doing so."

"She's an excellent rider," Drew assured him.

Jared grinned wryly. "So I learned."

"Surprised to see you here," remarked Drew. Since Beatrice had arrived, he seldom saw Jared without her. "Is Beatrice ill?"

"Not as far as I know. We were out late last evening, and I was merely lucky enough to slip out of the house before she awoke." Jared heaved a great breath. "Drew, never get involved with a woman," he advised.

Drew laughed. "Problem might be that you are involved with two women, both under the same roof. Used to think you were a smart fellow. However, these last weeks have made me reconsider."

"I fear you're right about my judgment, but it's far too late to undo what I've done."

"Never too late," judged Drew. "Send Beatrice back to her father. Spend some time with your wife."

"And what about taking revenge on my father?"

"Forget it," advised Drew. "What will you achieve? Can't get Eleanor back."

Jared called for a bottle. "I don't want her back," he confessed. "But I still feel as if my father betrayed me in a very elemental sense."

"He did," agreed Drew. "And now I believe he's aware of the seriousness of what he has done. He has certainly experienced the repercussions, none of them pleasant."

"As have I," said Jared, taking a deep drink.

"Just so, but you're also married now."

Jared snorted, lifted his glass, and emptied it.

"All right and tight, no matter how you choose to look at," Drew insisted. "Should put away past indignities. Make peace with your father and enjoy life."

"Ha! Enjoy life with whom? I cannot continue with Beatrice much longer, for she stretches my patience to its limits. I suppose I could form an alliance with a married woman, or find a ladybird who might offer some amusement."

"What about your wife?"

"You mean begin smelling of April and May, then set up a nursery with Cassy? It's far too late for that."

"Maybe not. Apology goes a long way," said Drew.

"Apologize? To that little mouse?"

"Should have seen your little mouse last night."

"What do you mean?" Jared asked suspiciously, unsure as to whether he wanted to hear what Drew had to say.

"She was overwhelmed by gentlemen as soon as she walked in the door. Never seen anything like it. Every dance was taken, more cups of punch than she could drink, and couldn't tell how many men were at her table for dinner. Heard some call her a Pocket Venus."

Jared didn't like the emotion, very much like jealousy, that boiled up in him. He couldn't be jealous of the little mouse he married. Then he remembered last evening when she came down the stairs, looking entirely different from the woman who had taken vows to be his wife. He had stood up for her mainly because he did not like Crawford criticizing anyone in his household. As far as Beatrice was concerned, she becoming altogether too bold and deserved to be put in her place. He was ashamed to admit he had used his compliments of Cassy partially to achieve that end.

However, he was not blind to the fact that Cassy had

been lovely, with her shining curls and her dress that shimmered in the candlelight. In contrast, she had made Beatrice appear as coarse as the most flagrant Cyprian.

Now he learned she had turned heads at the ball the night before. He felt uneasy envisioning Cassy being surrounded by men, passing from hand to hand as one dance followed another.

Jared took another drink. His senses were confused by more than liquor. On the one hand, he wanted nothing to do with his wife as she was merely a means to make his father suffer. On the other hand, he had to admit he found himself being drawn to her on more than one occasion and was inordinately jealous when he thought of her with other men. Perhaps it was merely the idea that she was his possession, and he did not want other men around her. He surely could not be becoming enamored of the chit.

By now the liquor had numbed the jagged edges of his discomfort. "I won't apologize, no matter how she looks," grumbled Jared.

"Think about it," encouraged Drew.

"No time to cast sheep's eyes at my wife," responded Jared, as he poured another drink.

Cassy had not meant to eavesdrop on Beatrice and Crawford. There was nothing they could say, she thought, that was of interest to her. Truth be told, she had no idea they were even in the house until she reached the drawing room door and heard Beatrice speak.

"I don't know what to do," complained Beatrice in a whiny voice she reserved exclusively for her father.

"You'll do as I tell you to do. Get Jared under your thumb," Crawford ordered.

"I've tried," said Beatrice. "But just when I think I have his complete attention, I find him with that little hussy."

"Then we may need to do something more."

"I'm doing all I can do," insisted Beatrice.

"If Cassy distracts him, then we must rid ourselves of her."

"What do you mean?"

"Don't play the fool," snapped Crawford. "We have talked before of doing away with the chit. I think the time has come."

"You don't expect me to . . . to kill her, do you?" Beatrice's voice sank to a whisper.

"Getting squeamish now that you might see some blood?" inquired Crawford, with a low chuckle.

"There must be other ways. Surely you know some-one who could do it."

"I'm teasing you," said Crawford. "When something happens to our dear little Cassy, it will be a tragic ac-cident, and we will be consumed with grief by her loss."

"That will be difficult to pretend," said Beatrice. "But I'll do whatever need be in order to have Jared all to myself."

"I must go," said Crawford. "I'll think on our prob-lem and let you know what I decide."

Cassy could hear them moving toward the door and tiptoed down the hall to the back stairs. A chill ran down her spine and goosebumps appeared on her arms as she considered what she had overheard. She did not doubt at all that Crawford would carry through on his threat to have her killed. He was desperate for money and had nowhere else to turn. A small matter of murder probably seemed trivial to him at this point.

She did not know what to do. Jared would not be-lieve anything she had to say about Beatrice at this point, particularly if it involved murder. Betsy could do nothing but worry, and Cassy would not impose that on her. Would Drew believe what she had to say? And, if so, could he do anything about it?

She would need to think on it, all the while being vigilant. What had been an embarrassing and irritating situation had now turned into something far more serious.

Cassy returned to her room and locked the door behind her. The life she had begun building for herself was once again in a pile of ashes. She must be on the alert for anything out of the ordinary if she wished to survive her marriage. She wondered about divorce and whether she could convince Jared to consider it. Although it was lengthy and costly and would put them both beyond the pale, anything was better than dying before she had begun to live.

That evening Jared sent Beatrice off with her stepfather, saying he had business to which he must attend. In truth, he had only an appointment with the bottle. Jared's drinking, which had escalated after his meeting with Drew, gave him too much relief from reality to ruin it by spending the evening with Beatrice.

He ate little of the dinner which was served in his suite, but partook liberally of the port Thomas had been ordered to keep in ready supply. Near midnight, he had some bread and cheese, then began to sip brandy.

Several hours and a bottle later, Jared heard the door in Cassy's suite close, followed by the rustling sounds that accompanied her arrival home. He wondered whether she had been overwhelmed with offers to dance again this evening. Had anyone guided her onto the patio and stolen a kiss, as he had with ladies many times in the past? His hand closed tightly on the glass.

The liquor had caused Jared to become maudlin, and he began feeling sorry for himself. He had suffered complete humiliation when he lost Eleanor to his father, and he had subsequently concocted a means of revenge to salvage his self-respect. However, it seemed his plan was falling apart, and tonight he was left drinking alone while everyone else was out dancing and laughing and enjoying themselves. Even the wife he had married had become something unexpected.

Drew had advised him what to do to make Cassy more amenable, but he couldn't quite remember through the alcoholic haze. He would go and speak with her, see if they couldn't agree to deal better with one another.

Jared filled his glass. Couldn't negotiate without a drink, could he? He stumbled to the door which led to Cassy's suite and opened it without knocking. The maid was gone and Cassy had retired for the night. There was a candle burning on the bedside table, and Jared moved as quietly as he could across the room.

Cassy had fallen asleep with a book still clasped in her hands. She wore a night gown trimmed with an abundance of lace. Her dark curls were tousled and her lashes lay like dark fans on her cheeks.

Jared slipped the book from her fingers and placed it on the table. He touched the lace around the low neckline of her gown, which felt as fragile as Cassy looked. At the moment, he forgot all that had gone on between them. He was merely a besotted man who suddenly found his wife too attractive to resist.

He lifted one of her curls from the pillow and rubbed the silky strands between his fingers. Then he stroked the softness of her skin down her neck to her bare shoulder and around the edge of low-cut lace.

Cassy murmured something and moved restlessly, but Jared was too foxed to take notice. She abruptly awoke with a start, jerking away with a slight exclamation. Could Crawford have already arranged for her demise? Was this the murderer leaning over her?

"Shsss. It's just me. Jared."

Cassy felt an overwhelming sense of relief. Surely Beatrice and Crawford had not talked Jared into doing away with his wife so quickly. "What are you doing here?" Cassy asked, pulling the bed linen up over her chest.

"Just came to . . ." What was it Drew had recommended? Ah, now he remembered. "Just came to apologize."

"In the middle of the night?"

"Couldn't wait," said Jared, reaching out for her again.

Cassy remained still. Could it be that Jared had decided he had been wrong and wanted to make a real marriage of the sham they were enduring? If so, did he deserve another chance? She had come to realize she foolishly harbored feelings for him even though he had made it clear he did not intend to make a life with her. And he had said he wanted to apologize. Was this what she had been hoping for ever since she had said *I do?*

"Must 'pologize," he mumbled again. He leaned across the bed, reaching for her. The glass in his hand tipped, spilling brandy on the pristine linens.

Cassy's expectations were abruptly dashed. "You are drunk!" she accused him in an affronted voice, pulling further away from him and the soaked bedcovers.

Jared pulled himself erect, weaving slightly. "I'm perfectly sober," he replied in a slurred voice.

"You are drunk, sir," repeated Cassy, furious that he

had approached her in such a state. "You will leave my room immediately."

"My house. My room," asserted Jared.

"I will not argue with you," said Cassy, climbing from the bed on the opposite side from Jared. She marched to the door leading to his room and swung it open. "Get out of my room," she ordered.

Jared only stared as if he couldn't believe what was happening.

"Get out of my room, sir, or I will call for Thomas to help you out."

"I'm here, madam," said Thomas appearing in the doorway.

"Good. Help your master back to his room," she ordered in a firm voice. "He is fatigued and needs to rest."

"Very well, madam." Thomas crossed the room, retrieved the glass from Cassy's bed, and then guided Jared to the doorway.

As soon as they crossed the threshold, Cassy slammed the door and locked it behind them. Anger sustained her for a time. Then, "I will not cry. I will not cry," she said, squeezing her eyes together tightly.

Sleep was impossible to attain in a brandy-soaked bed. The smell was overwhelming in the room, and she crossed to the window, opening it and breathing in the night air. How had she come to such a place in her life? She attempted to look up into the sky to see a star, but not one shone down on her.

Perhaps she should return to Jared's country house, where she might attain a measure of peace and perhaps added safety. She could do without staying the Season in town. She had lived a quiet life before she came to London, and she was certain she could easily adapt again.

Cassy sighed deeply. She sat on the window seat,

curling her legs beneath her, and stared out into the night. It was time to admit that her husband was a drunkard, she conceded, and there was nothing she could do about it. If he did not want her for a wife, he would certainly not welcome her advice concerning his drinking.

Tears gathered in Cassy's eyes. Her husband was such a handsome, intelligent man to have allowed himself to be caught in such a ruinous trap.

Cassy had agreed to ride in the park with Drew the next morning and was happy she had. The fresh air cleared her head and washed away a great deal of the unpleasantness of the night before.

"Have you named her yet?" asked Drew, indicating the mare Cassy rode.

"I know you'll think it ridiculous, but she's so dainty and regal, I'm going to call her Princess."

"Good name," agreed Drew. "Appropriate."

"You're certain? I would not like either of us to become a laughingstock," she said.

"Won't happen," confirmed Drew.

"Then I suppose you are Princess," said Cassy, patting the mare's neck.

"Saw Beatrice and her father out last night. Jared wasn't with them. Isn't ill, is he?"

"If he were, I'd probably be the last to know," replied Cassy. "However, I believe he stayed home. At least that is where he was when I returned." While Cassy was usually forthcoming with Drew about Jared, she could not share what she had experienced the evening before.

"Maybe he's regaining his common sense," suggested Drew.

"I think he was merely tired of the social round,"

said Cassy. "He will probably be back at it this evening.
Beatrice has an enormous number of new gowns, and
I believe she intends to wear them all before the week
is out."

"Would feel sorry for Jared if he hadn't brought it
on himself," replied Drew. "Look. The path is empty."
He glanced over at Cassy. "Feel like another gallop?"

"More than anything." She loosened the reins on
Princess and leaned over the mare's neck, urging the
animal forward.

Cassy and Drew experienced an enjoyable morning
in Hyde Park before turning toward home. They had
reached the town house and Cassy was beginning to
dismount when the saddle suddenly slipped sideways,
dumping her unceremoniously on the ground.

Drew and the groom were immediately at her side.

"Are you hurt?" asked Drew, anxiously.

"I don't believe so," replied Cassy, accepting his arm
to rise from the cobblestones. "Perhaps a bruise or
two, but nothing broken."

"Look at this, sir," said the groom to Drew. He had
removed the saddle from the jittery mare and held out
the girth for Drew's inspection. The leather strap had
been neatly severed nearly all the way through.

"You're lucky this didn't break while we were in the
park," observed Drew. "You could have been seriously
injured."

"It was cut, wasn't it?"asked Cassy, reaching out to
touch the raw edge of the leather.

"Afraid so." Drew turned toward the groom. "Keep
the saddle as is," he ordered. "Lord Carlisle will want
to see it."

"Jared will have no interest in this," contended
Cassy, as Drew helped her into the house.

"Don't misjudge him," warned Drew. "He will not

take it lightly. Know who would do something like this?"

Cassy thought of the conversation she had overheard between Beatrice and Crawford just the day before. They had not wasted any time in attempting to do away with her. However, she could not tell Jared her suspicions, for he would merely attribute it to jealousy.

"I do not like to think anyone would want to harm me," she answered, avoiding Drew's question.

"Will speak to Jared about it as soon as possible. In the meantime, don't go riding by yourself," Drew advised.

Cassy went directly to her room, where she ordered a hot bath to soak away her aches. She told Betsy she had fallen and there was nothing to worry about. However, as she stepped into her bath, she felt a chill that the hot water could not warm.

She could not ignore the evidence of the cut girth. Someone had meant to harm her, and from the conversation she had overheard, she had no doubt it was Crawford's doing.

She did not know how she could continue living in the same house with Beatrice, and with Crawford in and out as often as he was. Yet leaving would not solve the problem. They, or their agent, would merely pursue her until they achieved their objective. She must attempt to reveal their intent and, at the same time, endeavor to keep herself alive.

Cassy wondered whether she should tell anyone about what she had overheard and her suspicions concerning the cut girth. She supposed she could confide in Drew, but he might feel obligated to advise Jared of the situation, and that she did not want. James had just newly come into her life, and she could not burden him with her problems.

Cassy sighed, sinking lower in the scented water. She grew drowsy and her head rested against the back of the tub. Betsy slipped a towel behind her neck and tiptoed away. She would allow her to nap until the water cooled, then bring her a cup of hot tea. Cassy insisted she was going out that evening with her cousin, and Betsy knew nothing would stop her, but she could make certain Cassy was well rested.

"Where is she? Is she all right?" asked Jared, leaping to his feet. "I must see her."

"Think it best if you leave that for later." Drew had located Jared in the library and had told him about Cassy's fall. "Probably have a few bruises, but nothing more. She was ordering a hot bath the last I heard as she went upstairs. Wouldn't think she would like to be interrupted."

Jared paced back and forth across the room, stopping in front of the table holding a decanter and glasses. He reached out his hand, then pulled it back.

"Are you certain the girth was cut?" asked Jared.

"No doubt in my mind. Told the groom to keep it as it was so you could see for yourself."

"Could it have been a prank?" Jared wondered out loud.

"Serious prank, if it was," observed Drew. "Near thing. She could have been killed, depending upon when it broke completely through."

The decanter seemed to beckon to Jared, but he did not pour a drink. He needed to keep a clear head if he meant to make sense of Cassy's accident. "Did the groom mention any strangers being about?"

"Didn't ask. Your staff. Thought you should be the one to ask questions."

"And I'll do it now. Come with me and tell me what you think," he said, striding from the room.

Jared examined the saddle as soon as he arrived at the stable. As Drew had said, there was no doubt but that it had been purposely cut where it would be least discernible.

"When did you last examine this saddle?" Jared asked the groom.

"After her ladyship's ride yesterday, my lord. I took it off, stabled her mare, and cleaned the saddle. Nothing wrong with it then."

"And this morning?" questioned Jared.

"I didn't look at it closely when I saddled the mare. There was nothing to make me think something was amiss."

"Tell me, have any strangers been around the stable since yesterday?"

"None, my lord," answered the groom, twisting his cap in his hands.

"Besides Lady Carlisle, Lord Stanford, and myself, who else has been here since you cleaned the saddle?"

The groom stared at the ground. "Let's see," he mused. "There was a Mr. Howard, who come to call on Lady Carlisle. Then Mrs. Vance and her father come round. Wanted to see what kind of horseflesh you have in the stable, they said."

"And that is all," pressed Jared.

"Yes, sir. Well, no. Now that I think on it, your father, Lord Waycross, come by just this morning. Said Lady Carlisle had mentioned her new mare, and thought he'd stop and look her over. I brought her out and walked her round for him. He was pleased with the animal and left soon after."

"Any street urchins hanging about?"

"No, my lord. Nobody else that I know about what doesn't belong here."

"All right, Frank. If you think of anyone else, let me know."

Jared and Drew walked back to the house. "I'm at a loss," said Jared. "I can't believe any of my men would do such a thing. All of them have been with me for some time, and they couldn't find a better position with anyone else."

"Must be from the outside. Someone slipped in," suggested Drew.

"But why?" asked Jared, a bewildered expression on his face. "Hardly anyone knows Cassy, and surely not well enough to want to harm her."

"May be a mistake. Whoever did it got the wrong stable," said Drew.

Jared silently mulled over Drew's suggestion. "I think you may have hit on the solution," he said. "It's the only thing that makes sense. I shall see Cassy and tell her what we've determined." Jared felt a weight lift from his shoulders. He was irritated beyond all measure thinking there was a person who wanted to harm his wife. He had brought her into an intensely uncomfortable position by marrying her. He did not want to think he was responsible for threats on her life.

Jared wasted no time in knocking on Cassy's door.

Betsy answered the door. "Is Lady Carlisle awake?" he inquired.

"She's just getting out of the bath," Betsy advised him, blocking his way into the room.

"Will you ask if she will see me for a moment?"

"Who is it, Betsy?" said Cassy, appearing behind the abigail.

"I would like to speak with you about your accident today," said Jared.

Betsy looked from one of them to the other.

"Betsy, would you make certain that the gown I'm wearing this evening is free from wrinkles?" The abigail hesitated until Cassy gave her a nod. Then she retired to the dressing room.

As soon as Betsy left the room, Jared took a step toward Cassy. "Are you unharmed?" he asked.

Cassy took a step backward. She felt vulnerable being alone with him after the evening before, even though Betsy was only a room away.

"Damn it! I am not here to hurt you," he exclaimed, in a low voice. "And I would not have hurt you last night if you had but given me a chance to leave on my own."

"I've given you too many chances as it is," retorted Cassy, her color high. She drew the sides of the wrap she wore closer to her, which only attracted Jared's attention to the garment.

Try as he might, Jared could not keep his gaze from exploring the thin dressing gown Cassy wore. It revealed far more than it concealed, which was its purpose, Jared thought cynically. His wife did not resemble the starved waif she was when they first married. Her figure had filled out, and she carried herself with more authority than she had then. It was to be expected, he supposed, that she would grow into the role of lady of the house. That was one of the reasons, after all, why men married. Except for him, he reflected.

"It's best we stay with the subject," he said, drawing his hand across the lower part of his face.

"And that is?" she asked in a challenging tone.

"Drew told me you had taken a fall. I was concerned you were injured."

"I will have some bruises in the morning, and perhaps soreness in a place or two, but I expect nothing else," she said, relaxing her stance a bit.

"I questioned the grooms," he announced.

"Why did you do that? They will think I suspect them of wrongdoing," she complained.

"They will do nothing of the sort," replied Jared. "But if it will make you rest easier, I will reassure them you have complete confidence in them." Jared looked at her for a moment, then asked, "Do you know of anyone who would want to harm you?"

"No one," she answered, almost too quickly for his liking.

"Are you certain?" he pressed, feeling there was something she wasn't telling him.

"I said no, my lord. Isn't that enough?" she answered sharply.

Jared studied her again. "I suppose it must do," he answered, clearly unhappy with the results of their conversation. "I have informed Frank he is to fully inspect your saddle and bridle immediately before you ride. Drew and I believe this was merely a prank gone wrong. We think it was meant for someone else and that the person responsible confused the stables."

"I would hardly call it a simple prank when it could have killed me," said Cassy, thinking he was taking this far too lightly. Then she recalled that was exactly what she wanted him to do.

"I agree," he said. "I'm warning the nearby stables to beware of strangers and advising them what happened here. I hope it will be enough to keep anything of similar circumstance from happening again.

"By the way, Frank said there was a Mr. Howard who called on you. Is he someone you can trust?"

Cassy smiled for the first time since he had stepped through the door. "Yes, he is," she replied simply.

Jared yearned to ask who Howard was to her, but after their confrontation last night, he was treading lightly. "Good. He was the only person who had been at the stable I did not personally know."

"Who else had been there besides the grooms?" Cassy asked casually.

"Only Beatrice, Crawford, and, this morning, my father."

"Lord Waycross?" inquired Cassy with a smile. "I told him about my new mare and he said he would stop and see her. I wish he had informed me he was here."

"Evidently, he was in a hurry. Frank said he did not stay long at all."

"I wonder what he thought of her," mused Cassy. "I will probably see him this evening and I will ask him then."

"You're going out?" Jared asked in disbelief.

She regarded him quizzically. "Of course. I am not so poor spirited that I will allow a bruise to keep me at home."

"But . . ."

"Don't worry about me, my lord, or Beatrice will ring a peal over you. She does not like to be ignored," Cassy advised him as she walked to the door and opened it.

"I do not like your going out this evening. I hope Drew will keep a close watch on you."

"Drew is not accompanying me," she replied, nearly pushing him out the door.

He stopped in the middle of the threshold. "Don't tell me you are going alone?"

"I will be well escorted," she assured him as she closed the door firmly behind him.

Jared had kept away from the liquor that day and had been proud of his accomplishment. However, the interview with his wife and the upcoming evening with Beatrice caused him to turn toward the library and the bottle that he knew would be waiting there for him.

Ten

By that evening, Jared had generously sampled the liquor in the library decanter, but it had done little good. He was more than out of sorts and had considered telling Beatrice to go on without him, then decided sitting at home would do no good to anyone.

Beatrice seemed more hair-brained than usual, jabbering on about the latest *on-dits* as if he were truly interested in gossip about the *ton*. And the upshot of it all was that he could blame his predicament on no one but himself.

He had invited Beatrice to stay in hopes of using her against his father. Now it seemed his game of revenge was turning on him. Beatrice was becoming more of a nuisance every day with her endless prattle and empty conversations. What was worse was Crawford's acting as if Jared's house was a second home, popping in any time he wished with the excuse of talking to his daughter. If they had so much to discuss, perhaps he should take Drew's advice and send her packing to her father.

But tonight was already planned, and he would go through with it before he would admit Cassy had kept him from it.

"The carriage is at the door," he told Beatrice as she stood before the mirror admiring the ostrich feathers which adorned her hair. Jared silently cursed the person who had sold the infernal feathers to her. The longer she was in London, the more she looked like a doxy. She would do well to follow her stepsister's example, but that would never happen.

"I am ready," responded Beatrice, turning away from her image to clutch Jared's arm.

Just as they reached the foyer, a knock sounded and Regis pulled open the outside door. The man who entered was a stranger to Jared, but Regis greeted him as if he was expected. Jared stepped forward as Cassy descended the stairs.

Tonight she wore a blush-colored gown with an embroidered overskirt covered with deep rose flowers and tiny diamantés which sparkled with every step she took. Rose colored ribbons were threaded through her dark curls and a deep rose Kashmir shawl was draped casually from her arms to fall behind her in luxurious folds.

"James, how good to see you, and precisely on time," she said, a generous smile of welcome on her face for the man who had just arrived.

"I wouldn't keep you waiting," vowed the man as he took her hand in his.

"Aren't you going to introduce us?" asked Jared, unable to keep a sliver of misgiving from his voice.

Cassy made the introductions of James to Jared and Beatrice.

"Your cousin?" repeated Jared, taken aback. He was given to understand she had no family but her stepfather and stepsister.

"This must be a hum," said Beatrice. "I have never heard you had a family."

Cassy turned her gaze to Beatrice and gave her the sweetest smile she could manage. "I assure you James is truly my cousin, and a very welcome one indeed. Now, we must bid you good night or we will be late." The two disappeared through the door, a trill of Cassy's laughter trailing back to Jared and Beatrice, who stared after them.

It had taken every bit of strength Cassy possessed to appear normal during her short encounter with Beatrice. This was the woman who only the day before had talked about killing her as casually as ordering tea and who was possibly behind having her saddle girth cut to that end. Cassy would attempt to put it out of her mind this evening, for she felt safe with James. Drew and his family would also be at the soiree, and she would be surrounded by friends. Nothing could happen to her tonight.

"I tell you, I am doing all I can," whispered Beatrice to Robert Crawford. It was later in the evening, and they had hidden themselves in a small alcove off the main ball room at Lord and Lady Fitzhughs' home.

"Don't tell me you are unable to seduce Carlisle. You are living beneath his roof and have virtually unlimited access to the man. You must succeed with him. I am desperate for money," he complained.

"What of your plot to do away with my dear stepsister?" asked Cassy. "She has become such a spiteful cat."

"It will take time," responded Crawford. "I must be careful who I approach for the job. In the meantime, my creditors are pounding at the door and I have not a shilling to offer them."

"Then stop your incessant gambling," snapped Beatrice. "I was not brought into this world to relieve you of your debts."

"What else are you good for?" snarled Crawford. "Cassy was of more worth than you. She at least saw the house was run properly. You thought only of new gowns."

"Then perhaps you should ask Cassy for help, instead of planning her demise," Beatrice suggested sweetly.

"I have," he confessed. "And it did no good. She said I had gotten all I could expect from Carlisle and she would not ask him for more. I haven't gathered my nerve to approach him on my own. You are my daughter, and it is your duty to do all you can to help me."

Beatrice sighed. "I am trying, but I am meeting with little success. Jared does not respond to my enticements. Oh, when we are in public, he seems the most attentive of men. However, as soon as we are alone he withdraws."

"You must win out," he demanded. "Or you must make Cassy think you have succeeded in winning her husband. That should create such a disgust that it will drive her back to the country. Once that is accomplished, you will have free run of the house and perhaps more ready access to Jared's money."

"And if Cassy returns to the country, she might be easier to reach once you find someone to do away with her," said Beatrice, hoping she would be far away when the actual event took place.

"I believe that to be true," agreed Crawford. "Now you need only do your part." He rubbed his hands together, thinking of what might be if either scheme were successful.

"If it will keep you from badgering me, I will do all I can to become Jared's mistress," replied Beatrice.

"You must do it," reiterated Crawford. "Else I will be forced to flee the country or end up in Fleet prison for my debts."

"I will increase my efforts," promised Beatrice, weary of arguing.

"See that you do. I am counting on you," said Crawford.

"If I can prevail, it will be only a temporary cure. You must find someone willing to put out Cassy's lights in order for us to succeed. As long as Cassy is alive, Jared will never seriously consider me for his wife."

"I will do my part. You do yours," he hissed, before stepping back out into the ballroom.

Beatrice had disappeared for the moment, and Jared drew a breath of relief. It was tiring to be in her company for any length of time. The woman demanded attention every second, and it was no use attempting to avoid her demands. She merely became more insistent.

Jared was near the door, idly watching as more guests arrived, swelling the crowd far beyond what was comfortable. His boredom was banished at the sight of his wife and her newly found cousin. She had said nothing about coming here but, with things the way they were, he could hardly expect her to give him an agenda of her evening's activities.

He pushed himself away from the wall and approached the couple. "I never expected to see you here," he said, stopping before them. "I didn't know you were acquainted with the Fitzhughs."

"I've become good friends with Mary Fitzhugh," revealed Cassy, pleased to see the surprise on his face. "I promised we would stop by for a few minutes this evening."

"Has the lovely Mrs. Vance deserted you?" asked James, glancing around the room as if in search of her.

Jared's eyes narrowed. Was the man making a sorry jest to make him appear foolish in front of Cassy? He could not decide and elected to allow the remark to pass, turning his attention to his wife.

"I don't believe we've had the opportunity to dance before. Would you do me the honor?"

"James . . ."

"Is quite able to look after himself for the duration of a dance," said Jared, completing her sentence.

Cassy looked at James.

"Go right ahead," he said agreeably. "I believe I will sample the punch." Nodding to both of them, he made his way toward the refreshment tables.

"Are you still feeling no ill effects from your fall?" Jared asked, leading her toward the dance floor.

"Only a mild stiffness if I remain motionless very long."

"We shall see that does not happen," he remarked, taking her in his arms as the orchestra struck up a waltz.

Cassy had danced with an abundance of men since she had come to London, but none the like of Jared. He moved with a smooth grace and guided her around the other couples without demonstrating any of the difficulties some of her other partners had often evinced. His arms were strong about her and, strangely enough, she felt safe within his embrace. If only their marriage were a normal one, with no encumbrances to keep them from being husband and wife in the true sense of the word, she would be the happiest woman alive.

Jared felt more pleasure than he ever thought at having Cassy in his arms. As much as he had tried to keep her away, she had slipped under his defenses. He had said some hurtful things to her and she had not gone hiding, but had stood up to him stronger than ever.

If only things were different, perhaps they might make a go of it. But as it was, he was far too committed to punishing his father. And if that wasn't enough, bringing Beatrice into their home and treating her as he did had finished off any chance of making things right.

Jared pulled Cassy a little closer. She was his wife, after all, and they could dance as closely as they wished. She was light on her feet and followed his lead as if they had danced together for years instead of moments. Her scent wafted to him, light, yet teasing his senses so that an indefinable sensation stirred in his chest.

"I believe I spoke too soon," Cassy said, looking up at him.

"What do you mean?" he asked.

"My ankle is giving me some problem," she admitted.

"We will stop immediately," he said, suiting his actions to his words. "Can you walk?"

"I am not that bad off," said Cassy with a reassuring smile. "I merely need to avoid the dance floor for the rest of the evening."

"Let me help you to a chair," he said, nodding toward a small gilt seat placed along the wall.

"That is much better," said Cassy, as she eased herself down on the chair. "A few moments' rest and I shall be in fine feathers."

"May I fetch you anything? Punch? Water?"

Cassy shook her head. "No, thank you."

Jared felt suddenly tongue-tied, but forced himself to speak. "Cassy, about last night."

"Do not concern yourself about it," she said, staring down at her clasped hands in her lap.

"I cannot ignore it," he insisted, taking her hands in his. "I had no right to approach you while I was completely done over. I meant no harm."

"I know you did not," she said, allowing him to keep

her hands prisoner between his. "I have been on edge recently." She thought of the conversation she had overheard between Beatrice and Crawford and thought what an understatement she had made. "Beatrice and I are not getting on, then the accident this morning—if it was an accident—has put me out of sorts."

"As it should have," he agreed. "I intend to look into it further. In the meantime, I'd like one of my men to accompany you whenever you go out."

"I won't be followed around like a child," she protested, pulling her hands from his.

He leaned his head so close that his breath brushed against her ear. "You may not believe me, but I do not want you to come to harm."

"I should think you had best spend your time concentrating on Beatrice. She will not be happy if you ignore her for long."

"Cassy." Jared breathed her name with more than a little exasperation. "Beatrice is . . ."

"I don't need to hear anything about Beatrice," she said, standing swiftly, confused by the feelings his nearness caused. "I must get back to James. He knows so few people here, and I would be remiss in leaving him too long."

"Cassy." But it was too late. She was already making her way across the room toward her cousin.

Despite the threat that hung over her head, Cassy was in a lighthearted mood the next afternoon. She had awakened late after a good night's sleep and indulged herself by having breakfast in bed. Reluctant to ruin her good humor by meeting up with Beatrice or Jared, she had stayed in her room until nearly time for James to arrive.

"You look absolutely charming," said James when she came down the stairs.

Cassy was wearing a new gown of pistachio color with matching slippers peeping out beneath the skirt. The light, delicate shade of green went well with her hair and eyes, and she was confident she was *au courant*.

"Thank you. You might not have thought so when I first came to Town," she admitted candidly. "I have made some changes since then."

"And you are a complete success, but I'm certain I'm not the only one to tell you that."

"Well, the response has been favorable," she acknowledged, wryly.

"It certainly has," came a voice from the doorway. "My wife is an incomparable who is dazzling the *ton* this Season." Jared sauntered into the room, Beatrice following close behind.

"I'm certain she has always been an incomparable," remarked James gallantly.

Jared crossed to a table which held a decanter and glasses. "Sherry?" he asked, looking around the room. When everyone refused, he poured a glass for himself. Swallowing it in one large gulp, he poured another.

"We are going for a drive in the park. Beatrice thinks I need some fresh air. Don't you, my dear?" He lifted his glass in salute to her.

Cassy felt something shift inside when she heard the endearment, even though it seemed tinged with sarcasm, but she would not go into a decline and ruin her time with James.

"It wouldn't hurt," grumbled Beatrice, stung by his tone. "You are seldom sober enough to make a good companion."

Jared's expression turned menacing. "Then perhaps you should look for someone else to entertain you."

Cassy could see James was embarrassed by the squabble that had erupted between the two. She was not comfortable being in the same room with them, either. It was the first time she had heard Jared speak ill to Beatrice, and her stepsister appeared surprised at his reply.

Beatrice hastened to his side and placed her hand on his arm. "Forgive my impetuous words," she said persuasively. "I have no complaint with your company."

Jared stared down at her a moment longer. "Let us go," he said, setting the glass down on the table with a little more force than necessary. "You will excuse us." He gave a slight bow toward Cassy and James. The two of them departed as quickly as they had arrived. A few moments later the sound of the front door closing reached the drawing room.

"I'm sorry you had to see that," said Cassy in the quiet that had settled over the room.

"There's no need to apologize for someone else's gaucheness," remarked James, a trace of distaste apparent in his voice.

"I should not discuss it, but since you are family . . ." she trailed off.

James laid his hand over hers, and gave her an encouraging smile. "We are cousins," he said. "I hope there is nothing you hesitate to speak about with me."

"You should know that my marriage was arranged. I hardly knew Jared before we wed," she confessed.

"I wish I could have been here to help you," commiserated James.

"Do not blame yourself," she replied quickly. "You couldn't know. At first, I thought I could make it work, but I finally realized it was futile."

"Beatrice?" James asked.

"Not entirely. Beatrice was the intended bride, but when she wasn't available, Jared accepted me in her stead. Perhaps we could still salvage something, but as you can see, he drinks heavily and now Beatrice is involved. He's looking for revenge on his father for what he believes was a betrayal and is killing himself attempting to achieve it."

"You should not be forced to endure his coarseness," said James grimly.

"I cannot change the fact that we are married. However, I have determined to go on with my life as I see fit—just as he has done. My stepsister's being involved is one more embarrassment which I can do nothing about. I have considered returning to the country, but since you have arrived, I intend to finish the Season here in London. Not only do I intend to enjoy your company for as long as possible, but I don't want it to appear I have been driven away by my husband's actions."

"Remember, you now have another home where you would be welcome," said James.

"That means so much to me," replied Cassy, unshed tears glimmering in her eyes.

"Let us go out for some air," suggested James. "You should not be here alone after such an encounter."

Cassy felt better than she had for days. She had a family member to lend support when she needed it, something she had missed since the death of her mother. She wondered whether to ask James for advice on keeping herself alive, then thought they should enjoy one another before she burdened him with more of her problems.

"Shall we call on Lord and Lady Waycross?" she asked. "They are very agreeable people and I think you would enjoy knowing them."

"If you recommend them, they must be very amiable indeed," replied James, helping her into the curricle.

Beatrice was out of sorts as she climbed into Jared's phaeton, but she hid it from him as well as she could. It would not do to anger him again after such a short period of time, no matter how accurate her remark had been. Jared was no longer a comfortable companion, nor did he keep her entertained as he had previously. He was usually drunk and sullen when they were alone, exerting himself only to be pleasant when others were around.

She was beginning to think the plan she and her father had concocted was not worth the cost. Robert Crawford had insisted Beatrice go to Jared's town house when her husband had died. In addition to taking the expense of her upkeep off his shoulders, he advised her to get as close to Jared as she could manage. He wanted money, and he didn't care what she had to do to get it.

Beatrice had used every feminine wile she possessed and still had not been able to lure Jared into her bed or anywhere close to it. She had lived in his household long enough to assume he and Cassy rarely, if ever, shared a bedroom and could not understand why he had not taken advantage of the opportunities she continued to offer him.

She glanced at his profile as they drove along Church Street. He was a handsome man, to be sure, but his feelings must be pickled in the liquor he consumed in large quantities, for his eyes were as cold as the winter Thames whenever he looked at her.

"That was a pleasant interlude," she said, acrimoniously.

Jared did not so much as look in her direction. "As I said, I'm certain there are many men who would welcome the pleasure of your company."

"I do not want anyone else," replied Beatrice, fash-

ioning a pout on her full lips in case he turned toward
her. "But I could use more of your attention."

"You know full well I am married," Jared reminded
her. "And while I may be guilty of many things, I will
not take my wife's sister to bed."

It was plain speaking, thought Jared, but Beatrice
deserved it. She was beginning to press him for more
than he was willing to give. He had no desire to make
her his mistress, and if he did, he would not sleep with
her while Cassy was in the next room. He had subjected
his wife to many embarrassments, but that was one he
would avoid at all costs. At any event, Beatrice did not
appeal to him. She was offensive to him in manner and
dress, and it was all he could do to continue the farce
of escorting her about Town. He was finding revenge
was becoming more wearing on himself than his father.

Beatrice was unaffected by his blunt remarks. "I am
not asking to share your bed," replied Beatrice, although it was exactly what she desired. "I would be
satisfied for the present if you would treat me more
courteously. I have, after all, done nothing to put you
in your present circumstances and should not bear the
brunt of your discontent."

"You're right," agreed Jared. "But I cannot promise
anything better. Electing to spend time with me is your
choice. You are free to accept any offer that is made
to you. I won't object to whatever you decide."

It was not what Beatrice longed to hear, but she
would never have anything more while Cassy was alive.
The best of all possible worlds would be to rid herself
of Cassy, leaving Jared free to be with her. She must
urge her father to go forward with their plan of finding
someone to do away with her stepsister.

"I could not abandon you," replied Beatrice laying
a hand on his arm. "Particularly when Cassandra is
acting so peculiar."

"Is she?" asked Jared. "I wonder."

* * *

Cassy and James had been warmly welcomed when they called on Lord and Lady Waycross. She introduced James, and they took tea while they related the story of how they had come to find one another.

"Do you play?" James asked Eleanor in one of the conversational lulls, inclining his head toward the pianoforte occupying a corner of the room.

"A little," she replied.

"Would you do us the honor?" he asked. "I shall be happy to be page turner."

The two went to the pianoforte and began looking through music, chatting quietly with one another.

"How goes it with Jared?" Lord Waycross asked.

"He and Beatrice departed immediately before we did," said Cassy, allowing that bit of information to tell the tale.

Lord Waycross frowned and drummed his fingers on the arm of his chair. "I vow, I thought any son of mine would have more sense than to become mixed up with Crawford's gel." Realizing what he had said, he quickly spoke again. "You know I do not consider you related to Crawford. If only he had raised Beatrice as your mother raised you, then she could have married into a reputable family. However, I'm afraid Crawford's double-dealing is too ingrained for her to ever shake free of it."

"Jared does not seem to find her offensive," said Cassy.

"I wish you had known Jared before my marriage. He was a totally different man from what he is now. He enjoyed life and lived it to the fullest, with a spirit that touched everyone around him," reminisced Lord Waycross. "Liquor did not rule his every waking hour.

I do not mean to say he never took a drink, but I never saw him cup shot."

"Perhaps he will change his ways if given enough time," said Cassy.

"He's had more than enough time to come about," replied Lord Waycross. "I had hoped marriage would make him more responsible and sober, but it doesn't appear it has changed him in the least."

"I have considered leaving Jared in Town and returning to the country after James leaves," Cassy revealed. "Perhaps Jared would be happier if left alone with Beatrice." She was not yet ready to tell Lord Waycross that her idea to leave was prompted by the content of the conversation she had overheard between Beatrice and Crawford.

"They could not live together," he objected. "Your presence is the only thing that keeps the circumstances acceptable as it is."

"It would make not a whit of difference to Beatrice," replied Cassy. "She would no doubt relish being the object of the *ton's* latest *on-dit.*"

"I hope you will reconsider your plan, for Jared's reputation would be ruined, and I don't feel it would solve anything," said Lord Waycross. "Beatrice may fancy Jared for herself, but I don't believe he has any serious intentions toward her. If so, he would have followed through when Beatrice had her come out."

"You might think differently if you lived beneath our roof for a day," she responded more sharply than she had intended.

Lord Waycross reached over and patted her hand. "I know I am asking more than I should, but be patient with Jared for a little longer. It may take some time, but I believe he will come around."

Cassy sighed. "I will do my best," she promised.

"However, I no longer have the confidence that such a likelihood will occur."

James and Lady Waycross returned to their seats and the conversation turned toward more conventional topics.

"You seem to have gotten along very well with Lady Waycross," remarked Cassy, once she and James were back in the curricle.

"We found we had some acquaintances in common and were catching up on the news." James concentrated on passing a slow-moving town coach before speaking again. "Would you like to plan something for tomorrow?" he asked. "I'm all finished with my business and am free for the entire day."

"I'm afraid I must beg off," said Cassy. "Betsy insists we go shopping tomorrow to match a pair of gloves and purchase hair decorations for the gown I am wearing to the Campbells' ball."

"And I know how important that is," teased James. "Why don't I go with you? I would like to purchase gifts for some of my neighbors, and you are just the person to advise me what a pair of very young ladies would like."

"You would be bored beyond belief," said Cassy.

"I certainly won't," denied James. "Only tell me when you would like to depart and I shall be there."

Before they returned home, they had agreed upon a time to set off on their trip to the shops.

The next day Cassy and James drove to Oxford Street, anticipating the profusion of wares in the shopping bazaars.

"I hope you don't find this too tame for your liking," said Cassy, as they strolled along, with Betsy trailing a respectable distance behind.

"Not at all," he replied. "As I mentioned, I have several gifts to purchase also."

Cassy wondered whether one of them was for a special lady. James was a pleasing man with a productive estate, and she had thought he would have been snapped up by someone by now.

"It is crowded, though," said Cassy.

"We can leave anytime you like," said James.

"I have yet to find a new pair of gloves that is suitable," replied Cassy.

Suddenly, a commotion erupted around her. She was struck from behind and found herself falling, with cries from the ladies and shouts from the gentlemen adding to the confusion. Cassy lost her hold on James's arm and was thrown first one way, then another. As she fell to the rough cobblestones, a small body landed on top of her.

"Cassy, are you unharmed?" asked James as he and Betsy leaned over her.

"Yes." Cassy pushed herself up until she was in a sitting position.

"Are you sure?" questioned Betsy anxiously.

"I'm certain," she assured them as they helped her to her feet. She looked down at the child, who still lay on the sidewalk. "But I believe this young man may need assistance."

"Naw," said the boy, picking himself up. "Sorry I couldn't keep you from bein' hurt, but the knave was too quick for me."

"I'm fine," she reassured him.

The boy's gaze shifted to her side. "Don't think so, ma'am."

Cassy looked down and saw a red stain spreading across the pale blue of her gown.

Eleven

A stinging began on Cassy's side and she felt a bit faint.

"My God, Cassy! You're bleeding!" burst out James.

Betsy pulled out her handkerchief and pressed it to Cassy's side. "Get the carriage," she ordered, and James rushed to do her bidding.

The carriage was close by and took only a short time to arrive. James and Betsy positioned themselves on either side of Cassy as they made their way through the crowd of onlookers, with the young boy following at their heels.

"Is it true you saw someone push me?" Cassy asked the boy as the steps were being let down.

Betsy interrupted before the boy could answer. "We must get her home as quickly as possible."

Betsy's words galvanized James into action, and he helped Cassy into the carriage. The boy stood on the ground watching as Cassy was positioned as comfortably as possible against the soft squabs of the seat.

The faintness was becoming worse and Cassy blinked as she looked down at the small boy. His clothes were little more than rags, and he looked as if he hadn't had a good meal any time in his short life.

"Bring him along," she said, her voice not as strong as she wished.

"Who?" asked James.

"The boy. Bring him along," she repeated.

"There's no need to take him with us. I'll reward him," said James.

"No. I have questions I want to ask," she insisted.

James glanced at Betsy, who shrugged her shoulders. "If it will get us home faster, then do it," she said.

"Come with us," said Cassy, attempting a smile. The boy stood on the cobblestones staring at her, apparently unable to believe his ears.

"Please," said Cassy. "I promise you will not be harmed and there will be a generous reward for you."

At the promise of money, the boy climbed the stairs and settled himself as far in the corner as he could. He eyes were huge as he examined the luxurious interior of the carriage.

"Did you recognize the man who pushed me?" Cassy asked him.

"Not push, ma'am. Saw him with a knife in his hand, aimin' right at your back."

"Balderdash," said James. "He's making it up just to get in your good graces. Who would want to purposely stab you?"

"As you can well see, evidently someone did."

"You shouldn't be talking," said Betsy, accepting James's handkerchief and pressing it against Cassy's side.

"Talking keeps my mind off the pain," said Cassy. "Now, are you sure . . . what is your name?

"William," answered the boy. "But most just call me Little Will."

"All right, Little Will," said Cassy. "Tell me what you saw."

"I was just walkin' along," he began. "I noticed this thatch-gallows actin' shifty like. You can tell 'em once you've seen a few. He pulled out a knife just as he come up behind you. I ran as fast as I could and threw myself at his feet thinkin' to trip him up, but I was too late. He'd already swung the knife. He cursed somethin' awful and started to swing again. I kicked at him and lost my balance. That's when I fell on you. I'm sorry, ma'am." His eyes dropped to the floor of the carriage.

"There's no need to apologize, Will. I imagine you saved my life by falling on me." She smiled at the boy, and his face brightened.

The carriage pulled up at the front of the town house and, despite Cassy's protestations, James carried her into the house and up the stairs to her room.

"I'll send for the doctor," he said, laying her carefully on the bed before leaving.

Betsy was cleaning the wound by the time the doctor arrived.

"Good," he said, as he saw the progress she had made. "Well, my lady, you were certainly lucky. A little more to the left and the outcome might have been much worse. Keep the cut clean," he instructed Betsy. "I'll leave some powder to dust on it and some laudanum to give Lady Carlisle if the pain becomes severe. She'll probably have a slight fever. I'll call tomorrow, but send for me should she become worse."

"Doctor," said Cassy, "there's a boy downstairs in the kitchen who probably saved my life. Examine him, will you? He may have been hurt."

"Of course, my lady. I'll look in on him before I leave."

"Betsy, after Will has a good meal, see he has a bath and some decent clothes," instructed Cassy.

"Don't worry about the boy. He'll be fine as fivepence. You need to rest for a while," said Betsy as Cassy's eyes drifted shut.

* * *

The slamming of the door against the wall awakened Cassy with a start.

"What is going on?" demanded Jared, standing poised in the doorway for a moment before striding across the room.

"Hush," commanded Betsy, standing with her hands on her hips between Jared and the bed.

Cassy moved and gave a small moan as the pain in her side made itself known.

"See what you've done? You've awakened her," accused Betsy.

"Get out of my way, woman. I want to see my wife."

"It's seldom you recognize her as such. Why do so now?" responded Betsy, anger getting the better of her good sense.

Only knowledge that the abigail was speaking the truth and of Cassy's fondness for her kept Jared's anger under control. "I have heard she was injured," he said, attempting to speak calmly. "I would like to see how she is doing."

"It's all right, Betsy. I'm awake," said Cassy.

Betsy reluctantly stepped aside. Jared moved closer to the bed until he was looking down at Cassy. Even though he had been besotted, he remembered the last time he was here and the desire he had felt for his wife. He believed after what had passed between them she would hold him in disdain, but he had been unable to put her out of his mind no matter how arduously he flirted with other women nor how much he drank.

Cassy was propped up in bed against lace-edged pillows that served only to accentuate her frailty. She was more appealing than she had ever been, and it took a great deal of control not to gather her into his arms and plead with her to assure him she was unharmed. Instead, he did what men had been doing for centuries when they were confronted with insurmountable emotion.

"What the devil have you been up to?" he demanded in a gruff voice.

"Shopping," she replied succinctly.

He turned to Betsy. "Tell me what happened."

Betsy related all that occurred from the time they had stepped out of the carriage until the doctor had rendered his opinion on Cassy's health.

"You should not go about such dangerous places," he said, turning back to Cassy.

"I went shopping in a perfectly respectable area," she replied indignantly, annoyed to be spoken to as a child. "I was accompanied by Betsy and James. There is no way anyone could have predicted I would have been attacked." But there was a likelihood, she admitted, recalling Beatrice's and Crawford's conversation.

"James is inadequate to escort a lady," he scoffed.

"He is my cousin, sir, and as able as anyone. We were all taken by surprise, and it was over almost before it began," she said defensively, pulling herself up in bed. Her quick movement caused her to flinch and grow pale.

"See what you have done," reprimanded Betsy, as she moved to the bedside and filled a glass with water.

"I'll do that," Jared said, taking the glass from her hand. He put his arm behind Cassy's shoulders, gently supporting her while she drank. "I didn't mean to upset you. We can discuss what happened when you are feeling better."

"There is little more to discuss, except perhaps Will."

"And who is Will?" Jared asked warily.

"Actually his name is William, better known as Little Will on the streets. He's the boy who saved my life, so I brought him home with me," she announced.

"You what?" exclaimed Jared. "Wouldn't a reward have been sufficient?"

"Well, at least you and James agree on one thing," retorted Cassy.

"But you brought him home?" questioned Jared.

"It seemed to be the least I could do, since I owed him my life. Besides, I could tell he was hungry, and I thought I could see that he had a good meal."

"And has he?"

"I suppose," she replied. "I fell asleep before I could speak to him again."

"I'll check on the boy when we finish," he said.

"I should think we have little more to say," grumbled Cassy.

"I want to see the wound," Jared announced.

"You what?" said Cassy, staring at him as if he had grown a second head.

"I know a little about injuries. It isn't that I don't trust the doctor, but I'd like to see for myself that you've been adequately cared for."

Cassy shook her head in disbelief. "It won't do."

"Of course it will," he insisted. "What could be more normal than for a husband to be concerned for his wife?"

"We are not what you would call a normal husband and wife."

"Perhaps not in every sense of the word," he agreed. "But that does not relieve me of my duty to see you are well taken care of, and I will not leave this room until I see your injury."

Cassy examined his stubborn expression and nodded at Betsy. The maid folded down the bedcovers, then rearranged Cassy's gown until the white bandage which lay over the cut was revealed. She lifted it gently, but Cassy still grimaced slightly.

Jared did not like causing her further pain, but he

was driven to see the wound. He flinched when he saw the cut that marred her silky skin. His hands clinched into fists at his side, and he wanted nothing more than to have them around the neck of the man who had done this. His throat tightened until he found it difficult to speak.

"I've been thinking this might not have been a random attack," remarked Cassy, taking advantage of his silence.

"You think someone tried to kill you?" he asked in disbelief. "It was probably a common thief attempting to cut the strings on your reticule."

"I was holding it in front of me. The man came from behind. Little Will said the man had been following us for some time before he drew his knife and attempted to stab me in the back," she argued.

"I think Little Will took advantage of excellent opportunity to ingratiate himself with you."

"I don't believe that for a minute. And I intend to see he is well taken care of for saving me," she added as Betsy rearranged her gown. "Besides, I am not forgetting my cut saddle girth. Was that an accident also?"

"Assuming your suspicion is correct," said Jared, "who would want to see you dead?"

Cassy's unblinking dark eyes stared into his.

"Surely you do not suspect me?"

Cassy did not reply, but her gaze left his and moved to a point behind him. He turned to find Beatrice standing in the doorway, observing the scene between Jared and Cassy.

"Don't look at me," Beatrice said to Cassy. "I don't have the funds to hire a murderer even should I have the desire."

Cassy did not trust either of them. "A man would wait for payment as long as he knew a gentleman of means was involved."

Jared was newly affronted by the idea that he and Beatrice would plot her demise. "It is the laudanum speaking," he said, nodding toward the bottle on the table.

Beatrice shrugged and disappeared from the doorway.

Cassy leaned back and closed her eyes. "I am too tired to argue any further," she said, effectively ending the conversation.

Jared stood a moment longer staring down at her. She was so small and pale, and he could not think but that he had contributed to the events that had brought her to this point.

"Advise me if there is the slightest change in her condition," he ordered Betsy, before walking softly to the door.

As soon as the room was empty, Betsy came to the side of the bed. "You can open your eyes now. Everyone is gone."

"Thank goodness," replied Cassy.

"Now tell me the truth of what is going on," demanded Betsy.

Cassy told her about the girth being cut on her saddle, and though Jared thought someone had chosen their stable by chance, she was not convinced. After the events of today, she was even more certain both incidents were meant to do away with her permanently.

"I cannot believe it," replied Betsy, her hand clutched at her throat.

"Never say that you doubt me, too. Not after this," she said, motioning to her side.

"I do not doubt what you say. I just cannot believe someone wishes you harm." Betsy reached out and smoothed Cassy's hair as if to affirm she was all right.

"You must say nothing about this. I am attempting

to keep the knowledge confined. However, it seems to be slipping out to more people than I like."

"You might be safer the more people who know," suggested Betsy.

"Or it could make the people responsible even more intent upon doing away with me before they're found out," reasoned Cassy.

"Is there anyone you suspect? And don't tell me Lord Carlisle, for I'll not believe it. He may want his revenge, but I can't believe he's a murderer."

"He is going about with Beatrice, and she would like nothing more than to see me gone. She could marry Jared—and I'm certain she would arrange it one way or another—and have his fortune at her disposal. And you must not discount her father. Robert Crawford has been involved in all of this, beginning with my marriage. He would gain instant respectability and funds to support his gambling habit if Beatrice married Jared," argued Cassy.

"By the Lord!" exclaimed Betsy. "All three of them?"

Cassy shrugged. She did not want to tell Betsy that she had actually heard Beatrice and Crawford speaking of her demise. Betsy thought of her as her own, and she could not depend upon what the abigail would do if she knew for certain that the two were plotting against Cassy. "I can't rule anything out or else I could be exposing myself to the real culprit."

"I will allow no one else in this room," declared Betsy, full of determination.

"I cannot hide from the world," said Cassy. "I intend to go about my business as usual."

"You cannot parade about without any protection," argued Betsy.

"I will have Drew or James by my side, and I will take a footman, also. Of course, you cannot forget Will.

He has saved me once already." Cassy smiled at the thought of the small boy who had not hesitated to throw himself into the fray.

"It is nothing to make light of," objected Betsy.

Cassy winced as she shifted on the bed. "I do not, Betsy, you may count on that. I do not intend to allow anyone to end my life before it is fully begun." Cassy gave a small groan as pain from her side made itself known.

"Here, take some laudanum," said Betsy, pouring the medicine into a spoon and holding it out to Cassy. "And don't worry, no one will get past me," promised Betsy.

"I know I can sleep well," said Cassy, taking the bitter medicine, then sinking back onto the pillows and closing her eyes.

"She as much as accused me of trying to kill her," said Jared. It was the next day, and Jared had waylaid Drew as he arrived at the house with flowers for Cassy. "How could she think I would do that?"

"You were a stranger when the two of you wed," responded Drew. "I doubt whether you have made an attempt to get to know her. What should she think? You left her in the country the morning after the wedding and did not send for her until at least a fortnight had passed. You did not explain you were using her to extract revenge on your father. You invited her stepsister to live under the same roof with you, and you are constantly in her company.

"You're aware that Beatrice had hopes of marrying you at one time, and that she would do nearly anything to catch you into the parson's mousetrap. Cassy is the one obstacle blocking her way. Is it any wonder that she might suspect you or Beatrice had something to do with the attack?"

"I know it sounds sordid," admitted Jared, "but I would do her no harm. What do you think?" asked Jared.

"Known you far longer than your wife has," replied Drew. "So I don't need to ask whether you are involved. But put yourself in Cassy's place. Then maybe you won't resent her way of thinking."

"If she believes I would do this, then she must suspect I cut her saddle girth."

"Don't know what she thinks," declared Drew. "But if both incidents were deliberate, it makes sense it might be the same person. It's up to you to discover who precipitated both. Prove you had nothing to do with it."

"What has my life come to that I must prove to my wife I am not attempting to kill her?" Jared asked, more to himself than his friend.

Drew did not respond. Jared must answer his own question. It would do him no good if Drew answered it for him.

Drew picked up a bouquet of flowers from the table. "Must take these up to Cassy before they turn brown."

"Will you see whether you can talk her out of this mad idea that Beatrice and I are attempting to kill her?" asked Jared.

"Will do my best," promised Drew. "But can you eliminate Beatrice so easily?"

Beatrice found him still pondering that question when she arrived in the drawing room some time later. "You are in deep thought," she said.

"On occasion I find it useful."

"I hope I am the object of your deliberations," she

said, seating herself next to him on the settee, offering a coquettish smile.

Jared had no desire to rouse Beatrice's anger. Drew had caused him to look at Beatrice in a different light. He needed her in a good humor in order to learn as much as possible. Not that he thought Beatrice would personally harm Cassy, but there were men for hire who would stop at nothing if offered enough. He didn't think Beatrice would know anyone of such repute, but Crawford certainly would, and the two of them could be conspiring to rid themselves of Cassy. Beatrice had not hidden her belief that he should have been married to her, not Cassy. And after serious consideration, Jared could not preclude her from planning Cassy's *accidents*.

"I often find myself thinking of lovely ladies," he said.

Beatrice was pleased with his response. He had not been as attentive of late, and she feared she would lose him—if not to his wife, then to one of the Fashionable Impures who actively sought his protection. She wished her father would fulfill his part of their plan, but if today had been one of his attempts, he was as inadequate as ever.

"Tonight is the Elton ball," said Beatrice, wondering whether she should mention it after Cassy's experience.

"We shall continue as usual," commented Jared, before she could even ask the question.

A smile appeared on Beatrice's face. He must care for her, or else he would not abandon his wife immediately after she was injured. "I will wear something particularly designed to cheer you up," she promised.

Jared silently groaned. He was becoming exceedingly weary of Beatrice's propensity toward gowns whose colors and textures would damage a blind man's eyes. And if that were not enough, her hair decorations were even more atrocious.

"You need not go to any trouble for me. You make a simple gown seem elegant," he prevaricated, hoping to cause her to rein in her imagination.

Beatrice actually giggled. She hadn't done that since she was a green girl, but Jared's compliments overwhelmed her. "I must retire to my room to prepare for tonight." She patted him on the arm and left the room nearly skipping.

"What have I done?" he mumbled to himself.

He found out later, when Beatrice descended the stairs wearing a Bishop's blue gown, her hair covered by a huge turban of blue and gold satin edged with gold fringe, three large plumes undulating from its top.

That evening Drew met Lord Waycross at a musical and advised him of the attack on Cassy.

"For God's sake! Is she all right?" he blurted out.

"Doctor says she will mend all right and tight if she rests a few days," replied Drew. "Her maid is doing her best to see she does so, but it will probably be difficult."

"I don't think Jared would like us to call, but we'll send flowers and a note. Eleanor will be distressed when she learns," he said, searching the room for his wife. "And to think we were in the same area today. I was purchasing tobacco while Eleanor and her maid searched for some frippery or another."

"Odd coincidence, to be sure," Drew agreed.

"There she is," said Lord Waycross, as he spied Eleanor across the room. "She is talking to James Howard. Perhaps I should ascertain whether he has told her about Cassy yet. She has grown fond of Cassy,

and I know she will be upset to hear she's been injured. You will excuse me?"

Drew called for his coach and departed. He had no
desire to hear music this evening, nor the inconsequential chatter which passed for conversation at such
events. Something evil was twining itself around Jared
and Cassy and, as yet, he saw no way to prevent it.

The next morning, Cassy insisted upon seeing Little
Will. The boy looked far different from the last time
she had seen him. He had been given a bath and
dressed in clean clothes that fit him. His hair was as
golden as wheat in the field, his eyes as blue as the
summer sky. He was a lovely child and would grow up
to be a handsome man.

After speaking with him, Cassy realized her initial
assessment was true. He seemed more intelligent than
most children his age and could readily learn if given
the chance. Cassy wanted to help him better himself
and offered to see that he learned what he needed to
make his way in the world.

"Don't like the idea of sittin' indoors all day with a
book," he said when she mentioned reading.

"It won't be all day, and you will never get ahead
in life unless you learn how to read."

His mouth took on a stubborn expression. "I get
along all right."

"You have done very well indeed," agreed Cassy.
"But think how much better off you would be if you
could read and write as well as do your numbers."

Will stared at the floor, evidently thinking over her
proposal.

"You will be well fed and dressed," she coaxed.

"No ruffles," he demanded.

"Absolutely no ruffles," said Cassy with a solemn face. "Do we have a deal?"

"Dunno."

"No more sleeping on the streets. You will have a room all your own," she promised.

"Well," he said, still sounding a little dubious.

"You can be my page," she said, holding it out to him like a carrot to a stubborn horse. "You'll have a smart new uniform and will go everywhere with me."

"Dunno," he said again, but Cassy could tell he was beginning to yield.

Cassy had saved her strongest inducement until last. "You'll be able to ride with the coachman."

"Up front?" he questioned, his eyes wide.

"That's right," she assured him. "And perhaps in time he will allow you to handle the ribbons. But remember, you must learn to read and write in exchange."

"If I can ride up front, I promise," he finally bargained.

"Then we are agreed," said Cassy. She only wished her own life might be put to rights so easily.

Cassy was forced to keep to her bed for several days. During that time, Jared formed the habit of coming in each morning and evening to ask after her health. He was very formal with her, and she supposed he was still indignant because she had indicated there was a chance he could be involved in the incidents which had befallen her. And why shouldn't she? She knew beyond all doubt Beatrice was conspiring to get rid of her so that she might take her place, and since Jared was still going about with her, what was Cassy to think? If he wasn't in on the actual planning, he was allowing a situation to exist that made her more vulnerable to attack.

Cassy breathed a sigh of relief the morning the doctor allowed her to spend part of the day in the sitting room of her suite. "You must remain quiet, for we cannot chance that you will break the wound open again by going up and down the stairs or engaging in other activity. However, from the way the wound looks, it appears it will not be long before you will be going about as usual. Just be patient," he advised her.

"Be patient," grumbled Cassy, as Betsy helped her settle into a chair, then tucked a blanket over her lap.

"It won't be so bad," said Betsy. "You can have visitors now. At least, the ones you can trust."

"I've had a visitor every day whom I don't trust and have not enjoyed it at all," complained Cassy.

"Hush, now. I don't mean Lord Carlisle. Although I have been surprised he has been so regular in visiting you."

"You mean you're surprised he takes time away from Beatrice to see me, don't you? To my way of thinking, I would much rather he forget about me, for his visits do not cheer me up at all."

"Then perhaps Viscount Stanford would be more to your liking. I understand he is downstairs waiting to see you."

"Drew is here?" asked Cassy, all smiles.

"That he is. Do you want to see him or sit here and complain all morning?"

"Tell him to come up, please, Betsy," she begged. "I will not raise another fuss today."

A few minutes later, Cassy heard Drew's booted steps in the hall. He stuck his hand, holding a bouquet of flowers, into the room first. "Is it safe to come in?" he asked.

Cassy giggled at the sight. "Since you are bringing such lovely flowers, I suppose you may enter."

Drew pushed the door open and stepped inside. "But these are for Betsy. I must stay on her good side so she will allow me to visit."

"Gammon," responded Cassy. "Come in and sit down."

"Heard you're not the best of patients," commented Drew, after they had greeted one another and he had taken a chair nearby.

"Humph! I am doing as well as anyone could be expected to do. What would you do if you were restricted to your room for days?"

"You don't want to know," he teased. Then his face turned serious. "Went back to Oxford Street to see what I could uncover. A few people remembered the incident, but didn't get a good look at the man who stabbed you."

"I wouldn't expect they would. It was so crowded that day." She shuddered, remembering what had occurred. "But thank you for trying."

"Don't want to claim all the credit. Jared went with me."

"I'm surprised," Cassy remarked shortly.

"Shouldn't disregard him out of hand. He was in a pelt when he came from your room. He may not say it, but he's worried about you."

"And that's why he's sat by my bed continually since I was attacked," Cassy said sarcastically, "not that I would want it. But it might seem callous to some for a man to continue going about with another woman when his wife is still abed from an attempt on her life. And that the other woman could be involved in the attack makes it even more remarkable."

"Could be he's attempting to discover who's behind it," suggested Drew.

Cassy eyed him warily. "Do you really believe that, or are you merely endeavoring to placate my feelings?"

"Known Jared since we were both in leading strings and would need to catch him in the act to believe he would harm you. Hasn't had his head on straight since his father's marriage, but don't believe he's changed beneath the layer of bitterness and the liquor he consumes."

Cassy remained silent, listening, but not convinced of his words.

Drew allowed the silence to linger for a moment before continuing. "Don't think he considered what a marriage like the one he intended would do to you. Perhaps is just now realizing what a disservice he has done. Could want to right the wrong."

"Do you mean to say he actually wants to make our marriage work after all he has said and done?" demanded Cassy.

"Can't speak for Jared," said Drew. "Just my observations."

"I don't know whether I could ever be civil to him, let alone make a marriage out of the shambles in which we are mired. I have no idea what it would take to begin," she admitted honestly. "There is no question Beatrice must be gone from our lives forever, and I wonder whether he would be willing to give her up. He would need to make peace with his father and Eleanor, and then I must forgive him for all he has said to me." Cassy stared across the room, mulling over the seemingly insurmountable obstacles that stood in the way of her marriage becoming a real one. She shook her head and turned back to Drew. "But first I must identify who is attempting to kill me, or all this will not matter."

"Trust Jared to help," advised Drew.

"That may be impossible," she replied.

Betsy brought in tea, and for a time the two were occupied in filling cups and selecting cakes from the assortment cook sent up.

"We have become far too serious," said Cassy, once they were alone again. "Tell me all the *on-dits* I've missed."

Drew spent the rest of the visit regaling her with the antics of the *ton,* keeping her mind from the ugliness which loomed over her.

Cassy's close call with death and her discussion with Drew made her reconsider her present position. Life was so precarious at best that to continue her current course seemed untenable. Was there a way to make something whole out of the tattered remnants of her marriage? Drew had indicated Jared might be regretting the course their marriage had taken. She wondered whether he was right and whether Jared would be willing to sever his connection with her stepsister in order to put their marriage to rights.

Even if Jared agreed to give up Beatrice, that still left Eleanor. Cassy had no idea how her husband felt about his past love, since Jared never mentioned Eleanor when speaking of the rift between him and his father. The passing of time could have done its work, and it was possible Jared no longer loved Eleanor with the vigor he once did. His continued split from his father could be fueled by sheer obstinance, not from devotion to a woman. He was a stubborn man, but perhaps if Eleanor could speak with him, he would be convinced he should abandon the memory of his love for her. That would go a great distance in bringing the two men back together again, and perhaps leave Jared more time to consider his own marriage.

However, Jared's drinking was something else to address. If it stemmed from the fight with his father, then it was possible he could overcome it once he put aside the argument with Lord Waycross. Would he be willing to undertake the venture, or did the liquor have too strong a hold over him no matter what the situation with his father? There was far too much to think about, decided Cassy, her head spinning.

"Do you feel up to having another visitor?" said Betsy, interrupting her deliberations.

"It depends. If it is Mr. Simons who writes those extremely poor verses to my alabaster skin, I would prefer he be told I am not receiving callers."

"Mr. Simons has left numerous offerings of roses which are downstairs in the drawing room. However, he has not gathered the courage to call upon you in person."

"Thank God," replied Cassy fervently. "He is a very nice man, I am sure, but I hope he looks elsewhere for feminine companionship."

"I blame Lord Carlisle for making it seem you are open to attention to any man who comes your way," complained Betsy.

"It is not that bad," said Cassy. "Mr. Simons is merely playing the game. It is all the thing for a gentleman to yearn after a lady who is unapproachable. If I became receptive to his advances, he could probably not get away quick enough. So you need not worry I am going to be carried off on the back of a white horse. Now who is below waiting to see me?"

"Lord, I had forgotten. It's Mr. Howard. Do you want to see him?"

"I certainly do. Show him up. And bring some sherry—and apple tarts, if cook has them. He is particularly fond of them."

"You are looking in fine twig," said James when he entered a few minutes later.

"I am much better," she assured him with a smile.

"The doctor says I shall be up and around in no time at all."

"Do not rush it," he warned. "A few days more or less will not matter."

"It means you'll be closer to returning to your home, and our time together will be shortened."

"Perhaps there is something I can offer that will cheer you," he answered, leaning toward her.

"What would that be?" she asked.

"We have often spoken about your mother's home," he began. "How would you like to see it?"

"I would like it above all things," she replied.

"Then you shall do so," he stated. "Once you are well enough to travel and can get away from your commitments, we shall make a brief sojourn to my home. I will show you all about the grounds and the town where your mother once lived."

Cassy clasped her hands together in joy. "I cannot believe it. I have longed to know where my family came from, to feel connected to some place on this earth, and now my prayer has been answered."

James looked abashed. "If I had known it meant so much to you, I would have invited you much sooner, but I had no idea . . ." His words trailed off into embarrassment. "I just assumed you knew you were welcome and there was no need for a formal invitation."

"There's no need for an apology. I've been adapting to my new life and could probably not have visited any earlier. But now that I'm settled in, I think a trip to the country is just what I need."

"Excellent!" replied James. "It is just left to set the date."

"I will need to speak with the doctor, but as soon as he says I am fit to travel, we shall go," she decided. "Oh, I am so excited. I don't know how I shall get along until we leave."

"Do not expect too much," warned James. "While the estate is nothing to be ashamed of, I'm certain it cannot compare to Lord Carlisle's country home."

"It doesn't matter if it's a shack!" she burst out, jubilantly.

He looked at her quizzically, amused at her enthusiasm.

"Well, perhaps, just a little," she amended quickly. "But if that is all there was, I would still want to see it. You have no idea how solitary a person can feel when they have no connection to anyone or any place on this earth. To know where you came from is to help you know where you are going, and I have been lacking that confidence, particularly since I lost my parents."

"Then we shall make the trip as soon as you are well enough," he said.

"Thank you, James. I am truly grateful I found you." She quickly blinked away the tears that formed in her eyes. Gentlemen did not like watering pots.

Cassy lay in her bed that night thinking back on her conversation with James. It would not be long before she would see her mother's home. James had told her there were portraits of the family and perhaps some of her mother's belongings were still stored in the attics. Cassy could scarcely wait until they arrived at Derby. She would speak to the doctor the next day to see when he thought she might be able to travel.

It was some time before she returned to the problem with which she had been grappling when James had called. Or perhaps she had been purposefully avoiding considering whether she and Jared could patch up their marriage until it resembled one acceptable to them both.

The important question for Cassy was could she attempt a normal life with her husband after all that had happened between them? She would need to forgive how their marriage came about, with all the unpleasantness that had followed since, and concentrate on the few tender moments they had shared.

The candle had burned low before Cassy decided she would make one more attempt to save a marriage which had never been given a chance. She wanted children, and if that was all that came of their union, then she would learn to be content.

She resolved to appeal to Jared to put everything behind them and begin again. It might not be what either of them had planned for their life, but it would be more than they had at present. Perhaps in time a genuine bond would form between them.

Cassy was still awake when she heard Jared return home. It became quiet very suddenly, not his usual sounds of preparing to retire. She climbed out of bed, careful not to cause damage to the cut on her side. Tiptoeing across the floor, she eased the door open to Jared's suite. Her breath caught in her throat. Jared was sprawled half dressed across his bed. Bernice, clad only in her shift, was leaning over him.

Cassy clasped her hand over her mouth. Her stomach heaved and she felt she might be ill. Disgusted at the sight, she closed the door and leaned back against it, welcoming the coolness of the wood as it seeped through the thin fabric of her nightgown. That Jared would carry on with her stepsister while under the same roof with his own wife was abhorrent to her, particularly after he had sworn Beatrice was not his mistress. Tears streamed down her face, and Cassy realized she was grieving at the loss of the last bit of hope for her marriage.

Twelve

Beatrice straightened up when she heard the door close between Jared's and Cassy's room. She silently clapped her hands and twirled around, thrilled that her subterfuge had worked. Anyone seeing her with Jared a few moments earlier could have thought nothing else than that they were enjoying a romp in bed together. It did not matter that he was so drunk he was unable to find his way to his rooms and had to rely on her for guidance. Appearance was the only thing that signified when Cassy had peered into the room, and Beatrice had made sure there was no mistaking what was going on.

She glanced down at Jared and wrinkled her nose in disgust. She was bored beyond words at his constant drunkenness; it reminded her too much of her father and his friends. When she had Jared under her thumb, he would either stop his drinking or go his own way without her. After all, she would have his money. If he drank himself to death, the sooner she would have it all to herself.

There was no reason to stay in his room any longer, she decided. Jared would not awaken until morning, and she was certain Cassy would not repeat her trip to his room. Beatrice hastily donned her gown and collected her belongings. She had done all she could to forward the scheme to get rid of her stepsister. If

Cassy returned to the country after seeing her husband and stepsister together, then a tragic accident could be more easily arranged. She had narrowly escaped death twice. Surely her luck could not continue. Opening the door, she slipped out into the hall and returned to her room, pleased with the results of her night's work.

Overnight Cassy's misery strengthened into a resolve to ignore Jared and Beatrice. She had excused Jared's actions time and again, blaming them on the disappointment he had faced in losing Eleanor. But, as Drew put it, he was a grown man. It was more than time to get on with living.

Jared had chosen instead to wallow in his grief, to attempt to strike back at his father like a recalcitrant schoolboy, and by doing so had ruined her life along with his.

And was she any better? She had accepted his treatment, then watched while he formed an alliance with her stepsister, which had culminated in the scene she had observed last night.

Well, no more.

Jared awakened the next day with his head aching and his mouth dry as dust. Beatrice's scent was on his pillow, and he wondered what had happened the night before. He was afraid what Thomas would tell him if he asked, so he merely dressed in his usual meticulous style and made his way to the dining room, hoping coffee would make him a decent human being again.

He had spent the time since waking considering what he should do with his life. With a fairly clear mind and as honest an assessment as he could make, he realized he no longer felt the savage anger of betrayal toward his father. He was less eager to admit that the love he once felt for Eleanor no longer filled his heart, for that would mean that everything that had happened had been for naught, and he did not like to think he had wasted so much of his life. He wondered how he could have carried the grudge to such lengths.

The empty void resulting from the fatal love he had harbored for Eleanor was filled with the presence of a small, brown-haired woman who had stolen into his heart while he was unaware. Or perhaps drunk was more like it, he admitted with contempt.

But however it had happened, he knew it to be true. He loved Cassy and desired to waste no time in proving it to her. Nothing would keep them apart any longer. He would take her away from London with all its unpleasant memories, and they would not return until he had replaced every one with a delightful experience. His spirits lifting immeasurably with his decision, he dressed with care and made his way downstairs to find his wife.

Jared discovered Cassy in the drawing room. She was wearing a morning dress of yellow trimmed in brown, with yellow ribbons in her hair. She looked altogether charming. "I have been searching for you," he said.

"I'm surprised. I can't imagine how you could pull yourself away from Beatrice so early."

Dread swept over Jared, but he forced himself to ask the question. "What do you mean?"

"Last night, for some unknown reason, I decided to talk with you about redeeming what we could from the mess we've made of this marriage."

Jared felt a flare of hope that their thoughts were running in the same direction. He took a step toward her and opened his mouth to speak, but Cassy put up a silencing hand.

"I thought I heard you enter, but there was no sound coming from your room, so I opened the door slightly to see whether you were there. What I found was more than what I had bargained for," she said, her eyes trained on a spot across the room. "You were in bed, but not alone." She turned her eyes toward him, her smoldering gaze touching his. "Beatrice was with you."

Jared was frozen in place, his mind sparking with thoughts. He should have asked Thomas about what had happened the night before. At least he would have been prepared for Cassy's confrontation. Now he had no answer to what had happened, or evidently had happened, the night before. Had he made love to Beatrice without remembering it? He could not believe it of himself.

"Cassy, I . . . I don't know what to say. I don't remember being with Beatrice last night."

"If you're going to say you were drunk, don't waste your breath. That is no excuse, at least not to me. I will finish the Season here in London, mostly to be with my cousin. But as soon as James leaves, I shall be gone. I will not return to your country estate, but establish myself elsewhere, leaving you free to do whatever you want with whomever you wish without a wife looking over your shoulder."

"I will not allow . . ."

"The time is long past when you have any right to decide whether you will or will not allow me to do anything. I shall do as I see fit, and if you decide to attempt to force me into anything else, I shall make certain all London knows all your dirty little secrets." Without waiting for a reply, Cassy rose and left the room.

Jared lowered himself into a chair, feeling far worse than he had at discovering Eleanor and his father were marrying.

He stood, walked to the window, and looked outside. The perfect summer day seemed to mock his feelings. His hopes for his marriage were in ruins, and it was no one's fault but his own.

He suddenly turned, strode from the room, and climbed the stairs. He must get away, where he could think without the constant interruptions he experienced each day while in Town. "Thomas," he called when he entered his rooms. "We are going to the country."

A short time later, Jared descended the stairs. At that moment, Thomas was storing several portmanteaus in the coach. "Regis, I am going down to the country. I don't know how long I will be. Perhaps no more than a few days, perhaps longer. In any event, if anyone asks—particularly Mrs. Vance—I am away on business."

"Certainly, my lord."

Jared hesitated at the door, wondering whether he was doing the right thing. It was perhaps not best for making things right with Cassy, if he ever could. But he needed to make decisions about his own life before he could approach Cassy again about righting their marriage and attempting to make a real one of it.

He left the house and climbed into the coach, hoping when he returned he would have a plan of action for righting all the wrongs of the past few years.

Crawford barely missed meeting Jared as he sauntered into the drawing room where Beatrice sat, resplendent in a gown of amaranth. The purple color with a pinkish tint did nothing complimentary for his daughter, but he did not want to get her in high dudgeon so early in his visit, so he made no mention of it.

"Good morning, Father," she greeted him, her voice light and airy.

"You have met with some success," he guessed, observing her demeanor.

"Sit down and let me tell you what I have been up to," she said, patting the seat beside her. The next few minutes were taken up with Beatrice's telling of what had happened the night before.

"And you left before morning?" Crawford asked.

Beatrice pouted. It was an expression that did not suit her. "Is that all you have to say? Can't you offer me a compliment instead of a complaint?"

"Of course you did well," he replied, placating her. "However, it would have been much better had the household known you had spent the night with him."

"I could not do it," whined Beatrice. "The smell of liquor offended me more than usual, and he was lying across the bed. If I had stayed, I would have had to sit the rest of the night, and how would it look to his valet if he found Jared on the bed and me in a chair? It would have proved nothing."

"I suppose you're right," Crawford conceded.

Beatrice quickly took advantage of his acknowledgment. "And you have no right to complain about me when you allowed Cassy to get away on Oxford Street."

"I did not allow her to get away," he objected vehemently.

"Then you hired someone completely inadequate for the job, for it was certainly bungled," she remarked.

"I am telling you for the last time, I had nothing to do with the Oxford Street incident. It was probably the result of an attempted robbery."

"I will say no more," said Beatrice. "But I know it was your doing. You will simply not admit it because you were unsuccessful."

Crawford glared at her, but decided to allow the matter to rest. "Have you heard anything from either of them today?"

"Well, Cassy is still confined to her rooms from the knife cut, so I will need to visit my dear stepsister if I wish to discover her reaction to last night's little scene." Beatrice nearly purred with satisfaction. "As for Jared, I've neither seen or heard anything from him. We are to attend the Wilsons' soiree tonight, so I may not see him till then."

"I will arrange to be there, also. You can tell me about Cassy's reaction."

"Is it too much to hope she will be gone by the morning?" asked Beatrice.

"Cassy has more bottom than I credited her with. She may not be as easy to dislodge as we first suspected."

"Then it is up to you to get a better man for the job," said Beatrice.

"I have not yet hired anyone," he insisted, exasperated because she did not believe him.

"It does not matter whether you did or not. Concern yourself with finding someone competent," she directed.

"I am doing the best I can," he grumbled. "You must do the same. Once Cassy is out of the way, your position with Jared should be solidified in whatever manner it takes."

"Leave Jared to me," she said, a satisfied expression on her face.

"I will see you tonight, then," he said, patting her on the shoulder as he left.

Beatrice waited until she heard the door close behind her father. She was going to enjoy confronting her stepsister. Cassy had gotten entirely too full of herself lately. Straightening the skirt of her new gown, Beatrice ascended the stairs.

Betsy had just left to bring Cassy tea when she heard the door open. "Did you forget something?" Cassy looked up from her embroidery to see Beatrice instead of Betsy standing in the open door. "What are you doing here?" she asked.

"I've come to visit," said Beatrice, moving further into the room. "Aren't you happy to see me?"

"I would sooner see the devil himself," said Cassy, deciding to drop all pretense of getting along.

Beatrice widened her eyes in feigned surprise. "How could you say that when I've been so worried about your condition?"

"You are only worried I will cheat death," accused Cassy. "It would have suited your purpose splendidly if the knife had done its work successfully. Then you would have had the opportunity to have Jared all to yourself."

"I had nothing to do with your injury. I already have Jared, so why should I risk my own freedom in doing away with such a worthless creature as you?" Beatrice smirked. "You saw us last night, didn't you?" she asked.

Cassy did not reply, but merely stared at Beatrice, hoping she would go away. Instead, Beatrice moved closer, leaning over Cassy, the venom in her eyes burning brightly.

"I heard the door open," Beatrice continued. "I knew you were watching us, and I didn't care. It was time you realized just how . . . *close* Jared and I have become. Far closer, I'll wager, than you have ever been."

"But you are still not his wife," replied Cassy, unable to say any more.

"Not yet. However, with your propensity for accidents, I may soon have a chance."

"Are you threatening me?" asked Cassy.

"No. I am merely commenting on past events. But

you should be careful," warned Beatrice. "There is no telling when another accident will happen, and it could be your last."

"You had something to do with the stabbing, didn't you?"

"Of course not. It's merely my feeling that you might be safer in the country. Perhaps you should make plans to journey there."

"I will leave London at my own pleasure," replied Cassy. "You may hold Jared in the palm of your hand, but I will not allow you to drive me from my own home."

"It may be more prudent . . ." began Beatrice.

"Prudence be damned!" exclaimed Cassy, losing control of her temper. "Now get out!"

"What is going on here?" asked Betsy, as she entered carrying the tea tray.

"I'm merely visiting my stepsister," said Beatrice, stepping back from Cassy.

"She is not to have any visitors, especially not the likes of you," replied Betsy, mad as hops at this woman, who was no better than a strumpet in her eyes.

"I was just leaving," said Beatrice. "I believe I've said all I came to say."

"You've wasted your time," snapped Cassy. "If anything, this knife wound has made me more convinced than ever to continue my own way. If that conflicts with your plans, you should reconsider, for I will never, never buckle under to you again."

"It's time you left, miss," said Betsy, taking Beatrice by the arm and pulling her toward the door. Though the abigail was older, she had worked her entire life and was stronger than anyone would expect. Beatrice's rage mounted as Betsy walked her across the room.

"You will not get away with this! I'll tell Jared."

"Betsy does not work for Jared," Cassy reminded her.

"You had best look over your shoulder at all times, for you'll pay for this," threatened Beatrice.

"I've no doubt you'll try," replied Cassy wearily. "But I will be better prepared from now on."

Betsy closed the door as soon as Beatrice passed through it. "What was that all about?" she asked.

"Merely Beatrice up to her tricks again. Betsy, tell Regis I'd like a footman outside our door day and night until I tell him differently. There is no need to make it easy if anyone is plotting my demise."

"I will sleep easier," said Betsy.

The confrontation with Beatrice had taken more out of Cassy than she liked to admit. "I would like to lie down now," she said.

Cassy did not think she would be able to rest, but when her head touched the pillow, her eyes drifted shut, sealing out the ugliness that Beatrice had brought with her.

"What did you learn?" asked Crawford, when he met Beatrice at the soiree later that evening.

"That my stepsister is a stupid bit of baggage. Not that I didn't know it before, but it is far worse than I first thought," said Beatrice, slapping her folded fan into the palm of her hand.

"Quit complaining, and tell me what happened," instructed Crawford.

"Cassy will not be driven away. At least, that's what she informed me. She declared she will leave when she desires and will not be forced out by anyone, including me. She even had that woman of hers throw me out of the room," Beatrice admitted, chagrined.

Crawford gave a short laugh. "Must admit she's a

game one. But what of Jared? If he decides to send her away, there will be nothing she can do. Put your attention to him, and allow me to take care of Cassy."

"If only I could," replied Beatrice. "Jared is gone. I could get no more from that stiff-lipped butler of his than that he was away on business. I cannot believe he would simply leave without saying a word to me. He was to escort me tonight, and I was forced to travel here on my own."

"So Jared has flown," mused Crawford. "That is not good news. We must move quickly before he returns. I have saved the good news until last. I have found a way to see that Cassy is laid in the dust for good, and no one will be the wiser that it was not an accident."

Beatrice's despondent mood brightened. "Tell me," she demanded.

"I do not want the scheme to get out. It's too important to us," he said.

"You don't trust me?" she questioned, astonished that he did not. "I will remember this once I am Jared's wife and you come to me for money."

Crawford grasped Beatrice's arm and squeezed until she winced with pain. "Don't threaten me, girl. I'll not have it. Accept that I have a plan which will get us both what we want, and be prepared to comfort Jared on the passing of his wife." Crawford walked away without another word, leaving Beatrice to rub her throbbing arm and wonder what he had planned.

Cassy had no visitors the day after her confrontation with Beatrice. She was not surprised at Jared's absence after their argument. Betsy said the staff was buzzing about Lord Carlisle's quick departure—one moment he was there, the next he and his valet were climbing into the traveling coach. However, none of them knew

his destination nor when he would return except for
Regis, and the butler was not talking.

Cassy would have thought that Jared and Beatrice
were escaping to enjoy some time alone, except that
her stepsister was still in residence. Rumors were that
she was not at all happy with Jared's disappearance.
She had threatened Regis for not revealing Jared's destination, but the butler had steadfastly insisted he had
been ordered to disclose nothing concerning Lord
Carlisle's trip.

The next morning the doctor gave Cassy leave to
go downstairs if she wished. With the aid of Betsy, Cassy
made her way to the drawing room. She did not know
whether Beatrice was in the house at the moment, but
she would not allow Beatrice to keep her confined to
her rooms. Cassy was married to Jared. She was the
mistress of the house, and she meant to assert her
rights. If Beatrice had been involved in attempting to
harm her, she would soon find it had not worked in
her favor. Two close calls with death had merely
brought Cassy's stubbornness into play.

She looked up when Regis came to the door. "Mr.
Howard has come to call, madam."

"Show him in," she said, ridiculously pleased for
the opportunity to speak to someone without arguing.

"You look much better," James said in greeting
when he entered the room.

"Thank you. Except for some tenderness, I believe
I am healed. However, my spirits are low from being
confined to my rooms for so long."

"Then we shall take care of that," he promised. "If
you have nothing planned for the next few days, would
you like to visit your mother's home?"

"Oh, James," she said, tears gathering in her eyes.
"There is nothing I would like better, and I'm certain
it would cheer me up considerably."

"We shall do it then," he announced. "When would you like to leave?"

"I could be ready tomorrow, if that's not too soon."

"Good. I shall come by at ten o'clock. That should give you time for a good night's rest."

"I shall not rest at all just thinking about the trip," she said.

"Then perhaps we should cancel our plans if just the thought will not allow you to sleep," he teased.

"You have already promised, and I will not permit you to withdraw it. I have looked forward to this for as long as I can remember, and I shall not be cheated out of it. So pack your bags, Mr. Howard, for we are going for a drive tomorrow."

James laughed out loud. "I see you will not be thwarted. We should be able to make the drive in one day. However, if you become too fatigued, we will spend a night at an inn. You need not bring your abigail with you, for I have a maid who is experienced in waiting on ladies. We will travel lightly and quickly."

"How long do you expect to stay?" asked Cassy.

"This will need be a short stay, since I must be back in Town before Friday next. You will have time to look around and make yourself familiar with the estate. After the Season is over, I hope you will agree to come visit for as long as you like."

"I could not ask for a better cousin than you," said Cassy.

"Do you think Lord Carlisle will object to our plan?" James asked.

"He is not home," revealed Cassy. "I don't know where he went nor for how long, but even if he were here, I would go despite any objections he might offer."

"You are a woman who knows her own mind," said James. "A fit descendant of the Howard family."

Regis and the footman brought in tea, and Cassy had James describe the estate and the countryside surrounding it.

"I believe you will like it," he said, as he rose to leave.

"I'm certain I shall," she said. "I will be ready then at ten o'clock."

"I will see you then," he said, giving a small bow before leaving the room.

James had no sooner left than Beatrice appeared. "How sweet it is to see you and your newly found cousin getting along so famously."

"Don't tell me you have stooped to listening at doors," replied Cassy.

"You were making no effort to keep your conversation secret," said Beatrice. "I should think you would be traveling with your husband, rather than your cousin."

"I should think *you* would be traveling with my husband, rather than being left behind," mocked Cassy, watching Beatrice's face flush at the remark.

"Jared's decision to travel was too precipitous for me to accompany him."

"I understand no one knew he was going until he was ready to leave. I wonder why that was. It couldn't be that he wanted to get away from you, could it?"

"No more than he wanted to avoid your presence," shot back Beatrice. "You forget who was in his bed the night before he left."

"I've not forgotten at all," said Cassy. "That is why I am telling you to leave my house."

"What?" screeched Beatrice, her hands fisting at her side.

"I will be gone for a few days beginning tomorrow morning. When I return, I don't wish to see you here."

"You can't do this," shrieked Beatrice. "You have no right. Jared will not allow you to do this."

Cassy called for the butler. "Regis, would you witness this, please?" She turned back to Beatrice, who still stood, red-faced, in the middle of the floor. "I am mistress of this house, and I will decide who lives under its roof, particularly when my husband is not at home. I don't see Jared here defending you, so I am telling you once again. You will be out of this house by the time I return, or I shall have Regis set you out bag and baggage. I'm certain he will enjoy it for the way you have treated the staff while you have been here."

"It will be my pleasure, madam," replied Regis, bowing.

Beatrice took a step toward Cassy. "You will not get away with this," she bit out between gritted teeth.

Regis stepped in front of Beatrice, effectively blocking her from approaching Cassy any closer.

"You will not always be surrounded by people," Beatrice sneered. "Remember how your shopping expedition ended? It could be deadly the next time." She turned and stomped from the drawing room.

Both Cassy and James were prompt, and it was only a quarter past ten o'clock when the coach pulled away from the town house.

An hour or so later, Jared's coach arrived back in London. He had kept away from liquor when he returned to his country estate and had considered his life in a sober light. After much soul searching, Jared had decided he no longer wished to take revenge on his father. Perhaps Eleanor had been the wrong woman for him after all. She was beautiful—no doubt about that—but she was also extremely quiet and accepting. She would have never stood up to him as Cassy had on any number of occasions.

It was evident as soon as he allowed himself to think of it. He loved his wife and wanted nothing more than to spend the rest of his life with her. And, yes, he wanted to give his father as many grandchildren as Cassy desired.

But first he must show his wife he was serious about beginning their marriage anew. Beatrice must leave his house immediately. Allowing her to stay only indicated that he was involved with her. He cursed himself for not ridding himself of the woman before he left Town.

Jared returned to London as hastily as he had left it. He worried he had waited too long to resolve things with Cassy. She had seemed adamant she no longer wished to have anything to do with him and that as soon as the Season was over she would set up her own household. Jared marshaled his arguments as the coach raced back to Town.

He was to be disappointed, however, for when he reached the town house, Regis informed him that Lady Carlisle was not at home.

"Damn it!" he muttered under his breath. "When did she leave?"

"An hour or so ago," replied Regis.

"Surely she will not be gone long. She is still recovering from her wound," reasoned Jared.

"It's my understanding she will be away for several days," Regis informed him.

"Several days! Where the devil has she gone?" demanded Regis.

"I believe she is traveling to her mother's home with Mr. Howard. Her abigail would know more than I do."

"You mean Betsy did not go with her?"

"No, my lord. She remained behind, I understand, at Lady Carlisle's request."

It was highly unusual that Betsy was not with Cassy. "Something is not right here," muttered Jared. He turned and bounded up the stairs two at a time. When he reached Cassy's suite, he flung open the door so hard it bounced against the wall. Betsy, who had been sitting near the window sewing, leaped to her feet at his entrance.

"My Lord!" she exclaimed, addressing the heavenly host instead of Jared. "What's amiss?" she exclaimed, immediately thinking something had befallen Cassy and that Lord Carlisle was here to impart the tragic news.

"You must tell me that. Where is my wife?"

"She is with her cousin," said Betsy, regaining her composure. "They are going to visit Mr. Howard's estate."

"And you allowed her to go when she's so recently been injured?"

"Even though I have been with her since birth, I am only an abigail, sir. It is not my place to say what Lady Carlisle can do. I did ask to accompany her, but she insisted Mr. Howard had a maid who could attend her. She said I had been sitting with her too long and that I deserved some time to myself."

Frustration seized Jared. He wanted to waste no time in speaking to Cassy. He left Betsy and walked down the hall to the stairs. He was just descending when the door was flung open and Lord and Lady Waycross rushed in. Both were disheveled, as if they had left the house without a thought to their appearance.

"Where's Cassy?" demanded Lord Waycross, without extending any sort of greeting.

Even though he had decided he no longer wanted to carry on a dispute with his father, his manner was stiff and combative. "Why is it any of your concern?" asked Jared, reaching the hall.

"If she is with James Howard, I believe she's in danger."

"Come into the drawing room," said Jared, turning and leading the way. Lord and Lady Waycross followed at his heels.

"Jared, we must put aside our differences for the moment and concentrate on Cassy's safety," said Lord Waycross as soon as they were in the room with the doors closed.

"What is this all about? Why do you think she's in danger?" asked Jared.

"Eleanor, tell him what you told me."

"James is not what you think he is," said Eleanor. "Oh, he is Cassy's cousin, that part is true, but he is not the genial man you have seen." She halted and took a deep breath.

"Tell them quickly," urged Lord Waycross, "for we have no time to waste."

"I have known James before," she admitted, with downcast eyes. "James and I met at my come out. He swore he fell in love with me the first time he saw me. I was flattered, and we met as often as we could. He wanted to marry me, but my parents desired a title and security for me. James planned to improve his estate and make some investments in order to satisfy my father. He left London swearing to return as soon as his finances were improved so we could be married.

"I was just as happy that he had left, for I had discovered I did not love him as he did me. I went my own way, practically forgetting about James. After my marriage to Edward, James returned. He must have been watching the house, because he came to call while Edward was not at home. He swore he had never stopped loving me and was very near to having enough money to impress my father.

"I told him I was already married, but he said he

would not allow that to stand in his way. He went on to say that Edward was an older man who was prone to all manner of illness. I became afraid he would do something to harm Edward. Then James returned to his home, and I prayed he would forget about me.

"I had not seen him since until he came to visit Cassy. When they walked in together, I nearly swooned. When we were alone, he told me he had not given up on our marriage. He said Cassy was threatening his plan because his father had left half of the estate to her mother should she return. That part of the estate would now pass to Cassy, and he would be forced to buy her share if she desired to sell. James said he must find a way to eliminate Cassy's threat to the estate and his finances.

"He came by yesterday and revealed he had found a way to prevent Cassy from inheriting her part of the estate. James said Cassy thought she was going to see her mother's home, but he said she would never get her wish. I did not want to believe the worst of James, but I think he means to harm her."

"We came straightway, as soon as Eleanor related this to me," said Lord Waycross.

"I'm sorry for delaying. I did not want to think the worst of him," said Eleanor. Tears formed in her eyes and flowed down her cheeks at the thought she had inadvertently helped James in his plan to harm Cassy.

"Where is his estate?" demanded Jared.

"Just outside of Derby," replied Lord Waycross.

"They have a considerable start on us," murmured Jared. "Regis, have the bays harnessed and the coach brought around. Do it quickly."

"I'm going with you," said his father.

Jared stared at him for a moment. "Let me get my pistols," was his only reply.

Thirteen

A few minutes later, Jared and his father hurried out the front door and left London, headed toward Derby.

"I hope he takes the regular route and has not decided to take her to some deserted road," said Lord Waycross.

"He must make whatever he has planned appear to be an accident. He may even wait until he reaches the estate," said Jared, unwilling to think of James arranging Cassy's death.

"I know this isn't the best time," began Lord Waycross awkwardly, "but I want to apologize for everything. Eleanor, the marriage, not telling you before. You're my son. I never meant to hurt you." Lord Waycross lapsed into silence. He had done a poor job of asking for forgiveness.

"It is no longer important," confessed Jared. "It seems such an insignificant incident compared to what could be happening to Cassy at this moment. I don't love Eleanor and haven't for some time. Perhaps I never truly loved her, but was taken by her beauty. I'll never know, for Cassy has taken her place in my heart."

Lord Waycross felt a huge sense of relief. If only they could find Cassy safe from harm, he believed he would have his son back. If they were too late, Jared might be lost to him forever.

The men had traveled in silence for some time when they felt the coach slow.

"What is it?" yelled Jared to the coachman.

"An accident, my lord."

"Damn it!" burst out Jared. "We can't afford to stop, but I suppose we must see whether anyone is injured."

Jared and his father climbed down and surveyed the scene. A large tree limb had fallen across the road, and it looked as if the driver had attempted to drive around it. There was a swift-flowing stream alongside the road, and as the coach had endeavored to maneuver around the end of the limb, the vehicle had tipped over, splintering the shafts and landing upside down in the stream. Three of the four horses stood docilely on the other side of the limb, but no one else was in sight.

"Perhaps they have gone on by themselves," suggested Lord Waycross.

"And leave the horses? Not likely," judged Jared. "We are a far distance from anyone. They would have ridden the animals instead of walking. Let's look around," he said, walking toward the stream.

The water was brown from runoff, deep and swift-flowing due to the recent rains in the area. Jared thought he heard a voice, but the sound of rushing water was too loud for him to be certain. He could see no one from his present vantage point, so he walked beside the stream until he had a view of the entire coach. His heart dropped to the pit of his stomach, for between the front wheels, clinging to the coach, was Cassy. Her position was somewhat protected from the full force of the current, and she had been able to keep herself from being carried downstream.

"My God!" exclaimed Jared. He jerked off his boots

and jacket and waded into the stream. It dropped off suddenly, and he swam to the side of the coach.

"Hang on, Cassy," yelled Lord Waycross, "Jared's on his way. You're going to be all right. Just don't let go."

Jared worked his way toward the front of the wrecked coach, the current tugging relentlessly at his body. He finally reached the front wheel and pulled himself around it into the relative calm that lay in front of the coach. He reached out for Cassy as the water nearly pulled her hands loose from the spokes. His grip was firm and reassuring as his arms encircled her.

"Jared," she gasped. "I had nearly given up hope anyone would be here in time."

"Did you think I'd let you slip away when I finally realized what you mean to me?" He pulled her tightly against him, then felt the coach shift. "We must get away from here. The coach will be carried downstream any moment. Get behind me and put your arms around my neck," he ordered. "Can you hang on until we get to shore?"

Cassy pushed her hair out of her eyes and nodded. He turned and she locked her arms around his neck. Jared prayed he had enough strength to fight the current back to shore. The coach shifted again, and Jared knew there was no time left to consider what to do. He pushed off from the front of the coach and swam toward the shore. The current greedily grabbed at him, sucking him back into the stream. He cursed the liquor he had consumed over the past months, blaming it for draining him of the strength he so desperately needed.

Little by little, he came closer to the bank of the stream until he felt the bottom beneath his feet. He grabbed an overhanging limb and pulled himself the rest of the way to the bank. Lord Waycross reached out a hand and pulled him out of the water. Cassy allowed her hold to slacken and slipped down onto the grass. Jared collapsed beside her, breathing heavily.

Jared finally regained his breath. "Where is James?" he asked.

Cassy shook her head. "I don't know. He saw the limb blocking the road and ordered the driver to go around it. The coachman must have misjudged the distance, because the coach tipped a bit. James threw open the door and began to shove me out, I suppose trying to save me. When I saw I would fall into the stream, I tried to tell James not to push me, but he must not have heard. He gave me one last shove and I rolled down the bank into the water. The rest of the tree that was across the road was at the edge of the stream, and I was able to hold onto its branches. The next thing I knew I heard the horses whinnying in fright. Then the coach rolled down the bank and into the water, barely missing me. The tree was knocked free, and I grabbed on to the coach to save myself. I didn't see either the coachman or James. I suppose he could have been trapped inside." Her eyes filled with tears as she watched the coach being pulled along in the muddy current.

With Lord Waycross's and the coachman's help, they made their way back to Jared's coach.

"There are blankets in the coach. Take off your gown and wrap one around you. Here," Jared said, untying his cravat and offering it to her. "Use this to dry your hair."

"I am not going to take off my gown," Cassy protested.

"This is no time to be missish. You were injured not long ago. You could easily catch a chill, which could turn into something far worse."

Threatened with the possibility of further illness, Cassy climbed into the coach and did as he directed.

When she was finished, Jared wrapped the other blanket around himself, and they started back to London, with the remaining three horses tied to the back of the coach.

"How did you come to be here?" asked Cassy, once they had gotten under way.

"I returned to London only an hour or so after you left with James," said Jared.

"And Eleanor and I arrived shortly thereafter," injected Lord Waycross. "She was concerned about your trip with James," he said, and continued to explain the story as Eleanor had related it.

"We realized James had the means and opportunity to have arranged both the attempts on your life. You trusted him completely, and he was in a perfect position to make certain the third time would not be a failure," added Jared.

"Fortunately, we knew where the estate was and were able to start after you immediately," said Edward.

"I'm so grateful you did," said Cassy.

"As am I," replied Jared, looking at her as if he would never get his fill.

Cassy returned his gaze for a moment before glancing away. She was too tired to believe what she saw there.

It was evening before Jared, Cassy, and Lord Waycross reached home. They had been unable to find either James or the coachman, but Jared had located a single set of boot prints leading to where the horses stood. With one of the animals gone, they assumed the coachman had taken the horse and fled. If James had been trapped in the coach, they would need to wait until the water went down to see whether they could retrieve the body.

They had stopped in the nearest town and advised the magistrate of the accident. Jared left funds to pay for men to search for James and directions on how to reach him in London.

"I do not like to leave without some word of James," said Cassy.

"Staying here and becoming ill will not do any good. You would be best served by looking after your own health so you will be able to do what needs to be done when the time comes."

"I know you are right," she admitted, "but it seems so coldhearted."

"Murder is coldhearted, my love. Remember, that was his intent," said Jared, in a hard voice.

"I have been thinking on what you told me, and you must be mistaken. I can't believe James would harm me. I'm certain that Eleanor misunderstood. It must have been an accident," she insisted.

"There was no misunderstanding," said Jared.

"Then prove it to me," she demanded. "Let me talk to the man he hired to stab me or to cut the saddle girth."

"We haven't found him, and probably never will," admitted Jared.

"Then where is the coachman who drove us today? Surely he can tell us whether the coach overturning was an accident."

"He left before we arrived," said Edward. "That should tell you something. Any legitimate coachman would have attempted to rescue you, or at the very least gone for help."

"Perhaps he did," argued Cassy.

"Then where was he? The village was close enough that he should have been there and back before we came across you."

"Perhaps he was thrown into the water, too."

"We found his prints leading to the horses, and one of the animals was gone. No, he left, and we will probably never locate him either."

"Then you have no proof," she pointed out.

"Nothing concrete," confessed Jared. "But it is a certainty he was behind it all."

"Perhaps you can believe that, but I cannot," she said stubbornly.

Jared gave up on the argument. He knew he could not sway her from her opinion without solid facts to present to her. And it did not matter that she would believe no evil of her cousin. Jared was only grateful that Cassy was alive.

The town house was ablaze with light as the coach came to a halt at the front door. Betsy was waiting in the front hall, with Regis standing guard beside the door.

Jared lifted Cassy from the coach as if she weighed no more than a feather and carried her into the foyer. He set her gently on her feet and held her until she was steady.

"Take my wife upstairs and see she has a hot bath immediately," ordered Jared.

"As if I didn't know," muttered Betsy under her breath. She put her arm around Cassy and guided her toward the steps.

"Can you walk?" Jared asked. "I can easily carry you."

"I can do it on my own," declared Cassy, moving to the bottom of the stairs. She was still incensed that Jared and Edward thought James would harm her. During the ride to London, she had convinced herself they were all about in the attic and that James had died in a vain attempt to save her.

"I thought I heard someone," said Eleanor, hurrying out of the drawing room with Drew following close behind.

Cassy was grateful that her dress had dried and she had been able to don it before arriving in London. She would have been thoroughly humiliated if she had arrived wrapped in a blanket. "Drew, how did you get involved in this?" asked Cassy.

"He wasn't," said Jared. "At least, not when we left Town."

"Arrived shortly after you had departed," revealed Drew. "Had news, but found I was too late."

"You knew about James and his plan to harm Cassy?" asked Jared.

"I still do not believe it," avowed Cassy adamantly.

"Not only Howard, but Crawford as well," revealed Drew.

"What the devil does Crawford have to do with it?" demanded Jared.

"Weston heard it. Couldn't find you, so came to me."

"Heard what?" asked Jared impatiently.

"Heard Crawford and Howard plotting against Cassy. Crawford was to see the road was blocked so that the coach must try to pass on the river side of the road. James was to open the door and toss Cassy into the river. Knew it would be high from the rain and that she wouldn't have a chance once the current got hold of her. I came straightaway when I heard it, but missed you. Didn't know which road you were taking, so decided to wait. Nothing more I could do even if I caught up with you."

"Crawford and Howard," repeated Jared. He turned to Cassy. "Now do you believe it?"

Cassy could not continue insisting that everyone was mistaken about James. Her face crumpled as she accepted the bitter truth. "James," she wailed, leaning against Betsy, tears streaming down her face.

Jared wanted nothing more than to go to her and

hold her until the tears dried, but she might not welcome his comfort, and there were too many people watching for him to risk the embarrassment.

"You should go upstairs and change clothing," he said gently. "Regis, send for the doctor. I want him to check Lady Carlisle's wound."

"It isn't necessary," said Cassy between sobs.

"Humor me," he said.

Cassy had taken but one step when she heard a noise and looked up to see footmen carrying trunks down the stairs. She retreated to the bottom of the stairs and watched with the others as the footmen stacked a pile of trunks and portmanteaus in the foyer.

Jared stared at the trunks, then turned his attention to his wife. "What is going on? You aren't leaving, are you?" he demanded of Cassy.

"I don't have the strength," she answered weakly. Betsy wrapped her arm around her protectively.

"They are mine," said Beatrice, descending the stairs.

"It's an odd time to be departing," remarked Jared, his eyes narrowing.

"Both of you have requested that I leave," snarled Beatrice. "I do not want to stay where I am not wanted any longer than necessary."

Cassy looked at Jared. "You asked her to leave?"

"I did. And you?"

"Yes," she acknowledged, the shadow of a watery smile breaking through her tears.

Jared turned back to Beatrice. "What do you know about the happenings today?" he asked her.

"I have no idea what you are talking about."

"Were you aware James was attempting to harm Cassy?"

"How would I know that? I am barely acquainted

with Mr. Howard, and certainly not close enough for him to confide in me."

"What about your father? Did you know his part in the scheme?" pressed Jared.

Beatrice opened her mouth to answer when a knock sounded at the door. Before Regis could open it, Crawford burst in. He came to a sudden halt, not expecting such a huge welcoming committee.

He looked around, and then his mouth fell open. "What are you doing here?" he asked when he saw Cassy.

"You didn't expect to see her again, did you?" said Jared.

"I . . . I . . ." Crawford looked toward Beatrice for help.

"You should be more careful that no one is around when you're plotting murder," commented Jared, using all his willpower not to grab the man by the throat.

"You might as well tell all," said Beatrice in disgust. "They know everything anyway." When Crawford remained silent, she continued speaking. "James approached us. He asked us to help him get rid of Cassy and convinced us we would benefit by her death. He explained Jared would be free to marry me, and my father and I could live well on his money, while James's estate would not be threatened and he could pursue Lady Waycross. I believe he was also planning a deadly accident for Lord Waycross when he returned."

"He came to me earlier this week," said Crawford, finally deciding to talk. "He said he did not mean to fail again. It seems he had arranged for Cassy's saddle girth to be cut. When that wasn't successful, he plotted for her to be stabbed, but some street urchin interfered." Crawford stopped for a deep breath.

Jared made a mental note to see that Little Will

would have an education and a good start in life. "Go on," commanded Jared.

"James told me he had invited Cassy to visit her mother's home. We traveled the road earlier and chose a place where he could toss her into the stream from the carriage. It was my job to make certain the road was blocked in a manner where it was possible for the coach to squeeze by near the stream, but close enough so it would appear the door had come open and Cassy had tumbled out by accident."

Jared heard Cassy gasp, and wished she did not need to hear what Crawford had to say. However, it was the only way he knew of proving to her that James had attempted to murder her.

"I waited until I saw Howard send her flying," said Crawford. "I thought it had worked fine, and was ready to ride off when the coach slipped sideways on the soft ground. The coachman jumped as the carriage began to roll on its side. The shafts splintered and the horses broke free. I didn't see Howard again, and assumed he was either under the coach or in it. Either way, he was beyond my help. The coachman took a horse and went one way while I went the other."

"You didn't search for Cassy?" asked Jared.

"Why should I?" he asked, seemingly amazed Jared had asked such a foolish question. "The whole scheme was aimed at getting rid of her. There was no reason to rescue her just because Howard had done himself up."

Jared's fists clenched and he took a step toward Crawford, stopping only when his father put a hand on his shoulder.

Crawford turned to stare at Beatrice. "If only you had done what I told you, we would not be in such a mess."

"Don't blame your inadequacies on me," shot back

Beatrice. "If it weren't for your gambling, we would never have been brought to this in the first place."

"Don't turn on each other now," advised Lord Way-cross. "You will need to depend on one another more than ever."

"What do you mean?" asked Crawford, eyeing him suspiciously.

Jared and his father glanced at one another. "We think the two of you would be much more comfortable in another country," said Jared.

"What!" screeched Beatrice.

"By God, you can't do this to us," roared Crawford.

"We're not forcing you to do anything," replied Lord Waycross calmly. "We are only suggesting that the climate might be better somewhere other than England. And to help you adjust, we will contribute a sum of money to expedite your settlement elsewhere."

"I believe you'll find it much more comfortable than your life would be if you chose to remain here," threatened Jared.

Crawford stared at the two men confronting him. He knew they could deliver all of their implied threats and then some. Perhaps it wouldn't be so bad to get away from his debtors. And he would have money to start over again. He was certain his luck would change eventually.

"My estate?" he asked.

"I doubt whether there will be much left after your debts are paid," said Jared. "But if you will sign it over to me, I'll see your vowels are paid and your staff is taken care of."

"All right," Crawford acquiesced, "but I'll need a considerable amount to begin anew."

Jared nodded his agreement. "I'll send four of my footmen with you. You may collect your belongings and be on your way immediately. The money will be given to you once you board the ship. And don't try anything tricky," he warned. "My men will make certain you are on board and will be on watch so that you cannot leave it before departure."

Jared gave a sign to the footmen to load Beatrice's trunks on the coach, and the two were gone in a very few minutes.

The hall was strangely silent with Beatrice and Crawford gone. It was as if they had taken all the anger and animosity with them.

"We will go and allow you to rest," said Eleanor to Cassy. "I will see you once you are feeling more the thing."

"Thank you for everything you've done," said Cassy. "It was your revelations that sent them after me."

"Don't thank me," replied Eleanor. "I should have said something sooner, but I was afraid of losing my husband." She looked at Edward uncertainly.

"You had nothing to worry about. You will never be rid of me," he affirmed, taking her hand, placing it on his arm, and covering it with his own. Their love was apparent as they looked at one another.

Drew moved to Cassy's side, took her hand, and saluted it. "Must be going, too. Will call when you feel up to it," he said to Cassy. "Am grateful you are well."

"So am I," she said, squeezing his hand before releasing it.

"You must go upstairs," said Jared, after the others had departed. "It is long past time you had a warm bath and something to eat. The doctor should be here shortly."

Betsy put her arm around Cassy and the two women started up the stairs. Jared watched until they disappeared down the hall at the top.

"I am going down to breakfast," said Cassy the next morning.

"Are you certain you feel up to it?" asked Betsy, a worried expression on her face.

"Yes. And it is wonderful to think I will not be forced to face Beatrice over my buttered eggs."

"It is a relief," agreed Betsy.

"I'd like my new gown," instructed Cassy. "The sprigged muslin. It's most flattering, don't you think?"

"I do," said Betsy, taking the gown from the armoire. She hid her smile, thinking that Cassy's marriage might have a chance, after all.

"I didn't expect you up and around so soon," remarked Jared as she walked into the dining room.

"I feel very well despite everything that happened," she informed him.

"Allow me to fetch you a plate," he said, rising and holding her chair before going to the sideboard.

"Did you escape any ill effects?" she asked.

"A little water could not hurt me." He placed the plate before her and returned to his chair. "I have been thinking of us," he said, toying with his knife. He looked up from beneath his dark lashes, his green eyes brilliant in the morning light.

"And what is it you have been thinking?" she asked softly, her heart pounding faster than usual.

"I'm wondering whether we have a chance—whether you will give me another chance to make our marriage a good one."

"I'm uncertain what I want to do," she answered truthfully.

"I understand your feelings," he said solemnly. "I cannot apologize enough for what I've put you through. There is no excuse I can offer that will justify my actions since we married."

Cassy did not know what to say in return, so she remained silent.

"There is one thing I want to make clear, no matter what your decision. The night you saw Beatrice in my room . . ." he began.

"There is no need," she said interrupting him.

"Yes, there is," he insisted. "I was completely foxed that night. I vaguely remember getting to my room and falling across the bed, but that is all. I don't recall Beatrice even being there, and I swear to you nothing of an intimate nature has ever occurred between us. If you do not believe me, you may ask Thomas. I've told him to be perfectly candid should you ask."

"It isn't necessary. I believe what you say. I've learned Beatrice was far more devious than I ever thought she could be, and I would put nothing past her and Crawford."

Jared shook his head. "And to think I was the one who invited her into our lives," he said, his voice full of disgust.

"It's over and done with now," said Cassy. "We should attempt to put it behind us."

"I hope you won't decide to put me behind you, too," replied Jared, a wry smile on his lips. "That was a poor jest, but I am sincere all the same."

"Events have happened so quickly I have not had time to think," murmured Cassy.

"I understand, and I don't mean to press you. Perhaps we both need time to reflect," suggested Jared. "I believe I will return to the country. There is much I can do there, and this would be an opportune time to meet with my steward. At the same time, my absence will give you time to consider what you expect from our marriage."

"When will you leave?" she asked.

"There is no reason to tarry, so I will depart either

this afternoon or first thing in the morning. In any event, I will probably not see you before I leave, so I will bid you good-bye now."

"Watch for fallen trees," she warned. "I know first-hand that they can be harmful to one's health."

He smiled at her jest. "I shall remember."

Cassy attempted to continue as she had done in the past. She attended balls, routs, soirees, card parties, and musicals. Drew was often with her, as were Lord and Lady Waycross. They seemed to think she needed looking after, and Cassy did nothing to cause them to think differently.

Once James's body was found, they traveled with her to have him interred in the family plot on the estate. And although it was under unhappy circumstances, Cassy was finally able to see her mother's home.

The estate was a substantial one, with a large brick house and fertile fields and woodlands surrounding it. She met with the steward and the staff, assuring them their positions were secure. She did not yet know whether she would inhabit the house herself, but it would not be sold.

Even though Jared had apologized to her and she accepted that he was sincerely sorry for his actions, she was still deeply hurt by the manner in which he had used her. It was something that could not be wiped away with a few words, nor did she know whether they could live beneath the same roof.

She returned to London and the social whirl while waiting for her husband to return.

The summer was drawing to a close by the time Cassy received a note from Jared advising her he would return to town in a sennight. Cassy spent restless days and nights wondering what would happen when they met again. Before she was fully prepared, the day of his arrival was upon her.

He appeared in late afternoon and came to greet her before he rid himself of the dust of his journey. "My lady," he said formally, passing his hat and gloves to Regis. He took her hand, pressing his lips against her soft skin. "I hope I find you well."

"You do indeed," she assured him.

Jared looked much different from the last time she had seen him, and she was forcibly struck by how handsome he was. His skin was brown from the sun, and he looked altogether fit. The signs of dissipation were gone from his face, and his hand was steady as he held hers.

"The country has done you good," she said.

"It was peaceful," he agreed. "Yet I had plenty of company from the neighbors. I have not spent much time there lately, and found it amazingly comforting to fit myself back into the niche."

"I found it to be a pleasant place for the few weeks I resided there," replied Cassy.

"I hope you will return to enjoy it longer," he said, meeting her gaze.

"I . . . I don't know," she said.

"There is something else I have accomplished since you last saw me which might help you decide. I have not had so much as a drop of liquor since I last saw you," he announced proudly.

"You are to be congratulated," she said, her lips parting in a smile.

"It was not such a challenge," he replied. "I had used it to dull the pain I felt at the time and it secured a considerable hold over me. Once I realized I no longer hated my father nor loved Eleanor, the desire to numb my senses departed."

"You have resolved your differences, then?" she asked.

"We have," he affirmed. "I'm certain there will be some awkwardness between us, but time will take care of that. As for Eleanor, I know now we would have never suited."

Cassy wanted to ask whether he thought they would suit, but could not work up the courage.

"I apologize for not being here when you found your cousin," said Jared. "But I felt you might not welcome my company."

"I would not have objected, but there was no reason for you to be there. He was my cousin, and I owed him a proper burial no matter what he had done. However, he did nothing but cause you problems."

"Let us put that behind us," he suggested. "If you will excuse me, I am going to rid myself of the dust of my travels before dinner. I shouldn't be long."

"There's no rush," she assured him. "I told Cook to hold dinner until you arrived."

"I look forward to sampling her dishes again," he said, reluctant to leave her if only for the time necessary to change clothes.

Cassandra took stock of her reaction to Jared while he was above stairs. Her cheeks had flushed and her heart had quickened upon his arrival. The feelings of resentment and anger she had experienced while Beatrice was in their home no longer rose to choke her. Did Jared feel different about her, also? And would it be enough to rebuild their marriage?

Her thoughts were interrupted when he returned to the room. "It is enjoyable to be back," he said, coming to stand before her. "Although with the Season nearly over, it will be good to spend time in the country before the Little Season begins."

Cassy wondered whether he meant she should accompany him back to the estate. Perhaps she should let him know she had someplace to go in case he did not want to live in the same house. After all, she had stated earlier she would establish her own household once the Season was over.

"I have inherited the Howard estate," she told him.

His mouth tightened and he was silent a moment, assessing her expression. "Is it pleasant?" he inquired.

"I believe it to be," she said. "I left the steward in charge and advised him to continue as usual. I informed him I would return before winter set in so we might settle any questions he might have."

Jared walked to the window and looked out into the night. "Do you think to live there?" he asked, afraid to hear the answer.

Cassy admired the breadth of his shoulders and the fit of his jacket stretched across them. He had everything to commend him, and she wondered whether he would be satisfied remaining married to her. "I don't know. I've been waiting to speak to you before I make that decision."

He turned, looking at Cassy. It was cowardly not to face her when asking the most important question either would answer. "Are you thinking of leaving our marriage?"

"Is that your desire?" she said, answering him with a question, unable to commit herself first.

"There will be no divorce, if that is what you are thinking," he said gruffly. "I will not submit my family to additional scandal. What I have done these past two years is enough for a lifetime. If you cannot see fit to live beneath the same roof with me, then we will work something out."

"What are your true feelings?" she asked, afraid to expose her barely healed wounds to his rejection.

"If given my wishes, we would remain married. Only

this time it would be a true one in every sense of the word." He caught her gaze and held it. "I have given this considerable thought while I was in the country, and I've determined I was wrong about our marriage from the beginning. I thought I could marry you and then forget about you, but it wasn't to be. You would not leave me alone," he confessed with a wry smile. "You invaded my thoughts at inopportune times and remained there despite the copious amount of liquor I drank."

Jared crossed the floor to stand in front of her. He took her hands and pulled her to her feet. "I realized before I left that I loved you and wanted to spend my life with you. I want to give my father the grandchildren he desires, but not because he ordered me to do so." He smiled slightly and pulled her closer. "I would like you to be their mother because we both desire it. I want to give you the family you have always yearned for," he said, taking her hands and pressing them against the beating of his heart.

"That has been my wish since the death of my father," Cassy said. "My mother and I seemed incomplete without him. I know she married Crawford hoping to regain that feeling, but it was a dismal failure. I do not wish to go through life alone, but . . ."

"Trust me, Cassy. I love you. Give me a chance to prove we can become the family you covet."

She looked away, wondering whether to believe him and risk her heart. "Will you do something for me?" she finally asked.

"Whatever you want," he promised, hoping it would be within his ability to fulfill her request.

Her mouth went dry and she wondered how on earth she was going to bring herself to ask such a foolish thing. She took a deep breath, and spoke quickly. "Can we take our marriage vows again?"

Relief visibly surged through him. "I should have thought of it myself," he said. "And this time all our friends shall be present and we will celebrate for at least a sennight."

Cassy laughed at his enthusiasm. "I did not ask for all that," she said. "A simple ceremony will be enough."

"But not for me," he proclaimed, pulling her up and spinning her around until her feet left the floor. "I want everyone to know how much I love my bride, and how happy we are going to be."

"Then I will agree to give our marriage another try," she said, still laughing.

"Perhaps we should say a first try," he said with meaning.

She blushed prettily, and he could not stop himself from gathering her in his arms and kissing her as he had long yearned to do.

More Zebra Regency Romances

Embrace the Romances of
Shannon Drake